Something is out there,
getting closer,
moving in the darkness,
growing . . .

In Fluid Silence

DARK●MATTER

In the heartland of America, an agent for the Hoffmann Institute has disappeared. As he comes face-to-face with a centuries-old madman, his colleagues uncover a terrifying plot—one whose roots lie in Nazi Germany but may reach to the highest seats of world power.

DARK·MATTER

(One)
In Hollow Houses
Gary A. Braunbeck

(Two)
If Whispers Call
Don Bassingthwaite

(Three)
In Fluid Silence
G.W. Tirpa

(Four)
Of Aged Angels
Monte Cook
July 2001

(Five)
By Dust Consumed
Don Bassingthwaite
December 2001

(Six)
All Virtue Lies
G.W. Tirpa
April 2002

DARK•MATTER

IN FLUID SILENCE

G. W. TIRPA

Wizards of the Coast

IN FLUID SILENCE
Dark•Matter™
©2000 Wizards of the Coast, Inc.

All characters in this book are fictitious. Any resemblance to actual persons, living or dead, is purely coincidental.

This book is protected under the copyright laws of the United States of America. Any reproduction or unauthorized use of the material or artwork contained herein is prohibited without the express written permission of Wizards of the Coast, Inc.

Distributed in the United States by St. Martin's Press. Distributed in Canada by Fenn Ltd.

Distributed to the hobby, toy, and comic trade in the United States and Canada by regional distributors.

Distributed worldwide by Wizards of the Coast, Inc. and regional distributors.

DARK•MATTER is a trademark owned by Wizards of the Coast, Inc. The Wizards of the Coast logo is a registered trademark owned by Wizards of the Coast, Inc.

All Wizards of the Coast characters, character names, and the distinctive likenesses thereof are trademarks owned by Wizards of the Coast, Inc.

Made in the U.S.A.

The sale of this book without its cover has not been authorized by the publisher. If you purchased this book without a cover, you should be aware that neither the author nor the publisher has received payment for this "stripped book."

"Walt Whitman's Niece" quoted by kind permission of Woody Guthrie Publications. Copyright Woody Guthrie Publications, Inc.
Lyrics by Woody Guthrie. Music by Billy Bragg.

Cover art by Ashley Wood
First Printing: March 2001
Library of Congress Catalog Card Number: 00-190767

9 8 7 6 5 4 3 2 1

UK ISBN: 0-7869-2033-5
US ISBN: 0-7869-1680-X
620-T21680

U.S., CANADA,	EUROPEAN HEADQUARTERS
ASIA, PACIFIC, & LATIN AMERICA	Wizards of the Coast, Belgium
Wizards of the Coast, Inc.	P.B. 2031
P.O. Box 707	2600 Berchem
Renton, WA 98057-0707	Belgium
+1-800-324-6496	+32-70-23-32-77

Visit our web site at **www.wizards.com**

Acknowledgments

Thank you Mary-Elizabeth Allen and Keith Strohm for even trying to unravel my German, and thank you to the evil geniuses behind Dark Matter: Gary Braunbeck, Don Bassingthwaite, Mark Sehestedt, and the really evil geniuses Wolf Baur and Monte Cook.

For Richard E. Geis

Dark Matter So Far

Michael "Fitz" McCain retrieves a jar containing fragments of the brain of John F. Kennedy from a secret vault under the National Archives in Washington, D.C., moments before the building explodes.

Jeane Meara, an arson investigator for the Bureau of Alcohol, Tobacco, and Firearms, is sent to determine the cause of the explosion but finds her theories as unwelcome as they are impossible to believe.

Watching all this is the quiet form of Ngan Song Kun'dren, an experienced agent of the shadowy Hoffmann Institute, a private organization founded to investigate and stop the rise of the Dark Tide.

Now the Hoffmann Institute's newest investigation team, these three very different people are sent to Chicago. There they must learn to work together when a supernatural force threatens the life of a young woman and her unborn child—and threatens the sanity of her husband. As the restless spirits of Bachelor's Grove cemetery are laid to rest, Ngan, Fitz, and Jeane may be starting to like each other. . . .

i'm not him

Was it cold that day?

It was November. People were wearing coats.

There was that woman in the red raincoat. Did he see her? There were leaves on the trees, weren't there?

Was the side of the car cold? I can almost feel that thin, cold steel feeling of your arm touching, resting against the top of the car door.

The windows were down. The roof was off. I would have felt the wind, cool and dry. Did he feel that?

Right now—and there is a right now, a now that belongs to me, experienced by me, not him—right now it's warmth. It's the same temperature as my blood, as my body, my skin. I remember falling. I could feel that. I can feel the dense warm against my eyelids. It's incredible what you can feel with your eyelids. I never imagined I'd be where my most solid connection to the place I was in was the feel of it gently resting against my closed eyelids, but here I am.

Here *I* am.

Me. Not him.

If there's a difference.

What did he feel? There were stories. The softness of a breast every man in the world longed to feel, and there must have been others, though only one familiar and reassuring.

There was the smoothness of the desktop, wide and imposing. The smoother plastic of the telephone—a telephone with a dial. I can feel the tug at my cuticles—not pain but a comforting discomfort that was so mundane in a time that isn't really so long gone to be missed like that.

There was the feeling of a tiny hand in mine. Soft and warm and depending on him—on me? Depending on him. No one depends on me like that. No one with such small hands. A laugh from them must have brushed his hair, his ear, his cheek. He must have felt his children laughing.

He had pain. There had been an injury. I can feel the straight back of the chair that helped. I wouldn't have to feel that pain if it was an injury. That was his injury. That was his pain. Not mine.

He'd have felt the wind on his face. Sea wind. Salt wind. Wind from the ocean, across the deck of a yacht, not the wind coming down a mountain. The wind would have been cold and damp, not cold and dry. That was another difference. My cold wind has the water frozen out of it. That cold wind is mine, not his.

It might have been cold that day. He'd have felt the cold rim of the car door, even through his suit jacket. He would have felt her hand in his, though by then was her touch accusatory? Was it for the cameras and the illusion? She touched him by habit then, didn't she? Didn't her touch feel like habit then?

How could I know?

I can't know that.

That was him.

Could he feel the bullet enter his neck?

He must have. His hands went up and he could feel the blood, couldn't he? It would feel warm and thick and pulsing like what's pressing against my eyelids now. Is that what I feel now? Is that what blood feels like?

in fluid silence

His hands went up, but could he feel by then, or was it already over?

Could he feel the other bullet? The one that took his ear, the whole side of his head off? He couldn't have felt that, but I can almost feel it now. It would have been accompanied by wetness. Everything worth feeling is accompanied by wetness. There would have been blood and whatever else. I can feel his head exploding even though it wasn't my head. It was his head, burst like a balloon.

Her scream must have hurt his ear—the one still attached to his head. He could feel his eardrum vibrate with the panic of it. Panic can be a solid thing, like a moving wall. I can feel it. I can feel the wall of it—the wave rushing over, past, and through me. I can feel her screaming.

It pushed him back and to the left, and I can feel my head going there too, but goddamn it, it's not me. It was never me. That was him. It was him.

He felt the scream. He heard it, didn't he? And what the man in the front seat said. What did he say? I can't remember. It was simple words that anyone would say when they were sure, when the sounds and the feel and everything else made it clear that

Oh
My
God
They're
Going
To
Kill
Us
All.

They. Us. All. But not me. I wasn't there. That was him, that was them, the four of them, the two hundred million of them and more, but it wasn't me.

"They," he said. He said, "*They're* going to kill us all." I can hear it. The words echo in my head like a gift from his last second to his second life. That's not possible. I've read that. I've seen that in a movie, but I wasn't there.

I'm not him.

He would have heard the scream even as he felt it. What would that sound like? I can hear it. I can imagine it or remember it. It's the sound of everything coming to a sudden, complete halt.

A sudden.

Complete.

Stop.

Then silence like the scream of a lost child that ripped his heart to shreds even as it too came to a jarring stop. I can feel that too. How could I not feel that?

I can hear my own heart beating now. It could be the warm, dense something that's causing the roar in my ears, or it's stopping me from hearing anything—stopping any sound from coming in so my ears are compensating by listening to the inside. That roar, the rushing, could be the blood pulsing through my own skull. He would have heard his blood rushing out, not mixing through. Another difference between him and me.

But that would have been the last sound. He'd have had a lifetime of sounds stored for me.

The touch of a child's breath would have been only one part of the sounds of them. Laughter and tears and jokes that make no sense. They'd have called out to him or been talking to themselves, playing with toys when they didn't think he was listening, or, better yet, didn't care if he was listening.

He'd have heard her voice and his own and his brother's and another's. He would have heard a hundred languages spoken. I can hear them all like a chorus of sighs. Some would be happy to know where they'd both end up, others would recoil in horror.

I can still hear the blood rushing in my head.

I can hear words spoken in German.

"Sie sind hier unter falsches Beglaubigungsschreiben gekommen, aber Sie möchten irgendwie bleiben."

I can't understand. He wouldn't have—everyone knows he wouldn't have understood—but that doesn't make me him, or him me.

"Sie wollten, dass diese Landreise als jede andere unterschiedlich wären, aber in Ihre Lage, vielleicht sollte es eine Landreise für zwei sein."

in fluid silence

I heard those words. *For two.* That can't be—not really.

I've heard the sound of a voice from the farthest reaches of the infinite and the sound of a voice from beyond the grave. I've heard screams and whispers and lies and revelations.

So did he, I'm sure.

Mine make me different from him.

He heard the sounds of war. I've heard the sound of lies. Which is worse?

I've opened my mouth to make those sounds—the sounds of lies. Lies as bad as the ones told to me. Lies that tasted like aspirin dissolving on my tongue. I've told lies that tasted like the nape of a woman's neck and lies that tasted like nothing at all. I've told lies that slipped out without substance or with a reality solid enough for a taste.

I open my mouth now, and it pours in and tastes like *Potenz*. It tastes like *die Ausgang und die Anbruch des Welt*.

He would have tasted clam chowder. That was a joke from a long time ago: clam chowder. Good chowder.

He wasn't a joke, though. There was never anything funny about h—

I'm not breathing.

There's no air here.

If it isn't blood I'm in, it's certainly not air.

I'm alive. I have to be, but I can't be.

I'm drawing in what should be a breath through my nose, but all that comes in is more of the same dense, warm something that's pressing against my eyelids, roaring in my ears, filling my mouth with tasteless nothing. . . .

I can smell only memories.

Perfume, gunpowder, blood, rain on pavement, exhaust from a jet engine . . .

I can smell the food in the cafeteria at Yale. I can smell the three-bean salad that came with my lunch but that I didn't take because I hate three-bean salad. It smelled bad. It smelled like three-bean salad. The three-bean salad was me, but was the rest of it him?

The perfume was . . . ? What was her name? She had red

hair, or brown hair, or maybe blonde hair. She had a laugh he couldn't remember the sound of. It might have been more than one woman who wore the same perfume. It might have been Mar—

"*Sie können die Potenz riechen, können Sie nicht, Mikail?*"

I remember someone saying that. *You can smell the power, can't you . . .*

Michael?

Me.

Not him—me. I don't remember what the "power" was or what it smelled like. All I remember is . . . not Jeane's perfume. Does she even wear perfume?

And how do I know what he said?

How do I know what he asked me?

The words were clearly in German. It was German, wasn't it?

The world knew well enough that he didn't speak German, so it couldn't have come from—

Nothing could have come from him.

I open my eyes, and there's nothing.

I'm sinking again.

I'm deep.

I've pulled in a breath of something too thick to be water, so how could it be air?

When I expel it in a scream I hear nothing. I feel nothing rattle in my throat.

Silence.

Darkness.

Nothing.

I can remember him, and I can remember me, and I can't be sure which one was the movie and which was all too real. There was the thing underground, and the ghost in the cemetery, and the jar full of—

The jar.

That's what he'd felt.

Thirty-seven years.

Thirty-seven years as pieces of himself—out of his body, in

in fluid silence

the jar, in the fluid, in the dead, dark silence of a vault under a vault under a vault under a city full of vaults under vaults under vaults.

Thirty-seven years.

Will I be in here for that long?

Have I been here for that long?

Is that what I took out, what I handed off, what I never understood until it was gone? They must have put it in a vault of their own, deep and locked away where no one could use those pieces to make more of me.

That's where they got me. From that jar.

And that's where I've come back to.

Pieces, floating in fluid silence.

My hates have always occupied my mind much more actively and have given greater spiritual satisfaction than my friendships.
—Westbrook Pegler

*Last night or the night before that,
I won't say which night
A seaman friend of mine,
I'll not say which seaman,
Walked up to a big old building,
I won't say which building,
And would not have walked up the stairs,
not to say which stairs,
If there had not been two girls,
leaving out the names of those two girls.*
—Woody Guthrie, "Walt Whitman's Niece"

I teach you the superman. Man is something to be surpassed.
—Friedrich Nietzsche

Mein Langmut ist nun jetzt am ein Ausgang.
(My patience is now at an end.)
—Adolf Hitler, 26 Sept., 1938

chapter
ONE

Ngan couldn't tell which was more a mess, the man's office or his hands.

Fingers that were surely once graceful, long, and tapered were now bulging with arthritis. Veins made them look as if they were made of wicker. Spots of brown and even grey marred their color. They shook for no other reason than their owner was an old man, and old men have shaky hands. The nails were yellow for the same reason.

His office was as cramped as every office Ngan had ever been in. Offices, except in television shows, were always small. This one was lit by innocuous rows of color-draining fluorescent tubes. The faint buzz of them might explain, Ngan thought, why the world had gone mad, except that the world had always been mad.

There were stacks of paper everywhere. Most of them were white, with blocks of type making them appear grey. There were sheets and pads of yellow legal paper and other documents that hadn't started out yellow but had become yellow as years, then decades passed. Ngan could smell the decaying paper even more strongly than the oddly comforting smell of the decaying man. Considering the nature of the old man's work, the fact that so many years had passed was reassuring in itself.

The pile of paper in the center of the room concealed an old oak desk. There was a telephone there, almost quaint in its two-line simplicity. A clock radio on an equally cluttered credenza behind the desk was nine minutes fast. There was a stain in the middle of the faded tan carpet that must have been coffee from two or three years ago.

The walls were painted an institutional white that defied description, opinion, or any response at all. There were framed documents hung with little care on one wall. One was a plaque engraved entirely in Hebrew, which Ngan couldn't read. The smudged surface might have been gold but was probably bronze. There was a diploma, a very old one, written in French. The old man had attended the Sorbonne and had received the degree in 1950. There were others. Another degree, this one from New York University. A "Certificate of Appreciation" from Beth Israel Hospital. A certificate that had a very old photograph of an old woman proclaimed to all the world that she was a citizen of the United States of America. The woman's name was Tova Lieberman.

On another wall was a collection of photographs. There were children dressed in clothes that placed them in the late nineteen thirties or early forties. Those children must be in their seventies or eighties now. There was a photograph of the old man the way he looked maybe half a century ago wearing an Israeli army uniform.

In the middle of the collection of photographs was an eight-by-ten black-and-white photograph of an American soldier, obviously circa World War II. The man's face was smooth and innocent. His eyes sparkled with youth. His altogether ordinary features made him look like a child going to a Halloween party dressed as a soldier.

Ngan stepped forward and looked at the photograph more

closely, but it revealed no secrets about the young man. He heard a match strike behind him, and there was that sharp smell of sulfur.

"I would offer you one," Rabbi Ira Lieberman said, his voice thickly accented with a sort of generalized European that was disappearing from the world, "but I know you would say no."

Ngan smiled but didn't turn around. "I will accept someday," he said, "just to surprise you."

Lieberman moved so that his face appeared reflected in the glass, like an old ghost hovering over the young soldier. "It can be dangerous to surprise a man my age, Ngan, but I look forward to it."

Ngan could see a change in the reflection of Lieberman's smile, and though he was about to turn around, he stopped himself.

"That is Thomas Francis Green," Lieberman said, "Corporal Green of the Fifth U.S. Infantry Division. He was sixteen when that photograph was taken, a couple weeks or so after he lied about his age and enlisted in the army because the radio reports made it sound like the war was going to end. Thomas couldn't bear the thought of missing it. Do you believe that? A young man like that, from Cedar Rapids, Iowa?"

"He was a friend of yours?" Ngan asked, not entirely comfortable with the small talk but not wanting to rush the man.

Lieberman's face moved out of the glass, and he said, "I hardly knew him, but I will never forget him. Corporal Green made it into the army, made it to Europe, and did his part in driving the German occupation forces out of France. He saw things, this young man, that he did not want to see, no matter how much he thought he was ready for it or how heroic he thought he was being. He went to war for all the right reasons—if there can be good reasons to go to war. He fired his rifle in the direction he was told to fire it, marched in the direction he was told to march, and never shirked his duty to God and Country. He helped to save the world as much as any man ever did."

Ngan nodded, knowing the rabbi well enough to know there was a point coming in its own time.

"It was his unit that liberated Buchenwald on 6 April, 1945,"

Lieberman said, his voice still even and conversational. "That is where the paths of Ira Lieberman and Thomas Green crossed, in that part of Hell those poor boys stumbled into. They were told to hate their enemy, and they did, but until that day, they couldn't possibly understand what hate could mean, what hate could be capable of."

Ngan turned around and faced the rabbi, who was leaning lightly on a stack of papers on the desk. The old man's eyes twinkled from deep inside their wrinkled pockets, then blinked away smoke rising from the cigar. Ngan let a breath escape from his nose in a futile attempt to dispel the stench of the burning tobacco.

"He showed you some kindness?" Ngan asked feebly.

Lieberman smiled, showing yellow teeth and a sincere jocularity. "He and his friends freed me and the other Jews from Buchenwald. Is that 'some kindness'? I think it was."

Lieberman motioned to a chair, the seat stacked with books, and moved on stiff legs to a wooden desk chair.

"He sent you a picture of himself?" Ngan asked as he crossed to the chair and began to stack the books gently on the floor.

"His mother sent that to me," Lieberman said, then grunted as he sat heavily in the chair, "a few weeks after Thomas Green killed himself."

Ngan stopped, a book—*The Rise and Fall of the Third Reich*—in his hands. He looked at Lieberman, who offered a reassuring smile.

"There are things, I think," Lieberman said, "that once you see, you cannot un-see. Young Thomas Green was a hero, but the villains were worse than he thought they would be. They showed him things he was too good, too innocent to live with."

"You keep his picture then," Ngan offered as he sat, "to remind you why you do what you do."

Lieberman laughed, expelling a puff of cigar smoke into the cramped room. "I keep his picture," he said, "to remind others. I lived for three years in Buchenwald. That is not something you forget, Ngan. The work I do is fuelled by that today as it was fifty-six years ago."

Ngan nodded and returned the rabbi's smile.

"It is always good to see you, my friend," Lieberman said, leaning back in his chair, his round pot belly straining the buttons of his plain white shirt, his tie already loosened, "but I don't think you came all the way from Washington, D.C., to talk about Thomas Green, hmm?"

"I've come as far as Schiller Park, Ira," Ngan said. "They've moved me to Chicago."

Lieberman's face brightened. "Good news, this, yes?" he said. "This just happened?"

"I'm sorry to say I've been here for more than five months," Ngan admitted.

"And it takes you this long to come visit your old friend, Ira Lieberman?" the rabbi said, lifting one eyebrow in mock disapproval. "Such a shame."

Ngan smiled and said, "There were . . . unusual circumstances that required my attention, and the setting up of new offices."

"Unusual circumstances," Lieberman said around his cigar. "You and your unusual circumstances."

"There are always unusual circumstances, Ira," Ngan said. "It is such that brings me here today, I'm afraid."

Lieberman nodded and said, "I will be of whatever help I can, of course, but one day you should come see me just to talk. I do value your insights."

"And I yours, Ira," Ngan said with all sincerity.

Ira Lieberman's office was in the basement of a synagogue in the Chicago suburb of Skokie, Illinois. Few of the people who came to the synagogue even knew the office was down there. Lieberman didn't preside over any of the rituals that went on above him. He tended files mostly, and he held onto and disseminated information as necessary. Lieberman's work, like Lieberman himself, was growing old. Every year that passed made more and more of it obsolete. How long would it be before the last Nazi war criminal, the last war veteran, the last camp survivor was dead, claimed not by the bullet or the gas chamber or the gallows but by time itself?

"You have a name?" Lieberman asked.

"Hans Reinhold Erwählen," Ngan said in a clear voice. He wasn't surprised by the reaction the name elicited in Lieberman.

The rabbi's face turned pale, and the twinkle disappeared from his eyes. "Erwählen," he said. He took the cigar from his mouth and, hand still shaking, found an ashtray resting off kilter on a stack of spiral notebooks. He tapped ashes off the tip of his cigar and looked at Ngan. "This is a name I was happy not to have heard in a good many years."

"You know of him, then?" Ngan asked, unnecessarily.

Lieberman put the cigar back in his mouth and smiled at Ngan. The twinkle came back to his eyes and Ngan found himself sighing in relief.

"Hans Reinhold Erwählen," Lieberman said, "was a close friend and confidante of Adolf Hitler's—from the early days, mind you, before the burning of the Reichstag, before the war. He was a dangerous man, an ideologue. He actually believed all of it, was perhaps the architect for much of what became the Third Reich. He held this position and that with the army, the Gestapo, the Nazi Party. Hitler moved him around a lot, or he moved himself. There's reason to believe he was— Ah, I see."

Lieberman took a long draw from his cigar and coughed just a little as he exhaled the smoke. Ngan tipped his head to one side, waiting for Lieberman to finish. The rabbi stood and crossed to a row of four metal filing cabinets, each a different color, a different size, from the last. He opened the top drawer in the second cabinet and fished around in it as he said, "I can see why you would be interested in this one."

Ngan waited patiently as Lieberman lifted a plain manila folder from the cabinet and opened it like a book. He fumbled in his pocket and produced a pair of reading glasses, which he balanced carefully on the tip of his nose. He shifted the folder forward then back until it was obvious that whatever was written there was finally in focus.

" 'The Jewish scourge has bewitched this continent for centuries.' Erwählen himself wrote this in a Nazi newspaper in July of 1935. 'These wizards can be defeated with bullets, but it will take a sorcery of our own to put an end to the whole of them.' It might be the first time someone said, in so many words, that the goal of the Nazi Party ought to be the extermination of the Jewish people."

"By the use of sorcery?" Ngan said.

Lieberman looked up and regarded his friend with a devilish smile. "Hitler himself was obsessed with that sort of thing . . . among his many obsessions. You saw *Raiders of the Lost Ark*, yes?" He winked at Ngan and chuckled, then sat down again.

Ngan was not sure what *Raiders of the Lost Ark* was, but he smiled anyway.

"Hitler was a maniac in many ways, I think," Lieberman continued. "He pressed for research into things like the atomic bomb, the jet plane—which he built, by the way—missiles—which he also built—but also this magical thing, that old ritual, the other silly occult something. He had dreams of psychic assassins. He actually sent agents out—and this at the height of the war, mind you—in search of the Holy Grail. The Holy Grail . . . !"

Ngan smiled, wondering if maybe he knew more about Hitler's examinations into the occult and how successful he actually was than even Lieberman could guess. Ira Lieberman wasn't generally concerned with Hitler's failed attempts to retrieve religious and occult relics. There were very real, very living men who had taken scalpels and Lugers to six million Jews—men who were living in Argentina, Chile, Uruguay, or Cleveland. It was these people Ira Lieberman was concerned with, and Ngan, like any reasonable, compassionate person, was glad that someone like Ira Lieberman was looking for people like that. The Holy Grail would take care of itself.

"Erwählen wrote quite a bit about the necessity for research into the occult," Lieberman said. "He wrote even more on the superiority of the Aryan race and the evil represented by the Jews. He was dangerous not so much for what he did—I honestly haven't been able to find out much about what he actually did—but for what he believed. He believed, this one, very deeply, in this mad ideology. He wrote, he gave speeches, he served on committees, but I don't think he ever fired a shot in the war. He wasn't in any of the camps, at least not for very long. He was as consumed with hate as any Nazi—more so, perhaps, than the many opportunists who gravitated to the party when the winds of change began to blow in Hitler's favor."

Ngan nodded and said, "You never found him?"

Lieberman's face froze, his eyes stuck on Ngan's. Ngan was instantly embarrassed, his face flushed, and he tried hard to think of some appropriate apology, though he wasn't sure if he'd insulted the man or not.

"We never looked," Lieberman said at last. "After the war he disappeared, probably to South America. I have files from Israel that detail a cursory examination into his post-war whereabouts, but nothing conclusive was ever reported. All the leads to Erwählen tended to reveal paths to other Nazis—real war criminals responsible for torture, murder, the Final Solution—but never to Erwählen himself. Cooperation with other governments, especially Washington, in regards to this man was . . . limited."

"Limited?" Ngan asked.

Lieberman knocked ashes off his cigar again and smiled, then winked in a manner some might mistake as condescending, but not Ngan.

"The American military intelligence establishment was very interested in certain high ranking German operatives after the war. The Nazis had been fighting the Russians for some time, after all, and when the war was over and Russia became the new enemy, these people had use, yes?"

"I've heard that," Ngan said. "It is true?"

Lieberman shrugged and said, "They'll never say they did, but they did. And when they did, they set the same sort of false trails that surround Erwählen."

"So Erwählen started working for the American government after the war?"

Lieberman shrugged again and took another deep drag from his cigar. Ngan wondered how the man could keep from gagging on the awful smoke.

"I don't see why, honestly," he said. "Like I said, Erwählen was an ideologue—a sort of propaganda tool in some ways—but he wasn't a decision maker. His importance to the German war effort was minimal at best, and he wasn't involved in their intelligence apparatus. I honestly don't see what use he would have been to the Americans. Of course, he was no rocket scientist."

"So he just disappeared?"

"It was the end of the war," Lieberman said. "Europe was in chaos. You'd be surprised how easy it was to get out, to get to South America, or South Africa, or wherever you needed to go. Many of them just blended back into German society under assumed names. Germans weren't as quick to turn Nazi war criminals in to the Americans or especially to the Russians, as they were to give up their Jewish neighbors to the Nazis."

"So he could be anywhere," Ngan said.

Lieberman laughed and shook his head. He slid a photograph out of the file folder and handed it to Ngan. It showed a man in a simple black suit, a Nazi pin prominent on his lapel, standing next to Adolf Hitler on the famous balcony of the Eagle's Nest. In the bottom right-hand corner of the photograph was the year: 1944. The man next to Hitler was as old then as Ira Lieberman was now.

"He'd have been a hundred and thirty-three years old last month," Lieberman said, spreading his hands in dismissal.

chapter two

She took a cab because it would make sense for her to arrive in one.

Jeane Meara had been undercover before, but that had been a long time ago and then not for very long. She posed as a fertilizer salesperson in hopes that a certain KKK splinter group might want to build a bomb, but the suspected bombers were arrested for assault after a bar brawl before they could buy the bomb ingredients from ace fertilizer saleswoman Charlene Tisdale. A search warrant turned up child pornography in the house they shared, and that was it. Into the tender care of the Tennessee prison system they went head first. Jeane had never actually been in the same room with any of them, though in two weeks undercover she managed to sell more fertilizer than any of the real salesmen at the farm supply company in Rutherford County.

Jeane was determined to be rather less successful in that regard during this undercover turn.

The cab turned onto Fullerton Avenue from the

inbound Kennedy Expressway and went only two blocks east before coming to a complete stop. Traffic down Fullerton was unpredictable at best, and she opened her mouth to chastise the driver for his choice of routes, but she thought twice and stopped herself. It was the most direct route, and if traffic was bad here, it was likely bad everywhere. She was running early, and, maybe most of all, she still needed a little time to psyche herself up.

It was dark, but the street was well lit and the SUV behind them was doing a good job of lighting the back seat of the cab. Jeane opened the purse she'd bought earlier that day, after getting the word that the mark had finally called. There was a small compact there, which she took out and opened. She was sure her makeup was all right, though she wasn't used to wearing so much. She wanted to check it one more time, though, just as an excuse to look herself in the eyes again and remind herself that she knew what she was doing.

She tilted the little mirror up, and her left eye came into sharp, close focus. She blinked at herself and muttered, "I'm too old for this."

" 'Scuse, Miss?" the driver responded, startling Jeane. She fumbled with the compact and almost dropped it. "You say something?"

The driver's accent was unidentifiable—Middle Eastern, probably. His skin was dark and his hair black. He smelled strongly of Brut and tobacco.

"I'm sorry," Jeane said feebly. "Nothing. I was talking to myself."

"To yourself, huh?" the driver asked, apparently deciding she wanted to have a conversation. The cab moved forward half its length. "When I am alone, or when sometimes I am driving, I talk to God."

Jeane nodded and smiled. She looked into the little mirror again, hoping that if she appeared concerned with her makeup, the driver would stop talking to her.

"Do you pray?" the driver asked her, taking her off guard.

"I'm sorry?"

"Pray," he said again. "Do you talk to God?"

"I'm not, uh," she said, not comfortable with any aspect of the discussion. "I'm not really religious."

"Ah," the driver said as if he expected the answer. "Neither is God. He's just God."

Jeane didn't have the slightest idea what he meant by that. She turned her attention to the corner of her eye. She was sure that lines would appear spontaneously in the cab ride, but they hadn't. Jeane was thirty-nine years old and had the skin of a woman half her age. She smiled when she reminded herself that someone half her age would be considered a girl, a teenager.

"This is funny?" the driver asked, and she looked up, meeting his eyes in the rearview mirror. Jeane was relieved to see that the driver was amused himself. His eyes twinkled in the reflected light from the big vehicle still behind them.

"No, no," she said. "I'm sorry. My mind is wandering."

"You are thinking about the man you are going to meet tonight," the driver said with supreme self-confidence.

Jeane tipped her head to one side and smiled, then glanced away from the rearview mirror. She was oddly embarrassed that she wasn't actually thinking about the man she was meeting but was thinking about herself. It wasn't something she was prone to do, and she had never been too concerned about her age, but this was something someone younger should be doing. The mark would be expecting someone younger, whether he'd said "elegant" or not.

"How did you know I was meeting a man?" she asked the driver, as much because she was curious about what made him think that, as to take her mind off the fact that she was about to pose as a forty-year-old hooker.

"Oh," the driver said, still looking at her in the mirror as the cab pulled forward. The traffic was beginning to loosen up. "Oh, of course a beautiful woman like you is meeting a man."

Jeane smiled and looked to her right. The cab passed a children's hospital, and she suddenly felt guilty about smiling at a stranger's compliment after worrying that she was too old to pull off an undercover stint as a "classy, upscale kind of woman." That's exactly what he'd asked for. A classy, upscale kind of woman who would sleep with him for fifteen hundred dollars an hour.

She looked back at the rearview mirror and saw the driver's eyes again. The lust was evident in his dark stare, and Jeane's face flushed. She looked out the window again and saw a street sign that demanded quiet in a neighborhood of old brownstones that must have cost a million dollars each.

The SUV found a place to park on the street and pulled in. The back seat of the cab went dark, the driver turned his attention to the street, and Jeane closed the compact. She picked up her purse and dropped it in. A flash of reflected streetlight bounced off the gun in her purse, and she sighed, happy it was there, though if she had to use it, it would mean she'd failed completely.

She set her purse down on the seat next to her as the cab came to a stop at the intersection of Fullerton and Clark. The light was red, and a group of well-dressed young punks were crossing the street, obviously on their way to the club near the corner.

She looked down and smoothed the lap of her black dress and knew that if her face betrayed her age, her body certainly wouldn't. She was in excellent shape for all the right reasons—not vanity, but because she might need to use her body as a weapon. She had, and more than once.

She'd bought the dress that same day as well, at the same time she'd bought the purse and the shoes. The shoes were not at all comfortable and even less practical. She reminded herself again that she wasn't going to run around any more than she was going to shoot someone, but she didn't like the shoes anyway.

The cab crossed the intersection, and Jeane looked up. She met the driver's eyes again, and some of the lust had gone out of them, but he was attracted to her still. She'd seen that look before and had mostly discounted it.

"Not much further, Miss," the driver said.

She nodded and watched a couple of expensive high-rise apartment buildings go by. Ahead of them the crowded buildings of Chicago gave way to the open spaces of Lincoln Park. They turned right just before they got to the zoo, but Jeane could see the sign just ahead of them. She grabbed her purse again and sighed when she realized her palms had started to sweat. This wasn't the sort of thing she'd trained for, though since joining the Hoffmann Institute, most of what she'd been trained for didn't seem to apply anymore.

The cab came to a stop, and Jeane instinctively glanced at the meter. "Fourteen dollars, Miss," the driver said.

Jeane found a folded twenty dollar bill in her purse and handed it to the driver. "Keep it," she said, though the driver had made no move to reach for change.

She opened the door of the cab and the sound of the street flooded in on a wash of cool spring air. She stepped out, careful not to trip on the high heels. She straightened and took a step onto the sidewalk as she closed the cab door behind her. The cab didn't pull away immediately, and she looked back. The driver was looking at her, all pretense of trying to mask his attraction for her gone now. The look made her feel dirtier than she already felt, so she turned away quickly.

The cab pulled away slowly, and she could tell the driver was still looking at her.

The cab had brought her to the right place. Jeane looked up at the building, then glanced at her watch. She wasn't too early, so she drew her courage around her and went through the heavy glass door into the little lobby.

There was a doorman who looked up at her with bored, yellow eyes. His black skin was speckled with grey whiskers, and his teeth were startlingly white. He forced a smile and said, "Ma'am."

He was obviously waiting for her to say something, so she said, "Roger Fenton. I'm here to see Roger Fenton."

"Mr. Fenton is expecting you?" the doorman asked. His eyes flickered up and down her tight body, and Jeane felt herself cross her arms.

"Joyce Mannering," she said simply, using the name the escort service had told her Fenton wanted her to use. No one at the service knew why he liked that name.

The doorman smiled and picked up a phone from behind his little desk. He punched a number and waited patiently, offering Jeane a condescending smile.

"Mr. Fenton?" he said finally. "Yes, sir, Joyce Mannering. Thank you."

The doorman hung up the phone and nodded at a single elevator. "Press P, ma'am," he said.

Jeane mumbled a thank you and went to the elevator. The doors opened only a few seconds after she pushed the up button, and Jeane could feel the doorman's eyes on her the whole time. She stepped into the elevator and turned around. The doorman was looking at her, and it took his eyes a painfully long time to move up to meet hers. The elevator doors closed just as they made eye contact.

"Too old, my ass," she said when she was alone.

She pushed the button marked "P." The highest number below it was twenty-six. So Fenton lived in the penthouse. A penthouse on Lake Shore Drive. He could definitely afford the fifteen hundred dollars an hour.

The ride up the elevator gave her the last few minutes she needed to calm and gather herself. She sighed once, deeply, when the light above the door showed a blocky P. When the elevator doors opened, she was ready.

She stepped out onto a thick, freshly vacuumed carpet. A set of six-panel double doors with shiny brass hardware stood right before her. She turned as the elevator doors closed behind her, and she couldn't help feeling confined, even abandoned, knowing the elevator was already sinking out of reach.

To her left a richly framed mirror reflected a well-lighted picture of herself. She was beautiful enough to get what she needed from Fenton. The dress was working for her, and if all else failed, she felt confident enough that she could kick the man's ass. Still smiling from that thought, she pushed the little glowing button at the side of the double doors.

She could hear a faint buzz from inside and expected to hear a lock being drawn back, but the door just opened.

Fenton didn't lock his door. He opened it wide in the manner of someone who knew the person who had rang, though of course he didn't.

Roger Fenton was almost exactly average height, and his grey hair was well groomed. He was wearing a suit, which seemed somehow odd to Jeane, who'd fully expected him to answer the door in the nude, in drag, in leather—anything. The suit was tailored for him and looked it. His tie was a solid maroon color Ronald Reagan might have worn. He wore wire-rimmed glasses over large, deep brown eyes.

He smiled, revealing teeth only a bit less white than his doorman's.

"Joyce Mannering?" he asked, obviously knowing the answer.

Jeane smiled, let her eyes close halfway, and nodded.

"Please," he said, "come in."

chapter THR3E

Fenton was what Jeane liked to think of as a Post Industrial Gentleman. He was courteous and polite and refined in a gruff, American way. He moved quickly, but in a determined fashion. He was comfortable in his own home, but barely. He moved from room to room like a teenager moved through a mall—knowing full well where everything was, but aware that it was all put there by someone else.

His decorator might have used the term Post Industrial Gentleman as well. The place was too full of furniture that was too heavy for Jeane's more contemporary tastes. The furniture was all wood, varnished to a high gloss. Some of the pieces looked like antiques, but they were more likely new pieces designed to look like antiques.

The apartment was clean—professionally clean—and there was none of the mundane evidence of the place being really lived in. There was no clutter. There were no magazines or mail laying around. There were no television remotes balanced on the arms of chairs, no half-finished projects or empty glasses. When Jeane followed him into the surprisingly enormous living room, she saw that their shoes made footprints in the bone-white carpet as if it had been vacuumed every time someone walked across it.

There was no TV or stereo in the living room, no computer or any other sign of technology. There was a cabinet that might have been made two hundred years ago in Virginia but was more likely only a couple years old. Jeane guessed the TV was hidden in there. The penthouse was big enough that Fenton likely had an office here, so that's where the computer would be, a fax machine maybe, certainly a telephone.

One wall was dominated by French windows and double French doors that opened onto a narrow terrace. Beyond was the darkness of Lake Michigan at night.

Jeane kept her hand on the little purse and managed to remember to walk in what she hoped was an alluring fashion. The rug was thick, and the heels made her footing treacherous at best. She compensated by standing in one place.

Fenton stopped, realizing she wasn't following anymore. "We'll need to get some business out of the way, then," he said with a smirk.

It took Jeane a second to process what he was talking about, then she smiled and said, "That's okay. You have an account at the service, and they told me you understood the, uh . . . pay structure."

Fenton laughed. He had a pleasant laugh. He came closer to her, and she fought back the impulse to shrink away. He was handsome and obviously successful, smart and educated, but Jeane couldn't imagine having to sleep with the man. She knew too much about him already, and the sight of him left a bad taste in her mouth.

"We should start with a drink," he said.

He looked at her, waiting for her to say something. She could smell alcohol—not a lot, but it was there—on his breath. He hadn't had enough to dull his eyes or his senses. Maybe just one or two after a long day at work.

"Wine?" she said quickly, knowing she could fake her way through a glass of wine without getting drunk.

Fenton smiled and turned, crossing the room casually—he was at home after all—to a small bar set with sparkling clean glasses and an array of crystal decanters. "Red or white?" he asked along the way.

"White," she said, though she preferred red. For some reason she felt that if she'd asked for red it would have revealed too much of herself to him. She was in character, and her character drank white.

She scanned the living room, taking in details quickly: the three other exits, the white furniture, all leather, the coffee table with nothing on it, and the wall of bookshelves full of books both old and new.

"I have a reasonable Chardonnay," he said, and she noticed just the trace of an accent that might have been New York or Philadelphia, but a long time ago. "If that's all right."

"That's fine," she said, still not moving, "thank you."

Fenton walked behind the little bar and bent to retrieve the bottle. He placed it gingerly on the top of the bar and reached down again. He was looking somewhere under the bar when he said, "It's not chilled, I'm afraid."

Jeane shrugged, not realizing that he couldn't see the gesture. He looked up, and she had to shrug again. She smiled and knew it looked sincere because in a way it was. She couldn't help being amused that he seemed genuinely worried that a hooker enjoy her wine.

He returned her smile and said, amiably enough, "You can come in. I don't bite. I'm sure they told you about me at the service."

They had. They'd told her that his tastes tended toward the mundane. He insisted on white women with certain features. He liked women with large breasts and athletic bodies. He like certain facial features, blue eyes mostly, but he was flexible on that. None of the girls who'd gone with him reported anything violent or kinky. It was all very ordinary.

Jeane nodded and said, "The girls all said you were a gentleman."

This made him smile. He found what he was looking for under the bar—a corkscrew—and started to peel the lead off the bottle of wine. "The girls," he said quietly.

He started to uncork the wine, and Jeane ventured a few steps into the room. She stopped next to a long, white leather sofa.

Fenton nodded at the sofa and said, "Sit, please."

She sat, crossing her legs and making a point of not smoothing down her skirt. She figured she should show him some thigh to keep the illusion intact.

The cork came out of the wine bottle, and Fenton poured three fingers into a gleaming crystal glass.

"You look like someone," he said, putting down the bottle of wine and taking up a cocktail glass. He opened a leather-covered ice bucket and broke up some ice with polished silver tongs. "Marilyn Monroe, I think."

Jeane smiled. She'd heard that before but had always ignored it. Most of the men who'd said that had been the type who talked to her breasts, not her face. She assumed, and still did, that the comparison stopped there.

Fenton poured a good three shots of a golden-colored liquor into the glass, then dropped a few ice cubes into it. A few seconds later, Jeane could smell the whiskey in the air. He put one hand on the bar and leaned on it heavily. He took up his drink in his other hand and took a long sip, looking at her with eyes that were coldly appraising. Jeane had seen men look at cars that way.

"You've never had anyone notice the resemblance?" he asked.

She shrugged. "Men see what they want to see," she said, trying to make it sound chatty and succeeding well enough. "I've been told I look like Cheryl Ladd."

Fenton's brow wrinkled and he said, "No, no, definitely Marilyn." He set his drink down and came out from behind the bar, going to the bookcases. He went right for the book he was

in fluid silence

looking for and pulled off a tan, oversized hardcover. From where she was sitting she couldn't see what was written on the spine.

Fenton flipped through the book, looking for something in it as he came across the room to her. He sat down in a chair across from her, and Jeane suppressed a sigh of relief that he hadn't sat next to her. He found the page he was looking for and nodded. He set the book down on the polished coffee table and turned it around so she could see the photograph there.

On the left-hand page were two columns of text. On the right-hand page was a full-color photograph of Marilyn Monroe. Jeane had never seen this picture. She wasn't too interested in movie stars.

"Her hair is different, of course," Fenton said, "but there's a— Jesus, I forgot your wine." He stood up and went quickly to the bar as Jeane looked at the photograph.

Marilyn Monroe was standing on a beach, wrapped in a green towel. She might have been naked underneath. She was holding the towel closed with her left hand and holding a glass of wine—white wine—to her lips with her right hand. She was smiling and Jeane had to admit her own smile was similar. She had the same inward slope to her teeth she always thought she should have had fixed as a kid. Marilyn's nose was pointed in a way similar to Jeane's as well. It was obviously windy the day the photograph was taken, and Marilyn's bleach-blonde hair was disheveled and dirty. Her skin, like Jeane's, was freckled, but not too badly.

"I saw a movie," Fenton said, placing the wineglass on the table next to the book, "where there's a group of call girls who've all had plastic surgery to make them look like movie stars."

Jeane flushed and didn't want to look up at him. She looked back at the photograph in the book and noticed the simple caption: just the year, 1962.

"Don't get me wrong, of course," Fenton said. "I'm sure that's not the case—you don't look *that* much like her, but . . . Anyway, I meant it as a compliment."

"You don't have to—"

"I know," he said, cutting her off.

She looked up at him, and he took another long sip, pursing his lips. The look in his eyes changed, and all of a sudden Jeane really felt like a whore.

He smiled, and Jeane couldn't help thinking he knew he'd demeaned her in a very real, though very subtle way, and he was enjoying it.

"Have you been doing this for a long time?" he asked. "You aren't young—don't get me wrong, you're lovely and I enjoy mature, sophisticated, experienced women, but . . ."

"Six years," she said, making this part up as she went along, "give or take. I was a"—she almost said cop—"hairdresser for a while, but I got a divorce. He got everything, and there wasn't much, so after a while I got sick of living paycheck to paycheck."

Fenton nodded, obviously only pretending to understand, and drank some more.

"What about you?" she asked, leaning back, letting her dress ride another half an inch up her thigh. "What do you do?"

"That makeup you're wearing," he said. "What is it?"

Jeane knew to say, "Natura."

Fenton nodded and said, "I'm the chief operating officer of Natura Industries."

Jeane feigned being impressed. "That seems like kind of an oxymoron," she said.

Fenton's brow wrinkled again, and he was just about to say something when he swallowed the rest of the whiskey in one gulp.

Jeane felt uncomfortable in the silence. She knew she had to keep him talking. "I mean," she said, "Natura makes you think 'natural,' but 'industries,' well . . ."

He smiled and nodded. "You don't want to know what that really is you're putting on you face," he told her with a wink.

He put his empty glass on the coffee table, and she reached for it, brushing the rough skin of his fingers with hers. She picked up the glass and stood. Her dress clung to her legs a little and again she made no move to fix it.

"Can I get you another one?" she asked, letting her eyes settle on his.

"Thank you," he said.

She went to the bar walking carefully on her tall heels. She knew he was watching her walk. She pulled the stopper from the decanter of whiskey and poured a little more than he had poured for himself over the melting ice.

"Six years," he said. "That must be a lot of men."

She didn't turn around. Jeane put the stopper back in the whiskey decanter and took the top off the ice bucket.

"If you don't want to talk about it . . ." he said. "The other girls probably told you I would bring it up. I like to hear about . . . it's part of . . . what I want."

She dropped two ice cubes into the nearly full glass of whiskey and turned, a smile fixed on her face.

"It's okay," she said softly, not moving.

"You've been with all sorts of men," he said, looking at her body. "Men like me?"

"Sometimes."

"Rich men?"

"Sometimes."

"You don't know, though," he said, finally looking at her face, "before you get to their houses or hotel rooms, what they look like?"

She crossed to the chair and held the drink out to him. He didn't take it at first.

"Lean over and hand it to me," he said, his voice suddenly husky and threatening.

Jeane was sure she was smiling as she leaned forward at the waist. She handed the glass to Fenton and he took a long, unashamed look down the neck of her dress at her black lace bra. "No," she said, "It's not up to me."

He looked at her eyes, and she stood up. "You've had sex with niggers," he said.

Jeane had expected to hear something like that. Both Ngan

and the woman at the service had prepared her for it, but still she could feel her face turn red.

"Not if I can help it," she said, knowing it was what he'd want to hear.

chapter
four

Nothing about the experience was natural. Nothing about it made any sense in any logical framework.

It was a purely American experience, hurling through the air in a titanium tube that weighed 255,000 pounds. Regardless of the very real and obviously effective physics of lift and aerodynamics, it was simply counterintuitive. Ngan, who lived on a level almost everyone in the western world would consider impossible, fictional, even silly, recognized the odd reversal, but he couldn't seem to do anything about it.

The flight attendant was finishing her safety presentation, an act that made Ngan feel only less secure. If the airplane was safe to travel on, why was the mental preparation for a crash so important to the passengers?

". . . and, of course, your seat bottom will serve as a flotation device in the event of a water landing," the falsely pleasant woman concluded, ". . . however unlikely that might be between Chicago and Washington, D.C."

A few of the people in the cabin chuckled at this wholly inappropriate joke. Ngan was not one of them. Anyone with the slightest sense knew that a "water landing" was another way of saying "crash," and a floating seat cushion might best serve to make one's corpse easier to pull out of the water with a hook. The image made Ngan wish for a burial at sea. Add to that the fact that these supposed members of the crew apparently had no idea that they would, in fact, be flying over at least one of the Great Lakes, and Ngan felt somewhat less than reassured.

"Our flight time today will be one hour and fifty-three minutes," the flight attendant added. "Please sit back and enjoy your flight."

The plane turned onto the runway and the captain's voice came onto the overhead speakers. "Flight attendants, prepare for takeoff," he said. His voice was bored and that was only a little reassuring.

Ngan pulled his feet back in toward the edge of his seat and he felt the shoulder strap of his satchel catch on his left ankle. He took a deep breath, noting how it shook as he drew it in. He could feel his heart beating, and his palms were wet.

The plane sat at the end of the runway for what seemed like hours, but it was less than three minutes.

Ngan reminded himself that the plane was either going to fly safely to Washington or it was going to crash. If it crashed, he would have a few seconds, perhaps a minute, to gather himself, then he'd just be gone. His life, and a hundred and ninety or so other lives, would end. He could do nothing to affect the outcome, so there was no reason to worry about it.

That's what his teachers would have told him, and Ngan knew they'd have been right, but he couldn't just decide to stop worrying. This is what western psychologists call a "phobia."

The plane began to move, and it accelerated fast enough to push Ngan back into the rough, odd-smelling seat. He looked across the aisle at another passenger, a woman in an expensive suit. She was contentedly reading a paperback novel—one of the lawyer-in-danger variety that Michael and Jeane occasionally talked about. She was completely oblivious to the experience of flying.

Ngan looked back out the window as the plane came up off the runway. There was a moment when he felt completely certain that the plane would not make it off the ground, but of course it did. The ground fell away, and the airport stretched out below him. He saw planes parked outside of hangars, trucks scurrying around warehouses, then a street, a lot full of rental cars that looked tiny and grew smaller in pools of light from the lamps on poles that didn't look so tall now. Ngan knew he wasn't breathing, but he didn't bother trying to make himself start. He looked back at the woman with her face buried in the book. She was still reading, as if nothing at all out of the ordinary was afoot.

He looked back out the window. They were passing over high-rise office buildings. Ngan could see the expressway system like arteries in an open chest. There was a low rumbling noise, the sound of hydraulics and a thump. Ngan knew it was the landing gear retracting, but the blood drained from his head anyway.

The woman was still reading. Ngan found it impossible to believe.

He didn't find the experience of air travel at all pleasant, but it was at the very least remarkable. This woman, and so many others on the plane, took this extraordinary experience for granted. What could affect this woman? Hurling through the stratosphere—tedious. What would make her stop and look in awe like she should? It was awesome what they were doing, what people were capable of, all in the name of convenience.

A whirring sound came from the wings, and Ngan felt the plane drop. Again, the blood drained from his head, and he looked out the window, sure he would see the ground rushing madly up at them, but it wasn't. They weren't dropping, he reminded himself, they were just rising more slowly now.

A chime sounded, and Ngan jumped. This made him both amused and disappointed with himself. The chime meant they'd reached fifteen hundred feet. Ngan closed his eyes and took a deep breath. He held the breath for a three-count, then exhaled, again silently counting to three. He breathed in on a three-count, held it for three, then exhaled for three, repeating the sequence several times before being startled when the plane seemed to roll over a bump. The luggage compartment above him rattled, and Ngan went back to his breathing.

He had almost relaxed when another chime sounded. It had the same sound as a warning in a car. It had that unmistakable "pay attention" sound that Ngan could not possibly ignore. The blood rushed out of his head again but not as quickly and not as completely. They were at ten thousand feet now.

Ngan looked out the window and realized they must have passed through clouds when he'd had his eyes closed. Below them was a lumpy carpet of dark grey. The sky above and straight out was black and speckled with stars. The quarter moon was casting a pale shadow over the clouds, and the whole thing was simply surreal. Ngan had no sense of where he was, and that, maybe more than anything, unnerved him. Flying at night was like being in an elevator for two hours.

They began serving drinks, and the passengers who weren't already oblivious to their surroundings started to relax. Ngan was going to be on edge the whole way, but he forced himself to stop clutching the cold plastic armrest. He'd had a death grip on it the whole time, even during his breathing exercises. He let go and saw that it had made a red impression on his palm.

Deciding he would try to work, though he'd never been able to think too clearly while flying, Ngan bent to open his satchel. He fumbled around, trying to ignore his shaking hands, and found a pamphlet printed on thick, glossy paper. He pulled the pamphlet out, and a fear of a different kind washed over him.

"Something to drink, sir?" a woman's voice thundered over the background noise, startling Ngan yet again. He was growing tired of being startled.

He set a smile on his face and shook his head. The flight attendant moved on to the next passenger with total apathy. Ngan thought about changing his mind and asking her for a cup

in fluid silence

of tea, but he stopped himself. She had moved on, and it would surely be an inconvenience for her to come back.

Instead, he turned his attention to the pamphlet.

It was colorful, very professionally designed and printed. On the front was a clear photograph of a huge, rustic barn. Next to it was a silo and an American-style windmill. Trees scattered the grounds around the barn and were covered in light green leaves that made it obvious that the photograph had been taken in the spring. At the top, in clean but ornate script were the words Camp Clarity.

Clarity.

The word had several meanings, and Ngan knew what the retreat's organizers thought they meant when they used that word. Ngan had achieved brief flashes of real clarity in his life, and he couldn't imagine this place providing anything like that experience to anyone.

Ngan shifted in his cramped seat and opened the pamphlet. The plane shook as if in response. Ngan glanced out the window and saw the same uniform clouds below, and the same sprinkle of stars above. The noise was a dull throb that Ngan knew he'd be hearing for hours after they finally landed. He looked down at the pamphlet and squinted, trying to read the tight text there.

He reached up and turned on the little reading lamp above his head. Fake yellow light washed over him like muddy water, and he could see better but not well enough. He squinted at the text again and read the headline: *Motivational Excellence in an Exclusive Setting*.

Exclusive, indeed. The retreat was limited to white people, though the pamphlet never said that in so many words.

Ngan read the sparse text again, to himself, of course.

Welcome to Camp Clarity.

Below that headline was a photograph of the sun setting over rolling hills. Skeletal trees were black, silhouetted against the pink and orange sky. The ground was covered in freshly fallen snow. A thin, winding road disappeared into the distance, lined on both sides by the silhouetted trees. At the edge of the road was a tasteful sign that, in the same script as on the front of the pamphlet, read *Camp Clarity* and *By Invitation Only*.

The text below the photograph read:

Eight hundred acres in the peaceful rural setting of Southern Illinois is the new permanent site of our unique executive training program. Motivation and focus are the keys here, and only those professionals who have already achieved a measure of success in their chosen fields are invited to join us. At Camp Clarity, we don't make winners out of losers, we turn winners into masters.

Masters, Ngan thought. He closed his eyes, rubbed them lightly, then looked back at the pamphlet.

If you're reading this, it means you've been identified as the sort of person who is ready to achieve the highest level of personal and professional excellence.

As our guest you'll enjoy all the amenities of an all-inclusive resort hotel. Our program is demanding, both mentally and physically, but when your busy day draws to an end, you'll enjoy our first class, all-suite accommodations, heated pool, and full-service spa. Our team of world-class chefs creates cuisine that any five-star restaurant would be delighted to provide their customers.

Ngan sighed, imagining the scene around Camp Clarity's pool. White skin turning red while billionaires achieved personal and professional mastery. Regardless of the Institute's other suspicions, that alone would make Camp Clarity worth closing down.

Under the headline *Goals*, Ngan found the most telling and most chilling presentation.

You're a successful person. You've made money. You've tasted success and everything it has to offer. Or have you?

At Camp Clarity we provide you with the tools necessary to recognize the insignificance of the success you've already achieved. A bold claim? Do we mean to say that your success has been empty, that you should give it all away?

The answer the pamphlet provided was a ham-handed, uppercase NO! set in bold type.

The success you've already achieved will get you to Camp Clarity. What you learn at Camp Clarity will bring you higher than you've ever imagined. We can let you into the world of your dreams.

And then the most cryptic of all, a line that made the small hairs on the back of Ngan's neck stand up:

Ask the man who gave you this pamphlet.

Ngan sighed again and avoided looking out the window. He let his eyes wander over the edge of the tray table still hooked into the back of the seat in front of him. The man next to him fidgeted, his eyes closed as if he were trying to go to sleep. Another man was coming down the aisle of the plane, walking on uneasy legs in the light turbulence that Ngan was trying so hard to ignore.

The man was wearing a dark grey suit, well tailored, that looked like silk. His white hair was carefully combed back over his pale scalp. Ngan noticed his blue eyes catching the dim yellow cabin light. Something about the man, who had emerged from the first-class cabin trying not to look at any of the coach passengers, made Ngan look down at the pamphlet again.

He turned it over and looked at the photograph on the back. A white man in his early seventies smiled back, and Ngan flinched away from the image he'd looked at a hundred times.

Holding the pamphlet in his left hand, Ngan reached down for his bag with his right hand. The satchel had shifted again, and he had trouble opening the flap with it under the seat in front of him. He bent down farther, trying to get his right hand under the seat, so he grabbed the top of the seat with his left hand, crinkling the pamphlet a little.

"Oh," a strange voice said, "I see you know Camp—"

The man stopped talking the second Ngan looked up at him, sitting back in his seat empty-handed.

The man in the aisle was already pale, but what little color there might have been there drained when he met Ngan's eyes. The man looked *at* rather than *in* Ngan's eyes, and he drew in a sharp little breath that was almost a gasp.

The stranger in the seat next to Ngan didn't seem to notice the exchange and certainly wouldn't have worried about it if he had. He continued trying to fall asleep.

The plane bucked, and Ngan reached out with his right hand to steady himself. He grabbed the seat in front of him, and the turbulence passed. The man in the aisle looked away, grabbing the seats near him, though he seemed in no danger of falling.

"I beg—" the man in the aisle started to say at the exact same time Ngan said, "I'm sorry, I—"

Ngan smiled and nodded for the man to continue. The crystal blue eyes finally fixed on Ngan's, for just a second, and a look of unmistakable anger creased the man's brow. He turned away from Ngan, back to the front of the plane, back the way he'd come.

"It's all right, I . . ." Ngan said, but the man walked quickly away.

More turbulence shook the plane, rattling the luggage compartments and making Ngan grab the seat in front of him again. The strange man slid down the precise center of the aisle without so much as tapping the top of any of the seats he passed. Without a look back he disappeared into the first-class cabin.

Ngan was worried by the encounter. The strange man had obviously heard of Camp Clarity. There had been the unmistakable air of brotherhood and recognition in the man's voice. He must have stayed there and attended their seminars and exercises.

Realizing that the man couldn't do anything to him on a plane at thirty thousand feet with a hundred and ninety witnesses made Ngan feel safer than he'd ever felt on an airplane.

Remembering what he'd been doing when the man interrupted him, Ngan bent down again. He'd managed to open the flap before, and he found the file folder inside easily enough.

He leaned back, checking both sides for the man in the aisle, who was nowhere to be seen. The man might be confused, even embarrassed. Ngan found it safe enough to assume the man would limit his wanderings to the first-class lavatories for the rest of the flight.

Ngan opened the folder and took out a copy of the photograph of Hans Reinhold Erwählen and Hitler. As he'd done at least a dozen times in the last day or so, Ngan held the pamphlet

in fluid silence

over the old photograph and compared Erwählen's circa 1940s face with the little photograph on the back of the Camp Clarity pamphlet.

Under the picture in the pamphlet was the caption: *Hans Erwählen, Founder.*

Ngan looked from the pamphlet to the photograph and back again, then closed his eyes and sighed.

It was the same man.

The same man who hadn't aged a day in sixty years.

Jeane or Michael would have offered some explanation, to be sure. Michael, in fact, had offered one just before he'd been sent by the Hoffmann Institute to Camp Clarity three weeks before. Michael thought the Camp Clarity Erwählen was the Nazi's son, and the resemblance, though striking, was mundane.

Lieberman's file made no mention that Erwählen might have had children. He was never married and was always discreet in his personal life.

Ngan looked at Erwählen's blue eyes in the Camp Clarity photograph, and his thoughts went again to Michael McCain.

When the order to investigate Camp Clarity came down from Dr. Nakami at the Hoffmann Institute, there was only one clear choice. Jeane was a woman, and though there was nothing that said women were strictly prohibited, she would stick out like a sore thumb at the very least. Ngan, of course, was not white so therefore not welcome at all. It had to be Michael.

Discreet inquiries were made, and after what must have been a thousand phone calls, McCain got in touch with Tom Casale. Casale was an acquaintance of McCain's from D.C. and had been told about Camp Clarity by an acquaintance of his own. Casale had attended one session at Camp Clarity and was of great help in getting McCain in. Casale didn't know anything about the Hoffmann Institute and had no idea that McCain had ulterior motives. A few more days and a few more phone calls, and McCain was sent an invitation to attend Camp Clarity.

Three weeks later, Ngan wished McCain didn't have so many acquaintances.

Ngan had to entertain the possibility, however implausible or unpleasant, that McCain was dead already. Ngan had no evidence that he was dead, but he was two weeks off schedule, and this sort of silence was unlike him. All attempts to contact Tom Casale had failed as well.

Michael McCain awoke with something licking his face.

The name Sparky leaped to his dull, half-asleep mind. That was his dog's name, wasn't it? But Sparky died twenty years ago.

McCain opened his eyes and bright light seared them, so he clamped them shut. The dog stopped licking him for a moment, startled probably, then started up again. He was licking McCain's bare chest now, moving down toward his stomach. He could feel a thick, warm, viscous liquid covering most of his body.

He tried to push the dog away, but he couldn't lift his arm. He'd never felt so tired. His head spun, but it was beginning to clear. He opened his eyes again. The light wasn't so bad now. He'd just been in complete darkness for a long time.

Walls came into focus, sheet metal over thick wooden cross beams. The sheet metal was fairly new, and the treated wood still had a greenish cast to it. He looked down at the dog, and his body convulsed all at once—not from any physical cause but from the shock of what he saw.

It wasn't a dog.

At first he thought it was a little child, but within the first second or so McCain could see that this was no child. It was barely human, if it was human at all.

It looked like a little man, old, wrinkled, skin turning brown, streaked with grey. A wide flat nose dominated its face, and its cheeks were pinched and drawn back. Its wide eyes were closed. It had no hair.

Its tongue was as wide and as long as a big dog's, and it was busily licking a thick, honeylike liquid off McCain's quivering, naked body. When McCain flinched away, the thing looked up and opened its eyes, revealing black pits that seemed to absorb light. McCain opened his mouth to scream, but no sound came out.

The thing reacted to the non-scream by fluffing wings McCain had mistaken for a grey leather coat. The wings were like the wings of a bat.

McCain brought one hand up, his arm responding now, if weakly, and the little creature scurried backward. It bumped into a steel barrel and tipped it over. A loud clang echoed in the big, mostly empty space, loud enough that the little man covered its ears with hands that were tipped by brown, prunelike fingers. The golden liquid dripped from its twisted, bloated lower lip.

"Is this . . ." McCain managed to almost bark, ". . . hell? Am I in hell?"

The little man, who must have been no more than a foot and a half tall, folded his wings and said, *"Ich verstehe Sie nicht."*

McCain knew what he said, not realizing that he wasn't supposed to be able to understand German. He never studied the language in school, never spent any time in Germany or around Germans. But the little man had said: I don't understand you.

McCain wanted to know where he was, so he said, *"Wo bin ich?"* though he still didn't remember ever learning to speak German.

The little man tipped his head at McCain, as if the question made no sense. McCain went over the words in his head and was sure he'd said it right.

He propped himself up on one hand and felt rough concrete under him. He was suddenly cold, and he drew his arms and legs into him. The strange liquid spread over him like thick oil.

"Who are you?" McCain asked the little man. *"Wie heissen Sie?"*

"Nichts," the little man said, his voice surprisingly deep.

"Nothing?" McCain asked. *"Sie haben keine Name?* You have no name?"

The little man took one small step closer to McCain, who shied away, scraping his rear on the concrete before he came to rest against a low stone wall behind him. The stone was as rough as the cement floor. McCain's body started to tremble, shivering violently.

"Ich heiße Nichts," the little man said.

"Your name," McCain translated through chattering teeth, "is Nichts."

The little man smiled, and McCain screamed, then screamed again, only this time louder.

chapter 5IVE

"Welsh," she said, "I think."

That made Fenton smile. Jeane sat back on the sofa and glanced again at the photograph of Marilyn Monroe in the book still sitting open on the coffee table in front of her. Fenton stood up, taking his drink with him, and began to pace the room, more preoccupied than nervous. "You think?" he asked.

Jeane shrugged and asked, "Does it matter?"

It was Fenton's turn to shrug, though he seemed uncomfortable with the gesture. "My great-grandparents crossed over from England in 1893. My great-grandfather was in the whaling business. On my mother's side it was my grandmother who came over first, as a student from France. She married my grandfather in Nantucket."

"So you're English and French," Jeane said.

"And you think you're Welsh."

Jeane didn't say anything, didn't take the bait. She told herself that it was because she didn't think a call girl would necessarily be honest about her background

49

with a client. In truth, though, she just didn't want Fenton to know anything about her.

It occurred to Jeane that those two things were the same.

"Is that bad?" she asked, somehow thinking of the question even after it passed her lips.

Fenton stopped pacing and looked down at her. Framed by the bookcases, in his tailored suit, he looked strangely academic. His face was passive. Jeane plastered a smile on her face to which he had no response.

"Of course that isn't bad," he said. "Christian?"

"Sorry?"

"Are you a Christian?" he asked, starting to pace again and taking a sip from his drink.

"Lutheran," she invented on the fly, "but I haven't been to church in a while."

Fenton shrugged that off and said, "I can imagine. That's not important."

"And you?" she asked, starting to believe that drawing him out would be easier than she or Ngan had thought.

"Me?" he said. "I was Catholic."

"Was?" Jeane asked. "I didn't think you could stop being a Catholic once you started."

This made Fenton laugh, and he seemed to relax. He came back to the chair across the coffee table from her and sat down, crossing his legs with a subdued flourish. He looked at her eyes, suddenly engaged by her in a way that made Jeane's skin crawl.

"A man can decide," he said, "what club he wants to belong to."

Jeane nodded and tilted her wineglass up to him in a sort of salute. She almost drank the last of it, then took only a small sip and held the glass at her chest. His eyes glanced down at it.

"Why did you ask me before," she said, her voice quiet, "if I ever . . . ?" Jeane almost panicked, realizing all at once she didn't know how to say—

"If you ever went to bed with a nigger?" he finished for her.

She let her eyes stay on his but managed to keep her face blank. She took a chance by saying, "I don't like that word."

Fenton smiled and said, "They call each other that."

"I know," she said, "but—"

"But I'm a white man," he said. "A successful white man, so I have to censor myself, is that it?"

"I didn't say that," Jeane said. She knew she should back off, and tried. "It's not up to me. I'm sorry. It's your house . . . your dime. You can say whatever you want."

Fenton nodded, agreeing with her and amused by her at the same time. The look sent a chill down Jeane's spine.

"White men are the last minority in America," Fenton said, his voice conversational though the sentence seemed somehow rehearsed. "I have money, but I'm constantly told how to spend it. I have influence, but I'm never permitted to exercise it. Anything I say and do is suspect, and I'm constantly being asked to apologize for the transgressions of other white men who were dead a hundred and fifty years before I was born."

Jeane just looked at him, hoping he would misconstrue the look of anger on her face for something more seductive. He winked at her, which didn't tell her anything.

"I don't expect you to be pure," he said, his voice cold with condescension, "in either body or soul."

"I don't get paid for purity," she said, trying to make it sound seductive.

Fenton seemed suddenly agitated. He stood, tapping the side of his glass nervously. "You're not a Jew, are you?" he asked abruptly. "You're not Jewish, or Muslim?"

Jeane laughed a little, and he looked at her sharply, so she stopped laughing and said, "I told you I'm a Lutheran."

He stared at her for a long second, then looked down at the floor, tapped his glass a few times, nodding. "It's important to me that you be . . . white. I have to . . . You need to be white."

Jeane didn't say anything. She didn't know what to say, in character or not.

"It's all right," he said.

Jeane tipped her head at him, not sure what he meant. He looked back at her, and the supreme self-confidence was back.

"You can be proud to be white," he said.

"Who said I wasn't?" she asked, speaking quickly so she could get it out before she had a chance to get rattled or offended.

He looked angry, but only for a second, before saying, "Good for you."

"You sound like you're trying to convert me," Jeane said, hoping to convey with her tone that she was hoping he was.

"I shouldn't have to," he said calmly. "More wine?"

Jeane all at once remembered that she was still holding the all-but-empty wineglass. She had to make a quick decision. She needed to stay sober, but why wouldn't a real call girl go ahead and have another glass of wine? What would keep him talking?

She looked at Fenton's glass and saw that it was empty. "Yes," she said, "thank you."

She reached out the glass to him, and he took it. Their fingers didn't touch. He knew he didn't have to seduce her.

"Don't you make cosmetics for black people?" she asked him as he crossed back to the bar.

Fenton didn't break his stride in the slightest when he said, "We sure do. It's a lucrative marketplace."

"So they're your customers, right?" Jeane asked, knowing she was prodding him now. "Their money's green, so who cares what color their skin is?"

Fenton poured her wine in silence. She knew he'd heard her, but it didn't seem as if he was thinking about her question. He knew the answer already—his answer. He popped the cork back in the wine bottle and took up the whiskey decanter. He looked up at her and said, "That ridiculous rock star, what's his name? The one who likes little boys?"

Jeane didn't say anything, though she knew who he was talking about.

"He has a skin condition that makes him appear Caucasian, but only in irregular blotches," he said. "Afrolux, Ebonese—our products for the 'African American' community—they all cause this condition sooner or later."

Jeane tipped her head at him again, and he smiled while pouring his drink. "You . . ."

in fluid silence

He laughed, and it was a broadly jovial sound. "We thought it would be funny. You see, we never really tested that stuff as much as the real products, the white products. No one really ever complained, or if they did it was some incredibly impotent exposé in *Ebony* or something like that. No one gave a rat's ass."

He put down the decanter and picked up his glass, coming back around the bar with a glass in each hand.

"You turn them white?" she asked, going ahead and letting her confusion at the revelation more than seep through, letting it cover her outrage.

Fenton laughed, coming toward her slowly. "No, no," he said, "that's impossible. They're born niggers, and they'll die niggers. We just make them . . . blotchy."

Jeane forced herself to laugh, but knew it wasn't very convincing. Fenton stopped and held her wineglass out to her. She'd have to stand up to take it from him, so she did, assuming he expected her to do so.

"They want to be white, you know," he said, "but they also fear it more than anything."

Jeane took the wineglass from his hand and said, "Better hope Johnny Cochran doesn't find out."

Fenton laughed at that too, obviously not the slightest bit worried about that possibility.

"Eventually," he said, "they're going to want to fight. They're going to get so sick of it . . . L.A. a few years ago was close."

"Then what?" Jeane asked him. "A race war?"

Fenton smiled and looked slowly once down, then back up her body. His eyes all at once reflected the same lust she'd seen in the eyes of the cab driver and the doorman.

"You have no idea," he said. "Bullets whizzing through the ghettos. . . ."

"Bullets already whiz through the ghettos," she said. "Don't you watch the news?"

Fenton chuckled and stepped around the coffee table to stand no more than a foot in front of her. Another chill went down Jeane's spine, and she felt confined and weak in her impractical shoes and unfamiliar surroundings.

"I don't need to watch the news," he said, his voice husky, his version of seductive. "I make the news."

Jeane was just confused by that, so she sipped her wine.

"Is it true, what they say?" Fenton asked, letting it just hang there.

"Is what true?"

"What they say about niggers and Jews," he said. "You've had . . . experience, right? You've had an opportunity to observe the relative . . . differences."

He winked at her and smiled, obviously taken with his own cleverness. Jeane knew the question was meant to demean her as much as any racial group. The physical desire was still burning in his eyes, even seemed to be increasing. It wasn't quite an animal look. It wasn't that pure.

"Don't tell me you're shy," he said sarcastically, and Jeane realized it had been a while since she'd said anything.

"I'm not shy," she said, then sipped her wine to give herself another few seconds to think. She thought she'd feel dirty posing as a hooker. This conversation was making her feel orders of magnitude dirtier.

"I'd like you to tell me," he said. He reached out to her, and it took an enormous force of will for Jeane not to flinch away. He touched her cheek with the tip of one rough finger. She looked down, almost closing her eyes. His finger slid down her cheek half an inch, then fell away from her face. "You have very soft skin."

"Thank you," she said.

"That must be important," he said, "in your business. It must be important that you keep yourself in a certain condition."

Jeane nodded and looked him in the eyes again. He smiled and said, "You're not going to tell me. That's okay. Other women like you have, though I've gotten conflicting answers."

"Does it matter?" she asked him.

He looked very serious and said, "Tell me you prefer white men."

"I prefer white men."

There was something about the look on his face that said he

in fluid silence

didn't believe her. "What do I get for my fifteen hundred dollars an hour?" he asked.

Jeane shook her head and was about to tell him she didn't know, then realized she had to tell him something.

"What do you want?" she asked.

He reached out and touched her cheek again, this time his finger lingered longer. "I want the same thing you gave the last Jew who paid you. What do Jews want?"

Of course, Jeane had no way to answer that.

Fenton let his hand drop. He looked at her with cold eyes and said, "They almost killed them all, you know, the Jews. Hitler came very close. Since then, every country in the world has coddled them and given them whatever they want and more. In years past, all over the world, the dark people were treated the way the dark people should be treated, as lesser things. They used to have whites-only drinking fountains. Now they don't even have whites-only whores."

A wave of heat flooded over Jeane and her body tensed. Fenton leaned in closer, and she could smell the whiskey on his breath. Jeane had to push her bile down to stay in character.

"I need to make a living," she said lamely.

Fenton breathed out through his nose and said, "We all have to make a living."

His hand came up again, and this time she did flinch. He'd touched her lightly on the breast, and when she flinched, he flinched too. Anger flashed in his eyes.

"Do you let the Jews and niggers touch you there?" he asked, his voice a growl. "Don't I get what they get for my fifteen hundred dollars? My money's green Joyce Mannering. I want you to do me like you do all those damned ni—"

Jeane wasn't conscious of making the decision to punch Fenton in the face. She just did it. It was half a second, a tensing and releasing of muscles, a snap of her elbow, a sting on her knuckles.

Fenton went down hard, his right hand going up to his lip, his left hand dropping the glass of whiskey onto the perfect carpet. His right elbow bumped the table, and it slid away an inch or two.

It hit Jeane just as fast that she'd screwed it up. She'd known that she'd have to get herself out of there without actually having sex with him, but she hadn't planned on knocking him out. She knew also that she hadn't gotten any useful information out of Fenton. They already knew that he was a racist and a white supremacist, but they needed more than that. The black makeup conspiracy wasn't enough.

Damn it, she thought as Fenton hit the rug and rolled over slowly, I screwed it up.

Fenton came to his knees and looked up at her. Blood was in his mouth, had dripped onto the eggshell carpet. The smell of whiskey was thick in the air. The look in his eyes was wild now, animalistic, enraged.

Jeane was surprised that he was still conscious. She'd hit him hard, and she knew how to hit people.

"That was a mistake, bitch," Fenton said, then spat blood out onto the carpet.

Jeane knew he was right, but for different reasons.

chapter six

The little man spoke too fast, and McCain's ears were still ringing from his own screams, so he had trouble understanding the rough, gravelly German. He was able to pick up most of the words, but his head was spinning, and the half-muttered phrases just didn't register. He didn't know who this little man was, didn't know what he was doing in this strange place, didn't know what day it was, didn't know where he was, didn't know why he was there, and didn't know how he suddenly could speak and understand German.

He knew the strange, deformed little man's name was Nichts, but McCain was afraid to talk to him. He was afraid to even look at the creature. He thought if he recognized that the little man was even there, it would mean he actually existed, and McCain didn't want that to be true. He couldn't remember ever having a grip on reality, but he knew that such a thing was possible. He knew that there was a normal, real world that made sense, and though he didn't remember actually living in a world like that, he still longed for it.

The honey-colored semiliquid had mostly dried, but he was still cold. Something like twenty minutes had gone by since he woke up, and he wasn't feeling the slightest bit more normal. Still, there was something that was starting to come back from the recesses of his mind, something struggling back to his conscious self that was rebuilding itself neuron by neuron. This little man might not even be human, but something in the most basic part of Michael McCain realized that right here, right now, he was the closest thing to a friend he was going to get. Nichts was the only one there.

"Who are you really?" McCain asked, still not able to look at Nichts other than in flashlike glances. He wasn't aware of the fact that what he actually said was, *"Wer sind Sie wahrhaftig?"*

"Ich existiere um meinen Magister, der mich erschaffen hat, zu servieren," Nichts said.

McCain was instantly sure he didn't know what Nichts had said, then came to a chilling realization. "You exist to serve your master?" he asked in English, for sure this time. "Is that what you said?"

The little man tipped his misshapen head to one side and said nothing.

"Don't you understand me?" McCain asked. "You don't understand English?"

"Ich verstehe nicht, was Sie sagen," Nichts said.

"Sie verstehen nur Deutsch," McCain replied, deciding he'd better just accept the fact that he could speak German now.

"Ja, ja," Nichts said. *"Ich verstehen Sie nun jetzt."*

The rest of the conversation was conducted in German.

"I don't understand who you are," McCain said, finding that he could speak normally in the foreign language without having to translate his own words in his head.

Nichts looked at him with an indecipherable expression and said, "How could anyone understand who he is?"

Rather than try to understand that, McCain asked, "What kind of a person are you?"

"I am a homunculus," Nichts said.

in fluid silence

McCain didn't understand that word. Maybe there were gaps in his German vocabulary after all. "I don't know that word," he admitted, "but you don't seem . . . you're not . . ."

"I'm not human, true," Nichts said, "but you can't be concerned with me."

McCain almost sighed in relief. He'd found his opening. "Of course I'm concerned with you," he said. "Why wouldn't I be?"

Nichts stepped back and his wings came up against the sheet-metal wall. His eyes seemed to be trying to fend McCain off. McCain knew when to back off, so he did. He looked down at his still-naked body and scraped some of the yellow fluid off. It felt cold and thick, but not sticky on his hand. He flipped it off the end of his fingers and let it spatter on the floor. Nichts leaped forward, startling McCain back. The homunculus quickly and hungrily lapped the liquid up off the cement floor.

"What is that?" McCain asked.

He had to wait several minutes until Nichts licked up the rest of the fluid. The homunculus finally looked up at McCain with hungry eyes that made McCain think Nichts was going to start licking him again. Nichts didn't move any closer, but McCain pushed himself back up against the cold, rough concrete wall as far as he could go. Some of the skin on his back was scraped off, and it hurt, but he pressed in still.

"This is vril," Nichts said. "The master uses it to heighten you."

"Heighten me?" McCain repeated. "I don't know what you mean."

"Before you spent your time in the vril, could you have spoken my master's tongue?"

"So I was floating around in this stuff learning German?" McCain asked dismissively.

Nichts looked at him with open confusion and said, "You aren't done yet. The master will finish you, and you'll become one of the rulers of the Earth."

McCain chuckled, and his head cleared all at once—finally. He dug into one ear with the tip of his index finger and flicked off a glob of the yellow stuff Nichts had called "vril." It didn't seem to have any sort of power or energy to it. It was just . . . stuff.

"Why?" McCain asked. "Why me?"

Again, Nichts looked at him, confused. He stepped back another step and said, "You came here."

It was McCain's turn to offer a confused look. He didn't remember coming here—wherever here was. Something told him he shouldn't reveal that to Nichts. He was getting the sense that Nichts wasn't understanding the details of what was going on and would end up just getting confused. The little man seemed to think McCain had come here intentionally to be turned into some kind of "master." McCain's gut told him that wasn't the case, but it might have been.

He had to stop coming off like he didn't know what was going on.

"I'm having some trouble with my . . . with my memory," McCain said. "I'm getting flashes. It's starting to come back."

Nichts nodded and said, "It's a common side-effect of the vril immersion."

"How long was I in there?" McCain asked. He scraped vril out of his other ear and wiped it on the cement floor next to him. He then concentrated on getting it off his lower stomach.

"Thirteen days," Nichts said.

That didn't actually mean anything to McCain. Again, he thought it should, or had at some point in the past. Now, though, that was just a number that didn't seem either long or short. It was thirteen. It might have been a million. He wondered suddenly if Ngan would be missing him, then got stuck on exactly who Ngan was and why it might matter that he might be missing him. It was the first name McCain had thought of since emerging from the vril, so he felt he needed some more information—some idea who this man might be.

"What does Ngan think of that?" he asked Nichts.

Nichts shook his head and said, "I don't know Ngan."

"How could you?" McCain said quickly, reluctant to play the master race card, but hoping it would cover him if Nichts having heard Ngan's name would somehow be bad.

in fluid silence

Nichts glanced off to one side, and McCain followed his eyes. Next to Nichts was a line of orange plastic barrels that were stacked against the sheet metal wall in a row that must have been fifty yards long. They were stacked up three high. They meant nothing to McCain.

"Are you going to take me somewhere?" McCain asked Nichts. He was suddenly curious about how long he was supposed to sit on this rough concrete floor in some warehouse talking to a homunculus.

"Not yet," Nichts said. "I'll be told to when I'm told to, but I want . . ."

McCain didn't try to finish Nichts's sentence for him. There was something about the way the homunculus had started to state an opinion, a desire of his own, that made McCain sure the little man had never done it before, at least never out loud.

"Not long," the homunculus said.

"We stay here until then?" he asked as conversationally as he could.

Nichts nodded.

McCain didn't know how much time he'd have here, so he realized he'd better start getting some idea where he was, so he could remember it later when he made his . . . Would he have to make a report? Why would he have to do that?

He could see that he was in a big steel warehouse. There was the line of orange plastic barrels. Above him, maybe twenty or twenty-five feet up, was the pitched ceiling and skylights of mesh-reinforced glass. There were ceiling fans, but they weren't on. It was still cold inside.

McCain scraped the cold vril from his groin and turned his head. Nichts was looking at him but McCain made every effort to ignore the homunculus. It was partly a continuation of his playing along with this master race thing, partly embarrassment at his nudity and the fact that he was trying to clean himself, and partly because he had to examine the space around him.

He tried to look behind him, but all he could see was the rough concrete wall. He looked up and saw that the top of it was a foot over the top of his head. From the ceiling he could tell that he was maybe a quarter of the way across the side of the building. He knew he would have to stand to see the other three quarters of the way across.

He pulled his feet under him and tried to stand up. His legs were weak and shaky, and he couldn't do it at first, couldn't even begin to stand. He took a couple of deep breaths, concentrating on his numb, twitching legs for a few seconds, then he just stood up. He didn't have to use his hands. He rose up from the floor and was standing. Movement caught his eye, and he saw Nichts shy away and cower. Vril started dripping down McCain's legs, pooling at his feet.

The wall was the side of a square pool or tank that dominated the center of the warehouse. About a foot and a half from the top of the wall was the surface of a pool of golden liquid. It was obviously the same stuff that McCain was still partially covered in. The surface was still and reflected the nondescript ceiling, but it seemed to move slightly, bulging in the center, then dropping as if a wave was rolling up and down at regular intervals from the center of the square tank. The tank had to be at least twenty-five yards on a side, filling the center of the large open space. On either side of the central tank were two others, slightly smaller, also full of the odd liquid.

The stuff had no smell at all. The only thing McCain could smell was dust and the plastic from the big orange barrels. On the other side of the warehouse, kitty-corner from the first row of barrels McCain had seen, was another row of the orange barrels, also stacked three high. In the center of each of the short sides of the rectangular building were oversized rolling doors big enough to make McCain think he might be in an aircraft hangar. The concrete floor of the building was almost exactly the same size as a football field.

"How does this stuff . . . ?" McCain started to ask, then wasn't even sure what he wanted to know. "How did I . . . ?"

"I can't tell you that," Nichts answered.

McCain turned to look at the little man. The homunculus was holding a little black box. He turned it over in his hand, and McCain saw that it was a cellular telephone.

in fluid silence

"I do not know how any of this works," Nichts said, waving the phone at the vril. "All I know is that it does. I am here only because it does."

McCain nodded at the phone in the homunculus's hand and asked, "Is that for me?"

Nichts looked at it as if noticing for the first time that he was holding something. "I don't know how to use it," Nichts said. "I don't have anyone I can talk to."

"You were supposed to give it to me?" McCain asked.

"No," the little man answered, and his wings fluttered behind him. McCain decided that gesture meant the homunculus was nervous. McCain found it deeply unsettling, but he refrained from screaming this time.

"You want me to make a call?" McCain asked, and even as he finished talking, a phone number flashed across his memory, and he knew it was Ngan's. He knew he should call Ngan.

"If he knows I gave this to you," Nichts whispered, "he might destroy me . . . and you."

A chill ran down McCain's spine. His head went soft again, and his vision blurred. He sat down, stumbling halfway so that he fell hard on his rump, one leg twisted painfully under him. He put a hand up to his forehead, and he could feel his sinuses filling with fluid.

"Who will destroy you?" he asked the homunculus.

Nichts stepped forward, and McCain couldn't flinch away, though he very much wanted to. He felt the phone being placed in his hand.

"The master," Nichts answered. "The leader of the whole Earth, Hans Reinhold Erwählen. Promise me you won't tell him I gave this back to you?"

"*Back* to me?" McCain asked muddily.

"It is yours," the homunculus said. "Promise me."

McCain wrapped his fingers around the phone and said, "I promise, Nichts. I won't tell."

The directions Ngan had downloaded from the internet said the 14.33 mile trip from National Airport to the restaurant in McLean, Virginia, would take exactly thirty-five minutes. Anyone who'd ever pulled out of an airport in a rental car at night would know why it took him substantially longer.

The restaurant was different every time, and this one sounded promising. It was less than five miles southwest of the Central Intelligence Agency's Langley headquarters, but apparently that was far enough away for Vanessa to feel comfortable.

Vanessa Richards worked in some capacity for the Agency, but she had never told Ngan what that capacity was. At first he was afraid that she was a minor functionary like a human resources clerk or the lady who watered the plants, but she'd come highly recommended by the Hoffmann Institute, and she'd made available important, useful, and accurate information in the past. She always insisted on meeting in a public place, always in person. That had been easier before the Hoffmann Institute had moved Ngan from D.C. to Chicago. Ngan could only hope what she had to say about Erwählen would prove to be worth the trip.

He found the ramp to I-66 West and merged seamlessly into the late evening traffic. The Virginia countryside was decidedly underwhelming, and it was night, so Ngan concentrated on the road. He was well into the giddy, post-traumatic stage that always followed landing. Relieved to be on the ground, the car felt reassuringly small, mechanical, and controllable. He decided not to think about the flight back out in the morning. He was happy enough to be on the ground that he succeeded in relaxing.

He kept to the right lane and made a game of keeping the rental car at exactly sixty miles an hour. Cars passed him freely on the left as if he were standing still, but Ngan felt no compulsion to go faster. Despite his trouble getting out of the airport, he was still running early enough that he didn't have to hurry.

It occurred to him that he might have trouble finding a parking place when he found the restaurant—assuming he had no trouble finding the restaurant in the first place—and he might need more time.

in fluid silence

He increased his speed to sixty-four and smiled contentedly to himself.

The radio was off, and the only sound was the humming of the car and the pop of the tires over seams in the road. Ngan always liked the sound of driving at night. It was different than the sounds of driving during the day. The sounds were clearer, purer. Another car passed him, and the sound of it was like the wind through the glaciers near his home in Tibet.

"I miss that sound."

It had been forty-five years since Ngan had been in Tibet, and his memories of the place lay in the realm of half-remembered dreams. When he was younger he could remember more, but he always struggled with that time he spent away from the monastery. It hadn't been long, and he had been young. He knew it was real, had other proof of that, but his memory was clouded, heavy, and unreal. Now, even the mundane memories of the Monastery of Inner Light were taking on that same weight.

A car passed him fast on the left. The swish of it startled Ngan. He looked down at the speedometer and realized he was only going fifty miles an hour. Blinking, he forced his head clear and accelerated. He glanced at the speedometer again and was passing fifty-five when the cell phone in his vest pocket rang.

He fished the phone out of his pocket and touched it on. He could hear the sound of a frantic voice increasing in volume as the phone came closer to his ear. He slammed it to the side of his head when he realized it was—

"Michael!"

McCain didn't stop talking when Ngan said his name.

"... floating around in *Flüssigkeit. Ich* don't *gerade wissen und* this guy *hat Flügel*, Ngan . . ."

Ngan's heart skipped a beat at the sound of his name, but he couldn't understand all of what McCain said.

"... *und es gibt dieser* barrels all over the place, but I don't *weiß was sie sind.* So there's a lot of *dieser Stoff, falls Sie Sorgen haben.* If that's why *Sie haben hier gesendet* . . ."

Ngan passed a sign that read VA-7 West Leesburg Pike 1 mi., and he realized that was his exit.

". . . wherever it is I actually am, and anyway, *es ist mir bekannt, am welches Rückseite dieser Kerl standet,* and there's obviously a lot going on here that's not at all right, and I'm not sure what you have to do with all this, but I'm *sicher, Sie sind etwas verwickelt, um mich hier senden . . .*"

Ngan pulled off to the shoulder, and there was a loud series of crunching sounds as the tires skidded to a stop on the gravel. A passing car blew its horn for some reason Ngan couldn't quite fathom.

". . . so anyway, I'd really like you to tell me *wie Sie wissen, um eine Hölle wie dieser zu ankommen?* Do you want to know what?"

"Michael," Ngan said, "tell me where you are."

"Well I'll tell you what, *ich will die Hölle dieser Mißgeburt äußern, und ich will aus dieser Hölle entkommen,* so do me a favor. Will you do me a favor?"

Ngan closed his eyes when the car came to a complete stop and said, "Michael, please," three times as McCain continued without pause.

"Look up *das Wort 'homunculus' am Lexikon* because I'm talking to one, *und* he's *einer übele* little—hey, listen, sorry Nichts, *aber Ich* gotta *muss bei dir ehrlich sein, Mensch,* it's *nicht artig, ich stimme. Es tut mir leid, die Flügel sind* . . . well, the wings are what they are, and that's something, *aber die Zacken,* I'd *sage, und ah Hölle, anhören,* Ngan . . . listen . . ."

McCain paused finally, obviously confused, disoriented. Was that German he was speaking? There was a hiss that Ngan recognized. McCain was on a cell phone too. Ngan put the car in park.

"I have five senses, Ngan. *Ich kann sehen, hören, riechen, berühren, schmecken.* I'm cold, all right? *Können Sie mich* hear? Ngan?"

"I can hear you, Michael," Ngan said, displeased with the edge of panic he heard in his own voice. "Can you tell me where you are?"

"I told you where I am," McCain said.

Ngan's heart skipped a beat. McCain had spoken directly to

him for the first time. "You're still at Camp Clarity?" Ngan said, hearing the unintentional lilt of a question in his voice. "Are you still at Camp Clarity?"

"Clarity . . ." McCain mumbled, his voice now heavy with exhaustion.

"In Lesterhalt," Ngan said. "Michael, what has he done to you?"

McCain started laughing. It was a frayed, unsettling cackle.

"Can you get out?" Ngan asked.

"The neck," McCain said. *"Tasten Sie.* Right, Nich— Oh . . ."

"Michael?"

There was no answer. Ngan could hear another voice deep in the background but could recognize no words.

"Michael?" Ngan asked again, scared now.

"Listen," McCain said. "It's no big—"

McCain's voice was replaced by a hollow clatter then a sharp, sustained beep that made Ngan pull the phone quickly off his ear and wince with pain. He could hear the beep cut off, and he put the phone back to his ear and said, "Michael."

Silence.

"Michael!"

The line was dead.

Ngan tossed the cell phone onto the empty passenger seat of the car and took a deep breath. He signaled a left and waited for a truck to pass. He had to meet Vanessa Richards at the restaurant in McLean, but immediately after that, he knew he would have to find his way to Lesterhalt, Illinois. Something was horribly wrong with Michael McCain. Ngan had never known the man to babble, and he seemed not to know where he was, what he was doing, or even who Ngan was.

He pulled back onto the highway and squeezed the steering wheel tightly the rest of the way.

chapter 7EVEN

Of all the things Jeane Meara thought she'd find herself doing that night, fighting for her life was not one of them.

Fenton had come up from the floor fast and hard. He swore at her as he piled into her chest like a football player. The air went out of Jeane's lungs all at once, and she was pushed backward into the chair. On the way down she knew she couldn't stop herself, so she'd better make the most of it. When her backside hit the cushion, her right foot came up and into Fenton's groin hard enough to make him blow the air out of his lungs. She kept pushing him up until he ended up flipping headfirst over her to land in a jumble on the freshly vacuumed carpet behind the chair.

Jeane's brain went instantly to fight mode, though she kept open the possibility that her kick had taken all the fight out of Fenton and was prepared to stop. A sense of calm washed over her, and for the first time that night she was at ease, confident in her ability to handle the situation.

She didn't stop again to consider that she'd already mishandled the operation to the point of utter disaster. She might be able to convince Fenton that she was still a hooker, just a hooker who's very sensitive to racist rhetoric, but she'd never gain any of his confidence and would get no more information from him. As it was now, she'd gotten none.

"That was fun," Fenton said as Jeane stood and came around the chair.

He was laying on his back on the carpet with his hands under the chair. His lip was oozing blood but he was smiling.

"Look—" Jeane started to say, but stopped when the chair hit her in the face.

She fell back but not down and let the chair roll off her, though she knew she'd have a nice black eye in the morning. She hadn't the slightest idea how Fenton had managed to throw the chair. He was laying on the floor with no leverage. Though the chair wasn't impossibly heavy, it was too heavy for him to have thrown like that. He'd have been able to tip it over, but—

His fist smashed into her face, and this time she went down, sprawling over the coffee table and back onto the floor. She opened her eyes and saw the sole of his shoe coming at her. She rolled away and got to her feet without thinking. Running three steps, she found herself behind the bar before her eyes cleared enough to see farther. Fenton was standing next to the overturned chair and off-center coffee table. His chin was tilted down, and he was looking at her out of the tops of his eyes. His hands were at his side, and they were shaking. Jeane took a deep breath.

"I've never killed anyone before," Fenton said, his voice shaking and gruff.

Jeane could read his tone well enough. He'd never killed anyone before, but he fully intended this to be his first time.

She almost tried to apologize, tried to salvage the situation, but she knew all that would only make things worse. She had to get out of there and decided that if she had to kill Fenton to do it, she would.

"I think . . ." he said, taking half a step toward her. "I think I want to break your neck. I think that's how I'll do it."

He was between Jeane and the door. Behind her were the French doors that led out onto the terrace, twenty-seven stories above Lake Shore Drive.

She went over something like a plan in her mind, fast and efficient, as she was trained to do. She would make an obvious break for the door, let him come at her, then use his own momentum against him. She'd kick and hit him in the groin as many times and as hard as she could until he went down, then she'd run for it.

She kept her face blank but glanced in the direction of the door. His eyes followed hers as she stepped out from behind the little bar and ran straight at the door. He came at her, reaching out with both hands to grab her around the waist. Jeane stopped and her foot collapsed under her. The high-heeled shoes—she'd forgotten the damned shoes. She fell, twisting her ankle painfully, but it was a fortunate accident. Fenton didn't expect her to stop and certainly didn't expect her to fall. He tripped himself trying to compensate and sprawled clumsily to the floor.

Jeane made note of how slow he was even as she dropped her right hand to the floor and spun her legs under her, kicking off both shoes in less than one second. Fenton rolled over and grabbed her left arm just above the elbow. Jeane heard herself cry out at the touch—it was painfully tight. She grabbed one of the shoes with her right hand and swung it at the hand holding her arm. The spike heel came down hard on one knuckle, and a loud crack merged with Fenton's pained yelp. He let go so fast his hand knocked the shoe out of Jeane's grip.

"Bitch!" he shouted, "Nigger-loving whore!"

Jeanne snapped her head back fast into his face, and he grunted and fell back. She got to her feet, her pantyhose slipping a little on the carpet and her ankle blazing in pain, but she started to run. Fenton managed to grab one of her ankles and Jeane didn't believe he was actually lifting her over his head, but he was. She felt like a baby being thrown in the air. She flailed with her arms in the air. His hand came off her ankle, and she hit the ground just short of smashing through the floor-to-ceiling windows.

71

It wasn't possible. Fenton couldn't be that strong. He was a middle-aged rich yuppie racist. Dangerous on many levels—the systematic chemical poisoning of the African-American community not the least of those dangers—but he wasn't that strong. He couldn't be that strong.

"Whites only, Joyce Mannering," he said. Fenton was standing over her, his suit and hair all mussed. "The future will unfold according to a plan, you know, but you'll miss it. You could have been one of the mothers of the New World Order. You could have . . . Well, that won't happen now. Not for you."

He was picking her up again, and Jeane made herself snap out of it mentally and physically. She whipped her body up and to the side so fast her own head spun. She came out of Fenton's grip and landed with a wince on her bad ankle. She brought her other foot up, then down fast and hard onto Fenton's instep. There was a satisfying crack from the foot and an even more satisfying scream from the man.

Fenton didn't go down. He punched at her again, but the blow was so slow it almost made Jeane laugh. She ducked under it easily and brought an elbow into his belly that would have made anyone double over. Fenton flinched a little but remained upright.

"You haven't been punished yet," Fenton said. He grabbed Jeane by the hair and pulled.

She almost screamed but stifled it so it came out as a sort of disappointed growl.

"When Erwählen ascends, you will all be punished, and we will be purified."

There was the name. Ngan's suspect: Erwählen. They were connected, he and Fenton. They suspected that much at least, but that little confirmation was still not at all worth the damage this complete failure was—

Jeane made the final decision to kill Roger Fenton right then.

She had a gun in her purse, but she'd left her purse in the foyer. She'd have to get to the door to get her gun.

She twisted in his grip and could feel some hair come free of her scalp. It hurt enough to make tears cloud her eyes, but she was able to reach up between his legs and squeeze.

in fluid silence

He rumbled out a guttural curse and let go of her hair when she twisted. The second she was free of his unnaturally strong grip she ran toward the door and grabbed for the purse on the little table there. He was right behind her, grabbing at her feet the whole way, and she kicked his hands more than once.

"What's in there?" he snarled. He almost got hold of one of her feet, but her nylons were too slick for him to get a good grip.

She felt the cool patent leather of the purse in her hand and dived forward, twisting. She came to rest with her back pressed up against the door, and her right hand went into the purse. Fenton was crawling up her, his hands bent like claws, his eyes wild with rage and a sort of pure burning hatred she'd only seen once in her life, and there was the flash of a memory.

A little girl, then the man with the long hair and the eyes and the face that weren't human anymore and smoke and screaming and the realization that he wasn't what he said he was but the complete, impossible opposite. . . .

The gun went off with a ringing bang that was more like a ridiculously loud click in the confined space. Her ears rang, but she heard Fenton say, "That's it—a gun!"

Jeane's head cleared, and she realized she wasn't in Waco, realized that she'd found the gun in her purse and had shot through the bottom of it. Fenton was still on her, and she knew she'd missed. She squeezed the trigger again as Fenton batted the purse away. Another loud bang, and the purse and gun flew from her hand. The purse dropped to the floor next to them, but the gun flew back over Fenton's head and into the living room.

Jeane brought her knee up into Fenton's groin, and the man twitched and grunted. She did it again, and he rolled off her, but he didn't stop rolling until he got to his feet. He didn't bother looking at her. He looked back into the living room, scanning for something—the gun!—and seemed to find it.

Knowing she had to get to it first, Jeane grabbed him by the belt and lifted herself up even as she pulled him down, or tried to. Fenton locked his knees and didn't fall back, but Jeane was still on her feet next to him. They lunged at the same time, and Fenton would have gone farther except that Jeane was still holding onto his belt. He hit the floor face first, bouncing his chin on the carpet, but Jeane knew how to roll and still keep her bearings. She felt the back of her hand brush his, then felt the cold metal of the automatic on her palm.

Fenton scrambled to a standing position as Jeane continued her roll. They made eye contact when Jeane got to her knees. Fenton opened his mouth to say something, and Jeane squeezed the trigger. A rose of deep red blossomed on Fenton's stomach even as the sound of the gun going off assaulted Jeane's already stinging ears. Fenton was pushed back, lost his balance, and his arms pinwheeled. He hit the French doors and went through them as if they were breakaway movie props. The sound of the glass shattering was almost as loud as the gunshot.

Fenton slid across the terrace on his back and stopped when his head hit the concrete railing. Glass falling on the flagstone terrace sounded like rain. Jeane stood up, still holding the gun in front of her with both hands. She was breathing heavily, almost panting.

Fenton stood. Jeane tipped her head to one side, and they made eye contact. Fenton put his hand to his bloody shirt and said, with all the pure conviction of a three-year-old child, "I'm one of the *winners!*"

Jeane squeezed the trigger again, feeling a smile pull the right side if her mouth upward. The bullet caught Fenton high on the left shoulder and flipped him over the railing so fast that Jeane wasn't able too see the look on his face.

He didn't scream all twenty-seven stories down.

The man standing over Michael McCain was crushing the cell phone under very expensive-looking heavy black boots. McCain looked up at him. "I think I was done, anyway."

The man smiled, and McCain couldn't help but smile back. The man was sixty, maybe seventy years old, with distinguished lines creasing parts of his clean-shaven face. His white-grey hair was cut close and neatly combed back. His nose, eyes, and lips

in fluid silence

were small, fine, and his pronounced cheekbones gave him an aristocratic air. He was wearing a perfectly tailored charcoal-grey suit and a plain maroon tie made of shimmering silk. He wore no jewelry of any kind, even a watch. His eyes were crystal blue and sparkling with intelligence and something McCain hoped was wit.

"How do you feel, son?" the man asked McCain. He had a thick accent that made McCain realize the man was speaking English.

McCain had started to feel worse right around the time he'd stood up and looked over the pools of golden liquid. As he'd babbled—and he was babbling but hadn't been able to stop himself or organize his thoughts—he'd slid back down to sit, still naked and shivering, on the rough concrete floor. His head felt as if it were packed full of cotton, and his eyes hurt like he had a fever.

"Ich will heimgehen," McCain answered in German. *"Ich friere."*

"That will pass," the man said, "and when it does, you will have arisen."

McCain nodded, though he wasn't sure what he was nodding for. He heard footsteps behind the man and said, "Nichts?"

There was a rustle of leathery wings from the other side, and McCain saw the homunculus cowering next to the first line of orange barrels. He turned back to where the footsteps were coming from and saw four teenaged boys step up behind the man.

"Who are you guys?" McCain asked, pretty sure he was speaking English again.

All four of the boys glanced at the older man and said nothing. All four were wearing letterman jackets—a dull blue fleece with white vinyl sleeves. They wore numbers: two '01s, an '02, and an '03. McCain always felt old when he saw high school kids who were graduating after the turn of the century, and though he still wasn't sure where he was and what he was doing there, he felt old again. That made him smile.

"Have you been taking care of me?" McCain asked the man.

There was a metal-on-metal sound, a click, and McCain noticed that one of the boys had cocked the submachine gun he was carrying. How could McCain have failed to notice that the teenagers were armed?

The kid who'd cocked his weapon was smiling at McCain with a mouth full of braces. These were corn-fed Midwestern kids, football players, jocks, with dull expressions and a glint of cruelty in their eyes that McCain hadn't seen since he was in high school himself.

"I've been taking care of you," the man said, "yes."

"Are you the bad guy?" McCain asked him.

One of the boys stepped forward and aimed his weapon at McCain's head. McCain flinched and forced a smile and a rough, almost barking laugh.

"Bad guy?" the man asked, placing a still hand on the boy's shoulder and preventing him from splashing McCain's brain all over the floor.

"Arger Kerl," McCain translated, *"Bösewicht."*

The man smiled and said, "My name is Hans Reinhold Erwählen."

That name somehow rang a bell with McCain. He sat up, pulled one foot under him, and tried to stand. The boy with the braces reached out and pushed him back, and McCain's head hit the side of the pool. He swore, and pain and a flash of light exploded behind his eyes.

"That was uncalled for, Jerry," Erwählen said. "From a certain perspective Mr. McCain is correct. I am quite certain that any number of people in this naïve world would think of me as a villain. They will see soon enough, as will you, Mr. Michael McCain of Chicago, Illinois, that they were mistaken."

McCain put a hand to his throbbing head and closed his eyes tightly against the pain. The kid had pushed him hard. Very hard. He slid his hand to the back of his head and felt something warm and wet in his hair.

"Ah, see, now," Erwählen said, "he's bleeding. That will be a demerit for you, Jerry."

"Sorry, Mr. E," the kid said, his voice as dull as his cruel eyes.

"Yeah, Jerry," McCain said, his eyes still closed. "That was bogus, dude."

in fluid silence

"Man, shut the—" Jerry started to say, then stopped. McCain opened his eyes and saw Erwählen staring angrily at the kid, who was looking at the floor with a look on his face as if he might be relieving himself in his pants.

Erwählen met McCain's gaze and offered him a smile Ward Cleaver might have offered the Beaver. The sight of it sent a wave of cold trembling up McCain's spine, but he made himself smile anyway.

"No hard feelings?" he asked, glancing back at the boy.

The teenager Jerry didn't notice the look, just turned and walked over to the wall, still looking down, sulking. The other three boys kept their hands on their guns and their eyes on McCain.

Erwählen crouched in front of McCain, tugging gently at his pants as he sank slowly and effortlessly. It struck McCain as unusual that the man's knees didn't crack.

"I understand that you're cold," Erwählen said to McCain, the beatific smile still lighting his handsome face. "I understand, too, that you think I'm a terrible person, ruled by my hatreds, motivated by some kind of . . . what is it this year? Fear? Anger? I haven't been keeping up with my Oprah Winfrey."

Erwählen laughed, and the four boys—even Jerry—laughed with him. They sounded like toadies.

"I think it's fear," McCain offered, trying to return the smile.

Erwählen nodded and said, "Fear then. Still, it's not true. I'm not afraid, and you don't have to be either, Michael McCain—or shall I call you Fitz?"

"If you like," McCain said, confused at first then recognizing the nickname.

"So Fitz it is," Erwählen replied. "You're going to go back in for a while—"

"No chance in—" McCain said, stopping short when one of the boys stepped forward.

"No, Patrick," Erwählen said without looking back at the boy. The kid stopped and took a step back, but he kept his gun pointed at McCain.

"Hell of a goon squad you got there, Hans," McCain said.

To his surprise, Erwählen laughed, then winked at him and said, "The next generation of the master race."

McCain realized Erwählen wasn't joking, and it made him shiver.

"I know, Fitz," Erwählen said, "that you don't believe now, but that's because you don't understand. My little friend Nichts pulled you out too early. He'll be punished for that, of course, as he'll be punished for giving you the telephone."

Nichts rustled again but said nothing. One of the boys looked over at the homunculus with undisguised contempt.

"I spoil my children, as you see," Erwählen continued. "Forgiveness and a big heart are my weaknesses."

McCain didn't believe him. "You're keeping me here against my will," McCain said.

Erwählen smiled again, but all the friendliness drained from it. "Your will shall have to change, Fitz," he said.

McCain thought of a quick comeback but swallowed it. His head reeled, and he was having trouble lifting his arms.

Erwählen turned to the boys and said, "Pick him up. Put him back in the vril."

McCain said, "No," but they ignored him. He struggled, but they overpowered him. The kids were strong, and he was weak.

"You will see, Michael McCain," Erwählen said. "You will underst—" and his voice was lost when the vril filled McCain's ears.

chapter 8IGHT

Jeane got out of the apartment immediately after shooting Roger Fenton off the balcony. She took the stairs down six flights before having to stop. She sat on a step and breathed for six or seven long seconds. She'd blown the whole operation so badly that she was dumbfounded by the magnitude of her own failure. And she was the one they called Wonder Woman back at the ATF? She wasn't even Foxy Brown.

She gathered her wits and decided to keep going down the stairs. It seemed logical that one had two choices when fleeing a crime scene. You could either get out of there as fast as possible—before anybody showed up to throw you in jail—or you could hole up somewhere and wait for things to cool down long enough for you to leave after all the cops assume whoever did it is long gone. Jeane was always amazed by how rarely the bad guy was actually "long gone."

Taking the elevator would have been a mistake—cameras. The stairs should take long enough and get her closer to the back of the building. She'd have time walking slowly down twenty flights of stairs to think of a decent cover story in case she was stopped by the cops coming out. She considered ditching the gun, but it had her fingerprints on it, and as a former federal agent hers would be easy enough to trace. For that matter she still had fingerprints on a wineglass, and other things upstairs.

She stopped dead and looked at the door on the next landing. A large 12 was painted on it.

Damn it, she thought. I have to go back.

By the time Ngan made it to the restaurant—which was easy enough to find—he was in no mood to eat. He arrived before Vanessa Richards and was seated at a booth by a slight young Asian woman who smiled in the sort of sincere way that Ngan always noticed. He returned her smile and told her that he was meeting someone. Her only reply was a slight bow. She walked away quickly because a young couple had come in and was waiting to be seated.

He opened the menu, which promised "Siamese Cuisine," an old-fashioned way of saying Thai food, and sighed. The phone call from McCain had unsettled him all out of proportion, especially coming right on the heels of a flight, and Ngan felt his nerves stretched tighter than they'd been in years.

He was glad Vanessa was meeting him. Their relationship had always been strictly professional, of course, but they always shared the sort of casual conversations that most Americans take for granted but Ngan rarely engaged in. Vanessa treated him like a peer, in both age and work, though she was much younger than him and worked for an organization not at all like the Hoffmann Institute.

Ngan closed the menu and set it down on the strangely patterned table in front of him. The tabletop was like a kaleidoscope frozen in a not terribly interesting pattern. A tiny black-bud vase sat on the center of the table and held a couple of delicate white flowers—a touch of class at odds with the garish tabletop.

Ngan let his eyes focus on a spot an inch above the tabletop and made his breathing as slow and deep as he could manage. He lost all track of time, his mind closing off from the subdued bustle of the small restaurant. He could feel his palms sweating and concentrated on that physical symptom. His mind wanted to travel, literally leave his body for some other place—something Ngan had done often enough—but he held himself in, steadied his mind, and felt his body fall into place.

When he opened his eyes he saw that a small pot of tea had been set on the table, and two teacups sat next to it. One of the cups was full of steaming green tea. He looked at the door, and Vanessa Richards walked in as if she'd been waiting there for him to look at her.

Ngan watched her speak briefly with the hostess. Vanessa might have been a full twelve inches taller than the hostess, eight inches taller than Ngan. She'd obviously gone home before coming to the restaurant. At work she wore conservative suits. Now she was dressed in loose-fitting blue jeans that still showed off her long legs. Her sweatshirt told anyone who might have been interested that she was a graduate of Howard University. There were no rings on her thin-fingered, well-manicured hands. On her feet were brilliant white canvas deck shoes.

Vanessa looked up as she followed the hostess. She caught Ngan's eye and smiled. Her teeth were white, and though a perfectionist might have thought she should have visited an orthodontist her smile was delightful. Her skin was a perfect, uniform milk-chocolate brown. She wore very little if any makeup because she didn't need to wear any. Her hair was left natural, but cut close to her scalp. She walked with her back very straight. Ngan knew monks who had trained for decades to achieve the sort of balance she exhibited naturally in her walk.

"I know," she said in a voice husky and deep when she got to the table. "I have great natural balance."

Ngan smiled as she sat across from him, fluidly sliding into the booth. The hostess flipped over the other teacup and filled it with a practiced grace that came from having done it over and over again every night for years.

"It is a pleasure to see you again, Vanessa," Ngan said, still smiling.

The hostess put down the teapot and set a menu in front of Vanessa, then turned and walked away without a word.

Vanessa inhaled through her nose for exactly three seconds, then exhaled for five. It was something she always did before she started talking to Ngan. He assumed it was her way of steadying her nerves before she betrayed her oath and loyalty to the Central Intelligence Agency. He knew she wouldn't tell him everything she knew, but she always gave him accurate information and always gave him what she called his "One Thing"— one piece of information that would get her killed if anyone found out she'd told him. It seemed to be something like a professional courtesy she felt she owed the Institute. Ngan had no idea why, and he'd never asked her.

"We should look at the menu," Ngan said.

Vanessa smiled, opened her menu, but didn't look at it. "So they moved you to Chicago," she said, "the Windy City."

"Yes," Ngan said dryly, not looking up from the menu, "I have found it so."

Vanessa chuckled and looked down at the menu. Ngan glanced up at her for half a second, then looked back down at the menu.

"Here's one that has your name on it," Vanessa said, then read from the menu, "Kai Kung Nga Ngarm. Sounds good."

Ngan smiled and said, "I wonder if there is a restaurant where I could order a Vanessa Richards."

"No chance, honey," she joked. "I'm strictly home cookin'."

Ngan laughed with her, but he could feel himself forcing it. He couldn't help thinking that Michael McCain was being killed even as they joked about a restaurant menu.

"Volcano Chicken, then," he said.

Vanessa looked at him, smiling, then her face changed, growing just a little more serious. She'd noticed his anxiety.

in fluid silence

"What would Hans Reinhold Erwählen order?" Vanessa asked, winking at her own hamhanded segue.

"Royal Trout, I'd think," Ngan answered and was pleased when Vanessa laughed.

"Really, Ngan," she asked, not impatiently. "It looks like ancient dead to me."

Ngan shrugged and said, "Curiosity."

Vanessa smirked and took a sip of her tea.

"The Institute has wide-ranging interests," Ngan said.

Vanessa nodded, set down her tea, and said, "There are still people who think that was a volcano seven months ago."

Ngan shrugged. "It might have been a volcano. Volcano Chicken, perhaps, with too much red pepper and curry."

Vanessa smirked again and said, "There are people—very serious, important people—who want to move the capital. They think there's a baby Mount St. Helens down there."

Ngan shrugged again, and Vanessa rolled her eyes. "Black helicopters . . ."

"That wasn't us," Ngan said softly.

"No," Vanessa said, very seriously, her eyes cold and hooded. Ngan hated it when she got that look in her eyes. "No, that wasn't you."

"Erwählen was brought here after the war," Ngan said, bullying the conversation back to cover his own agenda in hopes that he'd get her to stop looking at him like that.

"Maybe he liked Siamese Cuisine," she joked lamely.

"I flew in an airplane to talk with you tonight, Vanessa," Ngan said with a falsely wrinkled brow.

Vanessa put out her lower lip in mock sympathy. "For me?"

Ngan smiled and said, "Anything for you, Vanessa."

"Seriously, Ngan," she said her eyes revealing real concern. "You need to find some way to get over that. It's, like, thirty-thousand times more likely you'll die in a car accident."

Ngan shrugged and said, "I know."

Vanessa nodded. "So I did some digging around after you called and found what little there is left to find. It was a long time ago, and records from that time were all on microfilm or some crap like that, and of course it was the height of the Cold War. . . ."

Ngan nodded but didn't say anything. Vanessa had many interesting contradictions. Politically, she was rather conservative. Conservative in the sort of Invade Cuba/Ted Kennedy-is-a-communist-bent-on-the-destruction-of-the-American-Way-of-Life kind of way that was getting thankfully rare in the post-Reagan era. Socially, she was as liberal as they come. A black woman, she certainly couldn't side with the traditional right, and she always seemed devoid of religion, so she never fell into the Christian right. She was committed to the mission of the CIA and was an enthusiastic, loyal agent. Still, she knew right from wrong and would not tolerate it when the Agency did wrong.

"He did work for the Agency after the war," she continued, obviously not happy with the whole idea of Nazi war criminals working for the CIA but aware of the fact that there was nothing she could do about it. "He advised on the Middle East and other things, but that's where things get fuzzy. I have to admit I'm not really sure what he did, and those records aren't in the places you can look without someone noticing you're looking. I saw some memos, though, that—"

The waiter appeared, as waiters are prone to, as if from nowhere. Vanessa didn't bother trying to mask the fact that she'd stopped in midsentence. The waiter noticed it, of course, and looked at her with eyes that tried to tell her he was sorry and he wished she would have kept talking because he was now curious about what she was talking about, since she obviously didn't want him to hear. Vanessa looked at him with eyes that said, more convincingly, get the hell out of here.

"You ready order?" the waiter asked, and Ngan couldn't help thinking the accent was fake, like Jerry Lewis as the Chinese waiter.

Ngan watched Vanessa glance at the menu and say, "Kai Kung Nga Ngarm."

The waiter didn't write anything down. He kept his hands behind his back. He looked at Ngan and asked, "And sir?"

"Volcano Chicken, please," Ngan said quickly.

in fluid silence

The waiter nodded and turned to go when Vanessa said, "And a limeade for me, too, please."

He made eye contact with Vanessa again, nodded, said, "Miss," turned, and walked away.

Vanessa watched him go, and Ngan watched Vanessa for twenty seconds or so before she turned to Ngan and said, "I saw memos that made it clear that some pretty powerful people really started to lose patience with this guy in the mid and late sixties."

"He did something wrong?"

Vanessa looked at Ngan silently for a long time, and he stared back at her. "This is your One Thing," she said.

He nodded for her to continue and took a sip of his tea.

"The nation of Western Sahara was having some trouble in the late sixties, and the Agency took sides. The bad guys were holed up in Guelta Zemmur and weren't going anywhere anytime soon. The Agency, based on your boy's advice, decided to poison the water supply in Guelta Zemmur. We don't do that sort of thing anymore, but there you go."

"So they poisoned the water," Ngan asked, "and something went wrong?"

Vanessa smirked and said, "Your guy decided not to stop with Guelta Zemmur. He was stopped literally minutes from poisoning the water for all of Western Sahara. When he was confronted by his superiors in the Agency, he told them he thought it was a reasonable opportunity to begin to lessen the . . . how did he put it? 'Overpopulation among the savages,' I think."

"Savages?" Ngan asked, puzzled by the term.

"Yeah, a real sweetheart," Vanessa said. "He was taken off the Saharawi situation and moved around from here to there, mostly doing what they call 'high-level consultation,' which means he sat in a room somewhere and thought about stuff."

"Thought?" Ngan asked. "About what?"

Vanessa sighed, shrugged, and said, "Whatever he wanted to, I guess. He'd advise on organizational matters, y'know: Back in Berlin these guys answered to those guys, the field commanders were authorized to do such and such, and the Agency

85

should do the same thing. Turns out he was a pretty crappy field agent. Some of the guys they brought over after the war were as loyal to Germany as any German, but weren't really ideologues. They worked the war like soldiers, or like cops. This guy, though, seems to have brought the racism, all that baggage, out of Deutschland with him and was prone, like in Western Sahara, to actually go ahead and act on it."

Ngan sipped his tea again and looked up to meet Vanessa's cool gaze.

"Why do you care, anyway?" she asked him. "He's dead."

"Is he?" Ngan asked.

Vanessa's eyes narrowed. She almost looked angry. "The Agency closed the book on him in '70."

"Closed the book on him?" Ngan asked. "1970?"

"It doesn't go on anymore," she said, "but . . . he was a Nazi, anyway, right?"

"The CIA assassinated him?" Ngan asked, legitimately surprised.

Vanessa smiled at him and closed her eyes, "We're in a public place, Ngan, and not that far from Langley."

"I apologize," he said, lowering his voice.

"That was thirty-one years ago," she said. "Why the interest all of a sudden?"

"And you're sure they killed him?" he asked, still speaking quietly.

Vanessa glanced to one side, then sat back in the booth and smiled. The waiter appeared again, set a tall glass of bright green limeade on a cocktail napkin in front of Vanessa, then turned and walked away.

"I read the memo that ordered it," she told him finally.

"But you're not sure they succeeded?"

Vanessa chuckled lightly, then picked up her limeade and took a sip. She smiled at the taste of it and put the glass down gently. "He wasn't hard to find, okay? Besides, he'd be dead now anyway, even if he got away from the Agency, which I'm sure he didn't. I saw a picture of him taken in El Aaiún in 1969; he must have been seventy."

Ngan had seen a picture of him taken in Germany in 1940, and he might have been seventy.

"I thought it was the A.D.L.'s job to find the hundred-year-old Nazis rotting away in Chile or someplace."

"I talked to the A.D.L.," he told her. "They told me the Central Intelligence Agency was suppressing information on Erwählen."

Vanessa smiled. "The Agency suppresses information on everything, Ngan. It's dried blood. Ancient dead."

Ngan nodded and looked over to see the waiter coming with their food.

chapter NINE

It didn't take long for Jeane to remove any evidence that she'd been in Fenton's apartment. She felt like a criminal, of course, which in the eyes of the law, she was. She'd killed Fenton in self defense and could probably prove it in court, but she could never justify why she'd been there in the first place. Likewise, she never got the feeling from anyone at the Hoffmann Institute, including Ngan, that they'd do anything to jeopardize themselves in order to defend her.

She was back in the staircase in only slightly better shape than she was the first time she'd started down. The police hadn't made it up to the penthouse yet, and she'd managed to get in and out fast enough. They'd probably come up in the elevator a second after she ducked back into the stairwell.

On the way down the stairs she thought of and rejected over a dozen possible cover stories. When she got to the first floor, she still had nothing and still had the gun in her purse. If she was caught with it, it would be all the evidence they'd need to charge her with murder, but for some reason she just couldn't stomach the thought of discarding it. Would she shoot a cop if she had to to get away? Would she shoot the doorman?

"I shot the sheriff," she sang to herself, "but I did not shoot the deputy."

She found the back way out, a cold steel door marked Emergency Exit Only—Alarm Will Sound.

The alarm was more like a fire alarm than a security measure, but Jeane didn't want to risk it going off. The building could be ringed by cops for all she knew, and those cops would be listening for exactly that kind of sound.

She fished in her purse and found a Swiss Army knife. It took a while to get the big metal box on the door off, but once she was inside it, she knew exactly which wires to cut to disable the alarm: the only wires. It wasn't exactly Fort Knox.

She sighed, hoping there wasn't a cop outside the door, and put her knife away. She debated pulling her gun, then decided not to. After taking a deep breath and closing her eyes, she pressed gently, slowly on the door handle and felt it click open. A high-pitched whine startled her, making her gasp, and her heart jumped in her chest—then she realized it was her cell phone ringing.

She snatched it out of the little purse before it could ring a second time and whispered, "Speak," into the phone.

"Jeane?" Ngan's voice asked. "Is that you?"

"Ngan," she whispered. "I can't really—"

"It's hard to hear you," he said, speaking loudly over dense background noise. "I'm driving back to National Airport. Michael is in serious trouble. My meeting here is finished, and I will need you to meet me in Lesterhalt."

"Lesterhalt?" she asked, daring to speak in an almost-normal voice. "In southern Illinois?"

Jeane had no idea where the town of Lesterhalt was, exactly, but she felt reasonably sure that she could find it on a map. Chicago was getting a little warm for her anyway.

"Yes," he said, a loud burst of static almost overwhelming

his voice, "that's right. Meet me there as soon as you can."

"Fitz is in trouble?" she asked, "You're sure?"

"Yes," he told her. "I think things are starting to go wrong."

Jeane closed her eyes and pressed the phone tight against the side of her head.

"Jeane?"

"I'll see you there," she promised. "Tomorrow."

"Good," he said, and broke the connection.

Jeane left the phone at her ear for a second, hearing Ngan say, "I think things are starting to go wrong," over and over in her head. He had no—

The phone disappeared from her hand, replaced by a blazing pain in the side of her head. Her neck snapped back, and she fell back and down like a sack of flour, scraping her right palm on the stairwell's concrete floor. Someone had punched her in the face—hard.

"Bitch!" Fenton barked at her.

She looked up, and there he was, suit drenched in blood. He was holding his left eye in with his left hand. It was hanging out of his black eye socket by a twisted cord that looked like blood-soaked yarn. He sneered at her, and she saw he was missing teeth. He looked like someone who'd just fallen twenty-seven stories to his death.

Except he wasn't dead.

"Fenton," she breathed, scuttling backward on the cold, rough floor.

"You," he breathed angrily, his voice low and bubbling, like his lungs were full of fluid. "You were going to kill me? You came to kill *me?*"

"No," she said, though she wasn't sure why. He kicked her, and pain blasted from her hip, up her spine, and into her already reeling head. Her vision went momentarily dark, and she fought against losing consciousness as best she could. She fumbled for the purse and blinked, trying to spot it on the floor.

"I am going to burn you," Fenton growled. "I am going to hurt you, bitch, and hurt you badly."

He kicked her again, and the pain made her sit up straight.

Something soft touched her back, and she knew it wasn't Fenton. It was the purse.

His hand grabbed her shoulder, and his fingers squeezed her so tightly she was sure they'd break the skin. She let him pull her up, all the while fishing in her purse for the gun. She could feel the hole already blown through the bottom, then felt the gun. She curled her hand around the trigger and opened her eyes, having just realized they were closed.

Fenton was smiling at her with a mouth full of blood and broken teeth. His left eye had finally fallen all the way out, and his face was a featureless mask of dark red blood. He pulled his fist back to punch her in the face, and she knew that, as strong as he was, he would kill her with that punch.

He started to move his fist forward, and she brought the gun up. She was fast enough by pure luck. She squeezed the trigger, and there was a flash followed by a loud, sharply echoing bang in the cramped concrete and cinder-block space. Fenton's fist exploded.

He screamed more in anger than in pain, and Jeane brought the gun up higher and fired again. Fenton's head burst into two big and several small pieces. His body poured down onto the floor in a pile of limp, twitching flesh.

Jeane didn't stop to put the gun away. Her ears were ringing and her vision was still blurred. She stepped forward over the body and fell into the door with enough force to open it.

She stepped out into the alley, and there was a three-inch drop from the door's threshold to the alley floor. She tripped and sprawled headfirst into the cool, wet alley. Gravel tore at her arms and chin. She swore but kept her hand on the gun.

Bringing one knee up, she scraped it, too, on gravel and bits of old broken glass. She was about to get up, then noticed something. At first, she thought that there must be something wrong with her eyes. The puddles in the alley were flashing alternating red and blue.

A foot fell next to her head.

"Fenton," she breathed, unable to believe it. He didn't have a head.

in fluid silence

A heavy shoe kicked the gun out of her hand, and she felt a knee press into the back of her neck. A stern, leather-gloved hand took hold of her wrist. The grip was firm but not as painfully tight as Fenton's. She blinked and saw the red and blue light still flashing.

A man's voice, but not Fenton's said, "Right there, lady," from somewhere above her.

"Got her?" another man asked.

She felt her hand yanked back, then another hand grabbed her other wrist. There was a clicking sound.

"Obarsky?" the second man asked.

"Hold on," the other man said. Jeane felt handcuffs click in place. "I got her."

"What . . . ?" Jeane managed to say, then blinked again. She was starting to come around.

She felt the man who'd handcuffed her lean in closer, then felt his breath on the back of her neck—breath that smelled like pretzels—as he said, "Hey, let's just go ahead and say yer under arrest, okay?"

"Damn it," Jeane whispered. Things were starting to go wrong.

chapter 10

Jeane was still groggy when she felt herself dragged across the alley, then lifted clumsily and stuffed into a car. The upholstery was vinyl—cheap, cold, and uncomfortable. Jeane lifted her head, closed her eyes tightly, then opened them. She was in the backseat of a police car. There was wire mesh in front of her, closing the backseat off from the front, where a shotgun stood barrel-up in a quick-release rack. There was a little computer with a blinking green cursor. The driver's side door opened, and something told Jeane to close her eyes and pretend she was unconscious. There was nothing she could say that would make anything better for her, but if she could hear what the cops had to say, she might at least figure out how bad off she was.

"C'mon, kid," the cop on the driver's side said, his voice impatient, annoyed. Jeane could see his hand on the door, his skin was pale, a little pink, and beginning to wrinkle. "Look, just get in and trust me fer once, would ya?"

It was a Chicago accent, North Side.

The passenger side window was rolled down, so Jeane could hear the other cop say, "Stan, this ain't goin' down like this, man. This is my ass, too."

The other cop was black.

"Look," the driver said, his voice friendly, reassuring, "I'll explain everything when we get outta here, okay? Nobody's gonna give a rat's ass we bring dis bitch by—"

"Stan," the passenger said, "there was a shot fired, man. We need to at least—"

"One time," the driver said. "We're supposed to be freakin' partners, Robby. You can do this one thing fer me. Yer gonna do one freakin' thing fer me ain'tcha?"

"Stan . . ."

"Aint'cha?"

There was a long pause, and Jeane could hear the sounds of the city around them: cars going by, a horn, an airplane passing overhead.

"Man," the passenger said finally, "I'm gonna regret this."

The driver laughed, a relieved sound. "You ain't gonna regret nothin', Robby. Cross my freakin' 'eart."

"Man," the passenger said, "just get in the damn car."

Jeane kept her eyes closed, but she could hear the cops slide into the car and close the doors. The radio squawked. The dispatcher quickly muttered something and was answered by another unit who reported that they were going to stop for coffee. The dispatcher acknowledged that.

"She still out?" the white cop—Stan, Jeane remembered—asked.

Jeane could hear someone shifting on the cheap vinyl bench seat in front of her. "Looks like it," the black cop said. "She could be fakin' it. You fakin' it?"

Jeane didn't answer. She kept her eyes closed and waited out the lengthy silence that followed.

The car lurched forward, and Jeane heard one of the cops shifting on the front seat again.

"Hey, man," the black cop said. "I go by Rob, okay? Not Robby."

in fluid silence

Obarsky laughed and said, "Yessir, Officer Rob Stewart, sir."

Stewart laughed, uncomfortably, almost devoid of humor. Jeane opened one eye and looked out the left side window. They were pulling out of the alley, onto Fullerton Avenue. A van pulled in as they crossed the sidewalk. The side of the van very nearly brushed against the side of the police car.

"Damn," Stewart breathed.

Jeane saw the driver of the van look at Obarsky and wink. The driver of the van was hard to see clearly in the dark. A nondescript white guy, maybe early thirties, wearing orange coveralls. As the van passed them Jeane recognized the logo painted on it. She'd seen it at the cosmetics counter. Natura. Fenton's company.

The van ground to a halt behind them, and Obarsky took a sharp left onto Fullerton. A silver minivan had to screech to a stop to avoid broadsiding them.

"Obarsky . . ." Stewart said, his voice impatient. "This is bad, partner."

Jeane considered saying something. She could open her eyes, sit up straight, and appeal to Rob Stewart. Obarsky seemed to be up to something. Stewart was uncomfortable, to say the least. Fenton must have—

But Fenton hadn't had time to call the police, especially not a specific police officer friendly to his cause. So was Obarsky working for the Hoffmann Institute? Was he sent to follow her, to pull her out if things went wrong? If that was the case, why was she in handcuffs? Also, wouldn't Ngan have told her about that? Agents should know whether or not they have backup. It had been obvious from the start of this now totally unsalvageable operation that she didn't have any backup.

Jeane had to admit she had no idea what was happening, and the best she could do was ride it out and wait for an opportunity to get the hell out of there.

She kept her left eye open just enough to tell that they were headed west on Fullerton, away from the lake, back toward the expressway.

"So where we goin'?" Stewart asked.

97

Obarsky took a deep breath. "Just up this way a little, then north on Halstead. Listen, Rob, this really ain't no big deal, okay? Promise."

It was Stewart's turn to take a deep breath. He didn't say anything.

The cool air rushing in through the open car window was doing wonders for Jeane's physical and mental state. She could feel herself coming around. She closed her left eye and let the air wash over her face. She listened to the police radio for some clue about where she might be going with these two cops or some mention of Fenton or a suicide or murder or anything.

"So," Stewart said after a very long silence, "I can't even look in her purse and find out her name?"

"Her name is Joyce, okay?" Obarsky said. Jeane had to suppress a shudder. Fenton had insisted on calling her that. She still had no idea why and less of an idea how Obarsky could have known that.

"Man . . ." Stewart said. "Look, Stan, she's all beat up, right, and she had that gun on her. And I heard a shot, okay? She could need medical attention. It ain't far to Northwestern."

"Hey, man." Obarsky replied. "She'll get to the hospital, okay, and we'll check out the gunshot and alla that, okay? I just gotta go by dis one place."

"I ain't askin'," Stewart said, his voice full of resignation, trepidation, and indignation. "Do what you gotta do, okay, but sooner or later there's gonna be a brother needs a little somethin'. . . ."

"I hear ya, bro," Obarsky replied jovially. "Done deal, my friend."

Jeane let her head roll onto the window as the car took a right off of Fullerton. She opened her left eye again and saw the street sign pass. They went up maybe a block and a half north of Fullerton on Halstead, then the car pulled off right and bumped over a curb.

"Stan . . ." Stewart said, sounding really nervous now.

Jeane got scared all of a sudden, and without really taking the time to consider her actions, she opened her eyes and said, "Where are you taking me?"

in fluid silence

"Jesus freakin' Christ!" Obarsky exclaimed.

Jeane caught his eyes in the rearview mirror. His head was almost spherical, his eyes looked black in the dark car. He had a tight crewcut, and there was a roll of fat around his neck. He wasn't wearing a hat.

"She's alive," Stewart said.

He turned in his seat to look back at her. He couldn't have been any older than twenty-five, a fresh-faced black kid with a shaved head in the style of Michael Jordan. He smiled, showing white teeth.

Jeane met his eyes and said, "Am I under arrest?"

Stewart's face sagged. Instead of answering, he looked over at Obarsky, who glanced at him, then stopped the car.

Jeane turned her head to look out the window. They'd come to rest behind an eight-foot wall of newly poured concrete with steel bars sticking out of it like the stalks of dead bushes. The tires crunched gravel as the car almost slid to a stop. It was dark, the whole area—obviously a construction site—lit only by the headlights of the police car.

"Am I under arrest?" she asked again.

"Yeah," Obarsky said, his voice sarcastic, bratty even, like a petulant teenager. "Yeah, lady, yer under arrest."

Stewart sighed and shook his head. Obarsky looked at him and their eyes met.

"Help me get her outta the car," Obarsky said.

Stewart just looked at him, hard. Obarsky returned the younger man's gaze, and Jeane knew within the first second that Obarsky was going to win. It didn't take much more than another couple seconds for Stewart to look away and breathe, "I will not lose this job, Stan."

"Yes, you will," Jeane said harshly before Obarsky could say anything.

Both of the cops glanced at her, the looks on their faces betraying their different feelings, different agendas.

"Help me get her out," Obarsky said flatly, then opened the door.

The dashboard began to chime, and the light came on. It

wasn't too bright, but it stung Jeane's eyes, and she had to blink to clear her vision. She could see Stewart looking at her. She tipped her head and said, "It's your career, Officer Stewart."

He looked away immediately and opened his door. Obarsky chuckled and got out, groaning as he straightened obviously stiff knees. Stewart slid out rather more fluidly and opened the rear passenger-side door. Jeane didn't make a move to get out.

"Come on, lady," he said, his voice calmer than his quivering eyes. "Just come on out." Then, more quietly, he added, "I won't let him hurt you."

Jeane was at a loss for words.

Stewart reached in and took her, surprisingly gently, by the right arm. She shifted in the seat and helped him pull her out. Behind her she could hear Obarsky's heavy footsteps on the gravel, walking slowly away from the car. Jeane stood up, Stewart holding her head so she wouldn't bump it on the top of the car door as she came through it. It felt good to stand, and all her minor injuries were starting to feel less urgent.

Stewart's grip became a little tighter, a bit more insistent. He turned Jeane around, and she could see Obarsky standing, weight on his right leg, holding a big steel flashlight up in his left hand. The light came on, and he kept it on Jeane's face. Purple splotches appeared over her already dim view of the scene, and she had to close her eyes. The handcuffs were tight around her wrists.

"Stand her up against the wall," Obarsky said, his voice taking on an edge now that might have been excitement or anticipation. "Over there. Facing the wall."

"Guys," Jeane said lamely, "come on, now."

Stewart was walking her slowly around the back of the car, not saying anything. Jeane wasn't wearing the uncomfortable shoes, and sharp gravel was poking into the bottoms of her feet.

"Damn it!" Obarsky shouted, his voice echoing off the newly poured concrete walls. "Move her ass over there!"

"Hey—" Stewart started to object, then pushed Jeane faster so she almost stumbled.

"Sorry, man," Obarsky said. "Just get her over there."

Five steps got them to within two feet of the wall. Stewart turned Jeane to face the wall, then let go of her arm.

"Look," Jeane said, "both of you. You guys could really get into a lot of trouble for this."

Obarsky laughed, and Jeane could see Stewart move, maybe instinctively—exhibiting his ability to tell right from wrong—between her and Obarsky.

"You want me to search her?" Stewart asked.

"No, Rob," Obarsky said. His voice was quieter now, but edgy, nervous. "That won't be necessary."

"Is that her gun?" Stewart asked.

Jeane opened her mouth to say something, to warn Stewart, but she couldn't get a sound out before the gun went off.

There was a bright flash—Obarsky was closer than she thought he was—and a loud, echoing crack. The wall in front of her and to her left was splashed with black-red gore as if someone had thrown a bucket of red paint on it. Jeane turned to her left in time to see Rob Stewart's headless corpse fall to its knees, then onto its chest like a rag doll.

Obarsky was standing only at arm's length from Stewart. He must have had the gun—Jeane's gun—pressed up against his partner's forehead.

Jeane's mind took all this in in less than a second, then switched into survival mode that made time seem to pass more slowly.

Her hands were still bound behind her back, so she knew without having to think about it that she would have to disarm, maybe even kill, Stan Obarsky with her feet alone.

Obarsky was looking down at the twitching corpse of his partner, so he didn't see Jeane take one long step toward him. He looked up, brought the gun up and pointed it at her just as she whirled into a high roundhouse kick, trying her best to compensate for the odd effect on her balance the handcuffs had. She succeeded well enough to make contact with Obarsky's hand. The gun popped out of his grip, and he said, "Bitch!"

Jeane's right foot came down on the gravel, and she continued to spin. Her momentum gave her the speed and power necessary to bring her left leg up just as high. Her stockinged foot smashed into the side of Obarsky's face hard enough to knock him back a step, but not down.

Twisting in midair, Jeane came down on both feet, facing Obarsky. The old, fat cop looked more surprised than anything. His left hand went up to his mouth, the flashlight beam waving wildly around the dark construction site. He put the back of his hand to his bleeding lip, and Jeane saw his right hand go to his service automatic, holstered on his belt.

Jeane kicked forward, snapping her knee and planting her stiff toes between Obarsky's treelike legs. The air burst out of his lungs, and the flashlight clattered to the gravel. The beam spun, causing a strobing effect that Jeane might have found unsettling if her brain were allowed to think that much.

Obarsky went down to one knee, and his right hand flipped the strap off the top of his pistol.

Jeane kicked again with her left foot, knocking Obarsky's hand away from his gun. He actually said, "Ouch!"

Hopping onto her left foot as it came down, Jeane kicked up, twisting her body sideways to plant the sole of her foot tellingly into the space between Obarsky's nose and his upper lip. His eyes went wide, and he went down backward, his head snapping onto the gravel. His elbow hit the flashlight, sent it rolling away, and the look on his face was lost on Jeane.

Jeane scanned the ground in the darkness and saw a faint reflection on the edge of the Sig Arms P232 .380 automatic she'd put in her purse for her first big undercover assignment for the Hoffmann Institute. She took two fast steps in that direction and spun as she dropped herself hard on her backside.

Obarsky sat up slowly and drew his gun. Jeane saw it come out of the holster just as her fingers closed around the gun. It, like her hands, was behind her back.

"Game over, Joyce," Obarsky grunted as he slid a bullet into the chamber of the gun. Jeane rolled forward, tucking her head in tight. She rolled the .380 through her fingers as she came around, and though she couldn't see what Obarsky was doing now, she knew he was aiming his gun at her.

in fluid silence

She made an educated guess with her aim and squeezed the trigger once in mid-roll. There was a flash and a bang, then a wet sound and another shot.

Jeane let herself roll to one side, and she came around to see Obarsky lying flat on his back. His gun was pointing up in the air, his legs, torso, and hand were twitching. With the easy action on his service automatic, his death spasms were making him fire blindly up into the air. Jeane set her jaw, hoping the dead cop's arm wouldn't fall over and cause him to finish his mission posthumously.

With her teeth grinding, her eyes twitching at every flash, and her ears ringing, Jeane counted a total of fifteen shots from Obarsky's 9 mm.

When it was all over and Obarsky's body was still, she lay there on the gravel and panted for a few seconds, listening to the bullets tinkle back to earth like rain. She let go of her own gun and struggled to her feet. Seventeen gunshots was going to attract attention, and Jeane did not want to be found lying on the ground in handcuffs next to two dead Chicago cops.

She sat down on Obarsky's chest and fumbled around behind her for what seemed like forever. Sweat broke out on her forehead, and she felt bad, physically. Finally she found the keys to the handcuffs and dropped them at least half a dozen times, swearing each time, until she managed to get the cuffs unlocked.

When her hands were free she picked up the gun, leaned into the police car, found her purse, and got the hell out of there.

chapter ELEVEN

Ngan was in Mark's Old Time BBQ in Lesterhalt, Illinois, just as the sun was setting. It had been a complex trip, but one that he still found amazing. The fact that he could come all the way from Washington, D.C., and still beat Jeane there by several hours was a good example of why he flew, no matter how it frightened him.

He read the stained menu with some degree of trepidation. The meal he'd shared the night before with Vanessa Richards had been quite good, prepared well by people who were proud of their work and eager to impress. Mark's Old Time BBQ was content to pass the last health inspection, limping along on "good enough" for so long that they had stopped even caring what good enough was.

There were only two other occupied tables in the diner that could have seated forty—as a yellowed sign thumbtacked above the door proclaimed. The décor could have been described as "a year's worth of restaurant auctions." Colors were mixed indiscriminately. There was no care taken with anything. Posters obviously given free by the distributors were tacked to some of the walls, sporting surprisingly unappetizing photographs of processed food with garish headlines like "Enjoy Freshly Popped Popcorn" and "Gyros: A Taste of the Mediterranean." It struck Ngan as particularly interesting that popcorn was not actually available at the restaurant.

He took stock of the other patrons, careful not to stare or even make his interest known. One table was occupied by a family that Ngan thought would be refugees if they happened to be in any country but the United States. The father was a rotund, greasy man in his mid thirties obviously employed in the lubrication of some machine or other. His hands were black. Seeing him stuff a beef sandwich into his mouth made Ngan wonder as to the nutritional value of motor oil and axle grease.

His wife was a profoundly sad woman packed into a too-small sweatshirt that advertised some country singer Ngan had never heard of. Her hair was long, stringy, and atypically untended for an American woman. She was roughly wiping the face of an angry-looking infant who was trying desperately to avoid the crumpled napkin in order to stuff Cheerios into his mouth with saliva-dripping hands.

The baby's older brother was a dirty-faced, emaciated boy who was pretending his soft drink cup was a gun. He was shooting the baby over and over again, annoying his mother but having no effect on either the baby or his father. A light of violence, anger, and need blazed from the boy's eyes. Ngan had seen that look in Tibetan refugee children—had seen that look in a mirror, but that was a long time ago.

Ngan looked down at the menu and read the description of a Francheesie with no little confusion before he took in the other table. It was a couple, no children. The woman was plump in the way that centuries ago had been considered attractive. Her top gave an unnecessarily detailed view of her ample cleavage and advertised chewing tobacco. An odd product to be advertised on a woman's top, though maybe not in southern Illinois.

The young man was a thinner, younger version of the greasy-handed father at the other table. He seemed unhappy, as did his girlfriend. It was a common enough ailment, and the observation didn't help Ngan get any sense of the peculiarities of Lesterhalt.

The waitress who brought him a glass of ice water and the menu was pretty, thin in a genetic rather than sculpted way, and limping. She forced a smile when she talked to him, and her eyes betrayed a curiosity she was apparently too shy to do anything about. Her name tag identified her as Sara, a name as nondescript as her face.

Sara was limping toward him from around the empty lunch counter, and he looked up at her and smiled. She didn't return the smile, just glanced at the door and a poster on the wall that read "Hot Dogs!" Looking at the empty table behind him, she took a little pad out of her apron. Ngan looked down at his menu, not wanting to embarrass her with unwanted eye contact.

"Ready?" she asked him, obviously forcing the word out through tight lips.

"I believe so, yes," Ngan said, still not looking up at her. "I would like the B.B.Q. beef sandwich."

There was a silence and Ngan glanced up. She was looking at him as if he'd just turned green and shot Roman candles from his eyes. Ngan looked back down at the menu and felt his skin crawl.

"Barbecue," she said, again trying to get the word out as fast as she could. "Not B.B.Q."

"Yes," Ngan said, nodding. "Forgive me."

"Anything to drink?" she asked. The unspoken subtext was: "Please don't make me have to ask you if you want something to drink."

"Water is fine," Ngan said, closing the menu and handing it to her. "Thank you."

Sara touched the menu with one shaking, thin-fingered hand, but didn't take it. Ngan didn't let go, and it seemed as if the air pressure in the room suddenly doubled. Ngan sensed that Sara had something to say.

The door opened, triggering the tiny rusted bell screwed to the peeled-paint doorframe, and Sara jumped, almost yelped. She snatched the menu from Ngan's hand and turned. She looked up when Ngan did, and they both saw the teenage boys swagger into the restaurant. She quickly looked down at the floor and limped away as fast as she could. Ngan watched her go. She got to one end of the lunch counter and stopped, seemed to realize she'd gone the wrong way, then quickly limped to the other side, where she tried hard to busy herself with something. She looked up at the boys, and her face paled.

Ngan looked over at the boys, who strode with teenage athletic confidence to the counter, still laughing about something that must have happened or been said in the parking lot. They were wearing the ubiquitous letter jackets, though the early evening sun was quite warm. One of them happened to glance Ngan's way, and he stopped so abruptly he almost fell over, taking his friend with him.

"Whoa, whoa, whoa," the one who saw Ngan breathed quickly, taking his friend by the arm.

The other boy looked up, and a look of anger passed over his face when his eyes settled on Ngan. "What the hell do we have here?" he asked, apparently addressing the first boy.

They both took a step closer to Ngan, turning to face him, their eyes dull but loaded with something Ngan thought might be disgust. The boy who'd first noticed Ngan had the number '02 sewn onto his jacket. The other one was to graduate in 2003.

"You take a wrong turn, slope?" '03 asked.

Ngan got the feeling it was a rhetorical question. He decided not to smile at the word "slope," though the epithet had always amused him. It apparently was begun as a description of a facial feature that maybe half the world's population had. It was a meaningless insult, but Ngan took it as it was intended.

"I am having dinner," he said, aware that anything he might say would be the wrong thing.

The boys looked at each other and smiled knowingly, greatly underestimating Ngan's grasp of the situation. "Not here, zipperhead," '03 said, fixing an expectant look on his face that he certainly meant to be taunting.

Ngan did laugh this time. He thought the term "zipperhead" might have originated in the Korean or Vietnam War. He had no idea what it was supposed to mean. It was just silly.

in fluid silence

"Oh," '02 breathed then. "That's funny? Did I say something funny?"

Ngan decided not to correct him, though it was in fact '03 who had said something funny. Instead, he gave a generic response. "I don't want any trouble."

The young couple at the booth on the other side of the restaurant had turned and were watching the exchange with faces so passive they almost looked dead. Of the dirty family, only the mother seemed to notice anything and even then only glanced up every other second as she continued to interfere with her baby's feeding. The father might have been blind and deaf for all he seemed to notice anything being said, and the little boy was now sitting on his knees, pointing the straw from his drink at the baby and making noises like TV explosions.

The two teenage boys looked at each other, smiled again, and walked quickly and with great determination to the edge of Ngan's table. Ngan sat straight as he always did, and laid his hands, palms down, on the sticky table in front of him. His eyes fixed on a point between the two boys, where he could take in both of them and register any movement from either.

"You don't want no trouble?" '03 said, dialogue repeated from a thousand movies. "Well, chink, looks like trouble found you."

Ngan was in Lesterhalt for two reasons. He needed to find Michael McCain and make sure he was safe, and he had to verify that the Hans Reinhold Erwählen who was running Camp Clarity was indeed the same man who'd advised Adolf Hitler in matters of the occult. These boys could help him do neither of those things directly, but a test of the stridency of their racism and the townsfolk's willingness to stand up to them would tell Ngan much about Erwählen's influence here.

"You are being rude," Ngan said, his voice steady, matter-of-fact, as if he were pointing out that it looked like rain.

The boys laughed again, a haughty laugh dripping with misplaced self-confidence.

Ngan concentrated on his hearing, so he couldn't see what Sara the waitress was doing. He could hear her breathing. She was afraid but unwilling to intervene. The little boy made a sound like a machine gun.

Ngan's eyes registered the movement, but it was the sound of the gun coming out of the teenager's pocket that best registered on Ngan's now narrowed senses. It was a small-caliber automatic that '02 pulled from the pocket of his letterman jacket. He pressed it against Ngan's bald temple, holding the gun a little to the side. The safety was off. The steel was cold against Ngan's head.

This was not funny anymore.

Ngan heard someone—probably Sara—gasp. The baby's high chair was pulled an inch or so closer in to his mother, squeaking on the cheap tile floor. Ngan could hear '02's heart beating. It was loud, strong, regular. The act of putting a gun to a stranger's head was hardly exciting him at all. Ngan knew from that sound that the boy was capable of killing him. It would only take a flinch. The tiniest twitch of a muscle, and Ngan would be dead.

Ngan listened for exactly that sound. If you listened carefully enough, if you were trained the way Ngan was trained in a monastery in the thin, magic-rich air of Tibet, you could hear a finger bend.

"If you're passing through, Charlie," '02 said, his voice as loud as thunder to Ngan's tuned ears, "you pass through. The sun sets on your yellow ass in Lesterhalt, it won't see sunrise."

Ngan didn't move. He was still in a way only a very few people were capable of being still. The gun came off his head, there was a hesitation, then it came back on again, a little less cold this time.

Ngan listened to the finger, waiting to hear it begin to tense. If it did, he'd disarm the boy first with his right hand, then go from there.

The boy didn't tighten his finger. The gun came away from Ngan's head, and he heard the boy slide it back into his pocket.

"This is a *white* town," '03 said.

Ngan said nothing, didn't look up. Rushing these boys into a confrontation would gain him nothing and probably result in their deaths. It was an insignificant victory for them, and Ngan was perfectly content to let them have it. He almost sighed when he realized that at that age it was possible to convince a boy of anything. Ngan didn't know for sure that they'd come under the influence of Erwählen. It cost more than Ngan could imagine either of the boys had to spend to attend Camp Clarity's workshops, but . . .

The boys backed off, and Ngan didn't look up. He knew all he'd see was self-congratulatory smiles.

"Time for you to be on your way, gook," '02 said.

Ngan stood, not looking at either of the boys. He could feel eyes on him, and he looked up and saw the waitress staring at him as if he were the devil himself. She turned away from his gaze so quickly that she knocked a coffee cup on the floor and it shattered with an echoing crash.

The two boys clapped and whooped loudly, and '03 said, "Good one, Sara!" as if the waitress had just scored a point in one of their games.

Ngan opened the door and stepped through without looking back. As the door swung open, the reflection of the little boy sitting next to his bored, silent father swung into view. He was pointing his finger at Ngan as if it were a gun, his thumb pumping up and down, pretend bullets ripping the funny-looking stranger to bloody shreds in the boy's polluted imagination.

The door closed behind Ngan, shutting the laughs of the teenage boys with it.

chapter TWELVE

McCain came awake in a way he'd never experienced before. Normally, it would take him as long as an hour of heavy, groggy, half-sleep before he'd be able to even climb out of bed. He would need to take a shower and really wouldn't be coherent until after his first cup of coffee. McCain was anything but a morning person.

His eyes popped open, and his mind was instantly clear, like a computer coming up from sleep mode. He went from black, blank, to full functionality in the space of time it took him to open his eyes.

McCain was laying on his back. Above him was a completely ordinary white acoustic tile sprinkled with tiny black holes. The tiles were held up by a grey metal grid. One of the two-foot by three-foot sections was a fluorescent light fixture that was dark. McCain was instantly aware of the fact that he could see details of the ceiling he ought not to be able to see in the nearly absolute dark of the room.

He turned his head to one side, feeling a soft cotton

sheet against his face. He sat up and scanned the room. It didn't take long. The room wasn't that big.

It had a sort of college dormitory feeling to it. The walls were blue-painted cinderblock. Again, McCain was struck by the fact that even in the darkness, he could tell the walls were blue. On the other side of the room, which was maybe half again as wide as McCain was tall, was a small, simple metal desk and a secretary's chair. On the desk was a reading lamp and a clock radio that wasn't plugged in. On the short wall behind him was a cheap, five-drawer dresser made of dark brown pressboard. On the wall in front of him was a steel door with an L-shaped steel handle. A strip of yellow light was visible from under the door, the only light in the room. The bed was an institutional twin-sized bed of the same design McCain remembered sleeping on in college.

He swung his legs over the edge of the bed, and when his feet touched the cold tile floor he realized he was wearing socks. McCain looked down and saw that he was wearing brilliant white, new sweat socks, comfortable cotton sweatpants, and an oversized sweatshirt that was so new the tag scratched the back of his neck.

He looked down at his chest and saw that the words Camp Clarity were embroidered onto the shirt in a delicate script. The sweatshirt and sweatpants were light grey and the embroidery a deep maroon. McCain looked down again and saw a pair of brand new canvas deck shoes sitting on the floor near his feet.

He reached down and pulled on the shoes, tying them with fingers he thought should have been stiff but were perfectly nimble. When his shoes were on, he stood and crossed to the door. His hand was two inches from the handle when McCain was startled by a faint noise behind him.

He turned and heard it again. It was coming from above, from behind one of the ceiling tiles. It occurred to McCain to be afraid, but he was happy to find that he wasn't. He watched as the tile shuddered under the weight of something moving around above it.

McCain turned back to the door and saw the light switch

next to it. The switch was turned down. McCain flipped it up. There was a stinging flicker, and the single recessed light went on. The tiny room was well lit by the single fixture.

The ceiling tile jumped a little. Whatever was up there might have been startled by the light coming on. McCain waited patiently, and after a second or two the tile was pushed aside from above, opening a single corner of darkness.

The side of a head then an eye appeared, and McCain offered the eye a smile. The eye in the ceiling narrowed, regarding him with suspicion.

"Nichts," McCain said, his voice even, clear, and friendly.

The little homunculus said nothing, but the single eye softened a bit.

"It's all right, Nichts," McCain said in perfect German.

Something tapped the floor in front of McCain, and he looked down to see a single drop of blood on the polished tile, then a second right next to it. He looked up at Nichts again, and there was a black line—a shadow, maybe—tracing down the little man's bulbous cheek.

It was a tear.

Another drop of blood.

McCain knew the tears and the blood were one and the same.

"Don't cry," McCain whispered. "It'll be all right."

Nichts's eye narrowed again, and another drop of blood tapped the floor.

"He punished you, didn't he?" McCain asked. "He punished you for giving me the phone."

The eye stared at him without a sound, but McCain knew Nichts was trying to say yes.

"Can't you come down?" McCain asked.

Again there was no answer. McCain waited. It took a long time—an hour. McCain remained perfectly still the whole time, and a corner of his mind marveled at his ability to do that— stand still like that for a full hour. Nichts stared at him the whole time. McCain wasn't going to beg Nichts to come down out of the ceiling.

Nichts pushed the ceiling tile back a little more—enough so he could crawl through. There was a puddle of blood on the floor below him that must have been five inches around.

The homunculus came out of the ceiling, and McCain smiled at the sight. He crawled out and hung from the ceiling tiles by the tips of his tiny clawed fingers and his even smaller clawed toes. He held there for the space of a few heartbeats, hanging from the ceiling by both hands and both feet. McCain could see the wings that had so unsettled him before, but he wasn't afraid now. How could he be afraid of this little man who had been his only friend?

Nichts unfurled his leathery grey wings, and it was as if the tiny breeze from them blew the last of the blocks from McCain's mind. He knew who he was, had a good idea where he was, remembered why he was there, and remembered clearly how he'd gotten there.

Memories of the dreams in the silence of the vril came back to him, too, and though they weren't always good dreams, the memory of them made him smile. The fact that he could remember anything at all made him smile. The fact that he could speak and understand German made him smile. The way he felt made him smile. He could feel a change, a difference in himself, and he knew it might take a long time for him to understand it—and maybe he never would—but he had been changed and changed for the better.

Nichts, still hanging from the ceiling, scuttled a few feet farther away from McCain and turned his head to look at him. McCain offered the little man a smile, but Nichts returned it with a scowl. The little man's already twisted face squeezed into itself. He'd stopped crying, but there was still blood on him.

"I'm better now," McCain told the little man.

Nichts regarded him silently for a moment, then dropped so he hung by only one foot, his clawed toes latched firmly into the acoustic tile.

"You called that stuff vril," McCain said. "What is it? How does it do what it does to people? How did it do this to me?"

Nichts dropped to the floor with his wings open and came

lightly to a rest just on the other side of the little puddle of blood from McCain. The homunculus reached out a gnarled little hand and touched the blood with the tip of one clawed finger.

"Your eye was bleeding," McCain said.

The little man looked up at him and said, "I was crying."

McCain didn't know what to say, so he said nothing. He remained motionless. Nichts touched the bloody finger to his own lips, and his face twisted into what McCain thought—hoped—might be a smile.

"I was not made to cry," Nichts said, looking up at McCain.

"I can speak and understand German," McCain said. "I can see in the dark, and I feel better than I've ever felt in my life. How is this done, Nichts? How does he do it?"

The homunculus looked at him blankly and said, "I can't know things like that. You feel the way you do because you are chosen of God. I am not even a creation of God."

McCain almost asked the little man what he was talking about, but he stopped when he saw another tiny drop of blood tap the floor under Nichts. The homunculus noticed McCain notice the blood and looked away, obviously ashamed.

McCain said, "I'm sorry, Nichts. He hurt you."

"He does as he pleases," Nichts said simply. "I was not intended to have intentions."

McCain wasn't sure what that meant, but he felt sorry for the little man anyway.

"You don't have anywhere to go, do you?" McCain asked.

Nichts looked up at him and said, "Go?" The little man's grey Halloween mask of a face looked almost as sad as it did confused.

"Why did you give me the phone?"

Nichts looked away and said, "I don't have . . . experience . . . with . . ."

"Compassion?"

"Thinking," Nichts corrected angrily.

A heavy silence passed.

"Vril doesn't have experience with being a liquid," the little man finally said.

McCain's eyes narrowed, and he regarded the homunculus with open confusion. Nichts didn't look up at him, so he didn't notice the expression.

"What do you mean?" McCain asked.

"The master," Nichts said, "has made it a liquid. It wasn't always. He has a way of making shapes. He is a great man, a powerful man favored of God."

"You've said that."

"It's true."

McCain smiled and said, "And it's true about me? That I'm favored of God?"

Nichts nodded, still looking at the floor, still bleeding.

"I don't believe in God," McCain said flatly.

Nichts looked up at him, his face as serious as any face McCain had ever seen, and said, "Then you're favored of Erwählen. And Erwählen's favor is enough."

McCain's heart sank. There were so many compelling reasons why that shouldn't be true, but there was a large part, a strong part of McCain's mind that grew increasingly excited, delighted, proud of that idea.

"Favored of Erwählen." Despite all McCain knew about Hans Reinhold Erwählen, he was beginning to believe that Erwählen's favor might be enough after all.

It had been a long time since he'd been favored of anyone. He was a man with no family, no ties to anything but a Hoffmann Institute test tube. Favored of Erwählen. Favored of anyone. Why not?

"Why not?" he asked the little man.

Nichts looked at him curiously and said, "You came here in opposition to him."

McCain nodded. He had. He had come as an agent of the Hoffmann Institute to investigate a conspiracy of white supremacists, then do what was necessary to disrupt their plans, but why should he? The Hoffmann Institute, Camp Clarity, the Nazi Party, Mothers Against Drunk Driving . . .

"I don't know why I came here," McCain said quietly.

The little man reared up, startled, and unfurled his tiny

batlike wings. McCain stepped back, surprised by the homunculus's strong reaction to what he'd said, then he realized Nichts wasn't startled by what McCain had said, but by the sound of footsteps outside the door, approaching.

Without a word, the homunculus hopped into the air, beat his little wings twice, and was back at the hole in the ceiling in the blink of an eye, hanging from the acoustic tile by his feet. He curled his body and crawled into the little space. McCain watched him go.

Nichts stopped and turned to McCain. "I don't get to decide," Nichts told him, the obvious implication being that McCain did get to decide, but McCain wasn't sure that was true.

Nichts looked at McCain as he pushed the ceiling tile back into place and disappeared. McCain could hear him scuttle away, even with the sound of footsteps now loud outside the door.

A light sound of knuckles rapping on the door came from behind McCain's head. He turned around and reached for the doorknob but stopped before his fingers touched it. He looked back and up at the ceiling tile that had served as Nichts's door into the featureless room. He glanced down at the blood and felt bad for Nichts, then was struck by the fact that he didn't feel bad for himself, though he was a prisoner of a fascist conspiracy.

He turned back to the door and grabbed the handle lightly. He was surprised that it turned easily. It wasn't locked. It opened smoothly to reveal the tall, grey-haired man he'd met before. It was Hans Reinhold Erwählen in a charcoal grey suit and maroon tie.

"Ah," Erwählen said, "Michael McCain. Good morning. Are you ready?"

"Ready?" McCain asked, meeting the man's genuinely amiable, crystal-blue gaze.

"Yes," Erwählen replied, "ready to begin your course of study here at Camp Clarity. We'll be moving you to more comfortable quarters, I assure you. You will be well taken care of."

A thought exploded into McCain's mind, and a waterfall of emotion followed it. Laced throughout the cascade was a vein of suspicion he'd once thought was an admirable trait.

Taken care of. Was it that simple? Was he that simple? Could that do? Was that enough to make him . . . ?

"You changed me," McCain blurted, his voice suddenly ragged, his breathing all out of its normal rhythm. "That shit you had me in, it—"

"It didn't do anything but make you better," Erwählen said calmly, smiling. "All it did was take what was inside you already and improve it. You are still Michael McCain. You're still the same man you were when you crept in here with your self-righteous agenda."

"I didn't . . ." McCain started to say, suddenly feeling like he had to defend himself. "You didn't improve my German."

This made Erwählen laugh. McCain was all at once delighted by the sound of Erwählen's laugh. He found himself smiling.

"An indulgence," Erwählen said, "the German. I hope it is my only one. A father could expect his children to speak his mother tongue, yes?"

A father.

McCain wasn't nearly that easily manipulated. No one with half a brain could be that easily manipulated.

McCain went to the tall man and fell into a warm, tight, reassuring embrace. A tear came to one eye, but McCain didn't cry. He didn't have to.

chapter TH1RT3EN

Through the peephole in the door of the motel room, Jeane's face looked puffy and distorted. Her lips looked even fuller than they normally did, and her makeup seemed badly applied. She was wearing sunglasses, but it was almost completely dark outside.

Ngan opened the door. Jeane smiled just a little, and said, "You always wear a suit."

Ngan stepped aside and motioned for her to enter. She nodded and stepped into the room, looking into the corners like police officers are trained to do.

"I was told," Ngan said, "when I first came to this country, that men wore suits."

"It stinks in here," was Jeane's disconnected reply.

She stopped in the middle of the room, looking down at Ngan's unopened suitcase sitting on the still-made bed. The TV was off, and the only sound in the room was an irritating rattle from the window air conditioner. The room was warm.

Ngan closed the door and said, "I believe it's vomit. Vomit and gasoline."

"You threw up?" she asked without looking up at him.

"No," he said, then, "Fenton?"

Jeane sighed and sat down on the bed. She was wearing loose-fitting blue jeans and a plain white T-shirt that fit her tightly around her large breasts. She was wearing new white tennis shoes, and her hair was pulled back from her face. She looked like a white Vanessa Richards. She was carrying a nylon duffel bag emblazoned with the logo of a shoe manufacturer. She dropped the duffel bag on the floor and looked up at him. He couldn't see her eyes behind the sunglasses. There was a bruise on the side of her mouth.

"It didn't go well," Ngan started for her.

She laughed uncomfortably and looked down, then took off her sunglasses. Both of her eyes were black.

"Back at the ATF," Jeane said, "there would have been a hearing. A series of hearings."

"Is he dead?"

Jeane nodded.

"Anyone else?"

"Anyone else dead?" she asked.

Ngan nodded.

"Two Chicago police officers."

Ngan sighed and crossed calmly to the other bed. He sat down slowly, not looking at her.

"Fenton has been using his cosmetics company to poison black people," she told him quickly. "The makeup turns them white . . . in patches."

Ngan nodded and said, "That is new information. I'll inform the Institute, and we'll see what can be done." There was a silence, then Ngan asked, "And?"

"He calls his hookers Joyce," she said.

"Joyce Mannering," Ngan confirmed. "A character from a film played by Marilyn Monroe."

Jeane looked at him sharply and let loose a laugh that was laden with relief, irritation, and nervousness. "He showed me a picture of Marilyn Monroe in a book."

"Did he?"

"Yes, he did," she said. "He told me I looked like her."

"You do," Ngan said with a humorless smile. "Don't you think?"

Jeane shrugged, irritated with the irrelevance.

"Did he mention Erwählen?" Ngan asked, sensing her impatience.

"In passing," Jeane sighed and looked down at her duffel bag. "Ngan," she continued, "I'm sorry. I don't know shit. I didn't find out anything. He was a racist, but you knew that. He had a thing for Marilyn Monroe lookalike hookers, but apparently you knew that too. I guess he had connections with the Chicago Police Department, but maybe only one, and that one's dead. He was a rich, white racist who thought he was one of the chosen people."

Ngan nodded and said, "Did you see anything unusual? Was there anything out of the ordinary about Fenton himself?"

Jeane laughed loudly for almost a minute. Ngan looked at her with a half-smile the whole time.

"I shot him off a twenty-some-story balcony," she said, "but he didn't die."

Ngan stopped smiling. Jeane wasn't laughing.

"I got the hell out of there," Jeane continued, "but he was waiting for me in the alley. He was all messed up, but he was alive. I shot him in the head, then, so I assume he's dead. I sort of passed out. That's when the cops got me. When we were driving away I saw a van from Fenton's company pulling into the alley. The driver of the van made eye contact with the white cop."

"And you shot this police officer?" Ngan asked.

"Yes, I did," Jeane said, "but only after he killed his own partner—a black guy, of course."

"You learned a great deal, Jeane," Ngan said reassuringly. He was sincere.

"Ngan," she said, "I'm telling you the whole thing was blown to hell."

Ngan shrugged and said, "It could have gone better, certainly. The Hoffmann Institute has ways of explaining away dead bodies, but not too many dead bodies and not too often. Still, Fenton's having survived a fall like that was serendipitous."

"You knew he could do that?" she asked.

"I suspected."

"You suspected," she said, "but didn't know?"

"We are investigating," he said. "We will 'know' when we are finished investigating."

"Did you send me there to kill him, Ngan?" Jeane asked, her voice stern.

"No," he said.

"Because if you sent me there to kill him—"

"I did not send you there to kill him," Ngan said flatly, "and neither did the Institute."

"How did he do that?" she asked, still not entirely satisfied with what she'd heard from Ngan. "How did he survive that fall? And he was strong, too. Too strong for a man his—for a man any age."

"You will have to believe me when I say that I am not at all certain how he managed that," Ngan said. "I honestly do not know, but again, that is why we're investigating."

Jeane stood suddenly and crossed to the cheap motel dresser. She drummed her fingers on the top of it. "This isn't just some yuppie KKK."

"Apparently not," Ngan said, "though we had suspected that is exactly what it was. This strength and ability to withstand injury is new. I have no doubt it's related to the fact that at the center of all of it is a man who hasn't aged a day in at least sixty years."

Jeane turned around and looked at Ngan. "You said something had gone wrong with Fitz," she said.

Ngan's face turned very grave, and he told her, "I received a telephone call from him when I was in Virginia. He was confused, delirious. He was speaking German and English mixed together so I couldn't understand him."

"They're drugging him in there?" she asked.

"Possibly," Ngan said. "I don't know. He has not been reporting in the way he was asked to."

"Jesus," Jeane breathed. "This is so bad."

"Not necessarily," Ngan said, though his voice made it obvious that he agreed with her.

in fluid silence

"Well, we have to get him out of there," she said.

"Indeed," he agreed, "but unfortunately you have not been invited, and I have been told that I am a zipperhead. This zipperhead status makes me unwelcome at Camp Clarity."

As if on cue, there was the sound of a car pulling up too fast into the parking lot. There was a squeal of tires, and bright white light spun in from the cracks around the drawn blinds. The car engine rumbled to a stop.

"Slope!" a voice shouted, low but with a squeaking edge to it. It was the sideline bark of a teenage athlete.

Jeane crossed to the window and slipped back the blinds just enough to see out.

"They're armed," Ngan, still sitting on the bed, warned her.

Jeane drew the .380 automatic from a belt holster at her back and slid the action back.

"Slopey-boy!" the teenager called out.

"They are offended by the shape of my eyes," Ngan joked.

"These are Erwählen's boys?" Jeane asked him.

"We told you not to sleep here, gook!"

"I'm not certain," Ngan said, "but I think it's a reasonable enough assumption. The Hitler Youth—after a fashion."

"Are they capable of killing?" she asked.

"Yes," Ngan said simply.

"Will they kill me?" she asked.

"Come on zipperhead!"

"Maybe not," he said. "You are white."

Jeane, her eyes serious and glimmering in the reflected light from the headlights and the motel room's yellowed lamp, looked at Ngan. She slid the gun back into the holster, leaving a bullet in the chamber.

"Very carefully," Ngan cautioned. "These are just boys, but maybe just boys in the same way Fenton was just a man."

Jeane nodded, turned the doorknob, and slipped out the door without opening it enough for the boys to see Ngan sitting on the edge of the bed.

The headlights were bright, and Jeane squinted, holding up a hand. The boys were driving a ten-year-old Camaro. The doors were open, and one teenager stood behind each of them. She couldn't see their faces, but she could tell they were wearing letter jackets. She couldn't tell for sure if they were armed or not, but she didn't think they were.

"Who's that?" she called to them, playing it cool at first.

"What the hell is this?" one of the boys—the driver—asked. "You with the chink?"

"I don't know what you're talking about, fellas," Jeane said, "but you're making a lot of noise out here, and people are trying to chill out for the evening."

The boy on the passenger side looked up at the sky, a deep indigo showing only three bright stars. It was after seven. The scattered old buildings of Lesterhalt stood out on the perfectly flat horizon in boxy silhouettes.

"You chillin' out?" the driver asked, mocking her.

"Tryin' to," she said. "What can I do for you boys?"

Both of them laughed, and the driver said, "You ain't half bad lookin' for an older lady, but you talk like a nigger. Your old man beat you up for that or something else?"

"That's not a very nice thing to say," she told him. "Why don't you guys go find something else to do tonight?"

The boys looked at each other, and the driver said, "Maybe we could do you."

Anger flooded through Jeane, and she wanted to punch this brat in the face. She choked it back and said, "Not in this lifetime, junior, but thanks for making an old lady feel special."

There was a silence from the boys that Jeane didn't like, then the driver said, "Are you rejecting me?"

Jeane didn't say anything, deciding on the fly to let him stew on it for a minute.

She saw the driver put his right foot up on the top of the door. The window was rolled down. He straightened his leg, and it looked like he was going to stand on the top of the door. Jeane's hand went to her back and curled around the handle of the gun. The boy sailed up into the air in such a high, long arc it made Jeane gasp. His jacket ballooned out behind him, and he stretched his arms to his sides. He seemed to fly, crossing

in fluid silence

the thirty feet between the car and Jeane in the time it took her to draw her gun.

The boy hit the ground in front of her, standing, and Jeane leveled her gun at him. She didn't even see his hand come up. It was just on her wrist as if he'd shot it out of a cannon. The boy's fingers tightened on her wrist, and it exploded in pain. Her fingers opened reflexively, and though she couldn't squeeze the trigger, she didn't drop it.

"Now we'll see who—"

The boy stopped talking, the braces on his teeth glinting in the light from the headlights, when a siren roared into life. Jeane had heard the sound before. It was a fixture of the Midwest and Great Plains. It was a tornado siren.

Instinctively she looked up. She could see more stars now in the indigo sky. It was clear. The warm spring air was still. The boy looked behind him at the car, then let go of her wrist and turned.

Jeane suppressed the sudden urge to shoot him in the back of the head. She'd been through a lot in the past several hours but managed to maintain some self-control.

He walked quickly back to the car. The passenger had already climbed in and closed the door. The driver didn't look back at her. He just slid into the car, slammed the door shut, and started the engine. The siren blared loudly.

"Hmm," Ngan grunted from behind her.

Jeane put her gun away, and the teenagers roared out of the motel parking lot, squealing off into the darkness.

chapter 4TEEN

McCain allowed himself to be pulled along by the flow of people. Erwählen had moved away and simply faded into the press of people that had appeared as if from nowhere. A siren was echoing in the distance, but the feeling of the people around him was one of excited expectation, a calm exuberance that McCain couldn't help but share. These men—and they were all men—couldn't wait to get to wherever it was they were going.

The corridor outside the little dorm room was as featureless and underwhelmingly ordinary as the little room itself. The walls were cinder block coated in thick layers of off-white paint. The floor was dead grey linoleum. There was a fire extinguisher, marked with the appropriate signage, hanging on the wall a few feet along the corridor. It had an inspection tag on it, and McCain found this completely reassuring. Someone had to come and inspect the fire extinguishers—someone from outside Camp Clarity. This was no prison, no evil genius's lair. This was just a place where people of like mind came to share ideas. McCain refused to think about the ideas. If the fire extinguisher guy could come and go, those ideas must not be so dangerous after all.

He thought of Jeane when he looked up and spotted a sprinkler in the ceiling tile above him. This place was built in accordance with fire codes. Jeane would have liked that, wouldn't she? McCain remembered that Jeane used to investigate arson for the ATF. That was before she had been railroaded into working for the Hoffmann Institute. She had been railroaded. She knew it. Ngan knew it. They all knew it. Jeane seemed happy enough. McCain might have been railroaded into Camp Clarity, but maybe he could seem happy enough eventually.

One of the men in the hallway bumped McCain's shoulder and startled him. McCain looked over at the man, and his heart jumped just a little. He was afraid. What kind of man did he just bump into?

The man was shorter than McCain, but not by much. He was younger than McCain by five or six years. His hair was long, tied in back by a rubber band. He had a beard as black as his hair. He smiled, showing small white teeth and his eyes were soft and friendly. McCain found himself returning the man's smile. This was a young guy, a guy with long hair and a beard. He wasn't some yuppie Wall Street guy or an old, grey-haired conspirator wielding political and economic power from a dark, smoke-filled room. This was a regular guy.

The siren faded away, and McCain continued to follow the tide of white men around corners, up a short flight of stairs, through a door into another corridor, then through a set of steel double doors. A brass plaque above the doors read **Fenton Auditorium**.

Beyond the double doors was a surprisingly large auditorium, with steeply angled rows of seats stretching maybe four stories up. McCain thought the auditorium could easily seat two thousand people. As surprised as he was by the crowd's destination, he realized he would have been surprised no matter where they'd brought him. Once he realized that, he started to look at the auditorium objectively. That lasted about two seconds, then he ignored it. It was precisely identical to every auditorium he'd

in fluid silence

ever been in in his life. The seats were upholstered in a rough maroon fabric that might have been burlap. The backs of the chairs were textured grey plastic. The carpet had a too-busy pattern of maroon and neutral brown that had a way of disappearing from the conscious mind immediately after the first glance. The walls were painted white, and attached to them were squares of the same maroon fabric as the chairs. McCain, like everyone else, assumed the maroon squares had something to do with acoustics, but he really had no idea why they were there and couldn't care less.

McCain followed the rest of the men as they flowed into the room and took their seats. There was the general murmur of conversation. McCain could see some men shaking hands. One laughed loudly, and there were a few amused chuckles. A couple of men coughed, and there was at least one sneeze. They were dressed in suits and T-shirts, flannel shirts, and polo shirts. They wore dress slacks and jeans. They had brown hair and blond hair and red hair. Some were bald. The only thing they all had in common was that they were all white, and they were all men.

So the men were ordinary, rounded up from any city or town in America. The room, like the hallway, was completely ordinary, down to the attention to fire safety and the maroon and grey seats. This wasn't some hidden volcano lair. Someone bought this stuff. Someone built it from blueprints using materials easily purchased from reputable manufacturers. Workers had been here—and inspectors, electricians, and plumbers.

A few rows down and to one side McCain recognized a familiar face, but he had trouble remembering the man's name. He was tall and thin with dark hair, wearing a navy blue suit and a gold pinky ring. McCain was sure he knew this man and should say something, but he couldn't—

Tom.

His name was Tom, and he had something to do with McCain's being here. Tom . . . Casale. That was it. Tom Casale.

McCain took his seat and was not at all afraid.

On the stage was a podium that had the simple script Camp Clarity logo on it. Behind the podium was a row of chairs—four of them. The back of the stage was a tall wine-red velvet curtain. Three men in suits stepped up onto the stage and smile-talked to each other as the audience settled in. McCain was two-thirds of the way up the auditorium and had a little trouble seeing the faces of the men on the stage at first.

The three men sat down and stopped talking to each other. They were facing out toward the audience and McCain could see their faces now. Two of them were senators. McCain had spent enough time in D.C. and always knew enough people who knew people who knew people. It paid to know who the players were.

One of the senators was a Republican from Illinois, the other a Democrat from North Carolina. The third man was Albert Barrington, the Secretary of Labor. He was a close friend of the President's and a well-known moderate. McCain had heard him speak at a Bar Association dinner in Baltimore. Barrington had talked about every American's right to work almost at the same time as he talked about a corporation's responsibility to its shareholders. He hadn't managed to walk the fence as much as work it like an Olympic gymnast on a balance beam.

A spotlight focused on the podium, and McCain couldn't help but look back at the source of it. At the top of the auditorium was a teenage boy working the spotlight. He was standing stiff, at attention, and his face had a sort of alien glow, a look McCain had never seen on a teenage boy: reverence. McCain turned to the stage, then back to the teenager.

Jerry. The kid's name was Jerry. As if the boy could hear McCain's thoughts, he looked down. Their eyes met, and McCain smiled. Jerry nodded, his face blank, noncommittal, then looked back at the stage, tipping the spotlight just the tiniest bit.

McCain faced front and saw Secretary Barrington stand and move to the podium. Applause thundered through the room. He squinted into the spotlight then turned to the audience with a practiced smile. He waved, caught the eye of someone in the audience, and smiled and winked at whoever it was. He set his hands lightly on either side of the podium and exhaled lightly. It echoed in the microphone, and McCain smiled. It was a way to determine if the microphone was live without looking silly saying "testing one-two" or starting to talk without anyone being able to hear.

"Gentlemen," Barrington said, waving one hand to still the applause, which faded on command. "Thank you very much, all. It's great to see so many familiar faces here, back for your second, third, even fourth course of study here at Camp Clarity. We all know what we're here for today, who we're going to have a chance to hear speak."

Barrington stepped back, put a hand in a pocket, letting the audience stare quietly at him.

"I don't have words," he continued, stepping back into the microphone, his eyes fixed on a point far in the back of the auditorium. "I just do not have the words to describe what this man has meant to me, what he's meant to my life. He's shown me . . ."

There was a pause of the perfect length, then he said, "But you all know that. He's meant the same to you, or you wouldn't be here today. I'm not going to yack all day. I'm here to introduce *Herr* Erwählen, and that's exactly what I'll do. Gentlemen, our teacher, our savior, our leader, and the great shining beacon of the New World Order, Mr. Hans Reinhold Erwählen."

The room exploded in applause. McCain's ears started ringing. The row in front of him stood, and McCain found his view of the stage blocked. He stood up, clapping, in time to see Erwählen step out from behind the curtain, smiling, his white teeth reflecting the spotlight. McCain smiled. Someone in the audience whooped.

Erwählen shook Barrington's hand, and the secretary looked at him as if Erwählen were his father. Erwählen clapped him on the shoulder, and Barrington moved to stand next to the two senators. When Erwählen got to the podium the three men sat down, and McCain could tell it was rehearsed. Rehearsed, but flawlessly executed. The room was still echoing with applause.

Erwählen put one hand up, and the audience was quiet at once. He raised his other hand, and they sat.

"Thank you all very much," he said, smiling that beautiful, warm smile. *"Vielen Dank zum allen.* I'll speak in English to honor the country that has been so good to us all—the country that will be so much better to us in the years to come."

An excited laugh spread through the audience.

"Let us take this opportunity to discuss the African savage and his role in the world we have all set about to create."

The audience settled in to listen, some of them leaning forward, eager to hear.

"The African people," Erwählen said, in casual, conversational tones, "are genetically inferior to the Aryan races. We know this to be true, though there are so-called scientists who will try to convince us that it is not. We're told over and over again that the differences between black and white are cultural, or social, not genetic. We're told that the American black is angry, that he has been kept down by white society, that it is white society's fault that he loots and burns his own neighborhood . . . on and on and on. We know differently.

"You have all spent time exposed to the vril, to the power that chooses its vessel. It chose you, like it chose me, because we are worthy. It chooses only the best of any species, as was the case since before recorded time. Vril has never chosen a colored man, and it never will.

"They're different, aren't they?"

There was a murmur of agreement from the audience, and Secretary Barrington nodded in an exaggerated way that showed he was playing to the last row.

"There are differences in the chemistry of their bodies, as much as the tenor of their souls. From their pigment to their endocrine system, their nutritional requirements and the diseases they find themselves in danger from that pass us by. We evolved differently, separate from them, and stayed separate until the days of the slave trade when ill-mannered white masters indulged themselves with the help."

This got a laugh.

"They are fine athletes, aren't they?" he went on. "They run fast, lift heavy weights, have amazing physical endurance, but name one that was responsible for a fundamental breakthrough in science or engineering. Name one black Newton or Bell or Ford."

Erwählen paused for effect, and McCain took the time to try

to remember the name of the man who invented peanut butter. George something . . .

"There was George Washington Carver, of course," Erwählen said, "who brought us all the miracle of peanut butter."

A wave of self-satisfied laughter followed, and McCain shrugged, feeling a little foolish. He was pretty sure Carver was responsible for more than peanut butter, but Erwählen's sarcasm played well to the audience.

"So much for the African-American contribution, eh?" Erwählen said, smiling through the laugh that thundered through the auditorium.

"You can teach a black man to bend to different cultural rules, of course," Erwählen said. "You can teach a dog to shit on a newspaper."

Another laugh.

"You can dress a black man in a suit, and he'll make a passing lawyer, maybe even run for office. You can put shoulder pads on him, and he will win your football game for you, but what does that mean? He's strong and easily adaptable, can be tamed, even domesticated. The African can run and jump and carry things, sing and dance and tell funny jokes, but a black man cannot lead. He cannot do that. A black man does not have that spark that truly sets us off from the cheetah, who can run, the monkey, who can jump, the elephant who can carry. A black man can sing like a bird, dance like a firefly, and, like a parrot, tell funny jokes he's heard elsewhere. What animal leads? What jungle dweller invents, creates, sets himself in the front and says to the world, 'I am master of all I survey and I will do anything—*anything* to back that up.' "

The audience applauded again.

"If you own a football team . . ." Erwählen paused, scanned the audience then said, "Ah, yes, there you are James. You can use them, train them to perform on your field, but would you put one at the head of your board of directors, or make him CFO?"

The grey-haired man Erwählen was looking at shook his head, smiling.

"I didn't think so." Erwählen looked back up at the audience and asked, "Would you trust him with the future of your business, your home, your nation, or your world?"

A murmur of "no's" washed through the audience.

McCain thought of a guy named Freddie Mitchell. Freddie lived in the dorm with McCain their first year at Yale. He was in pre-med, and he was good. If he wasn't at the top of his class, he was pretty damned close. A week before he was sent to Camp Clarity McCain had read in an alumni newsletter that Freddie had been named to the faculty of Johns Hopkins School of Medicine. Freddie Mitchell was black, and his father was the comptroller of a successful publishing company in Philadelphia.

"We are not the chosen of God," Erwählen said, his voice heavy, filling the auditorium with sheer importance. "We created God. That is something no African savage could do."

The audience laughed again, and a chill ran down McCain's back. A sweat broke out on the back of his neck when they started clapping and he joined in. His head spun when he stood with them, and his heart raced when Erwählen smiled.

chapter FIFTEEN

"It must be some kind of signal," Jeane said as the tornado siren wound down, echoing into silence. "They must use it to call people in."

"They?" Ngan asked.

She looked at him and scowled. He knew what she meant—he always knew what she meant—but he liked to pretend he didn't. He liked Jeane to say exactly what she meant. It was an irritating trait.

"The Nazis, the Klan, the GOP," she said. "You tell me."

Ngan smiled and folded his arms across his chest. He looked up at the clear night sky and said, "A curfew, maybe, enforced by Erwählen."

"No lynchings after seven?" she quipped. "Maybe they're regrouping—rallying in the face of the yellow peril."

Ngan laughed loudly but said nothing.

"Are you cold?" she asked him.

"No," he replied, "I am worried."

"About Fitz?"

Ngan sighed and said, "He could be dead already."

A car drove by, fast, heading the same direction the teenage boys had roared off in. "We could follow the crowd, go find him, and get him out of there by force."

"Against the fascist army of armed teenagers?" Ngan said quietly. "If that was all, I would have gone in after him myself."

"What else is there, Ngan?"

"Erwählen," he said simply.

"You're afraid of him?" she asked, not believing he could be.

"Of course," he said quickly. "There is reason to believe that Erwählen is a sorcerer of no small skill. The style of magic he has at his disposal is not entirely familiar to me. I cannot know for sure how dangerous he might be."

Jeane let a long breath hiss out her nose. "A sorcerer?" she asked.

"There might be some other name for what he is," Ngan answered. "He might call himself a thaumaturgist, perhaps a wizard."

Jeane shook her head. "I'm going to go ahead and assume you're joking about that, okay? I mean, Fitz has disappeared into this rich white-guy asshole training camp, and you're telling me the Great and Powerful Oz is behind it all?"

Ngan narrowed his eyes, tipped his head, and said, "The Great and Powerful Oz? Is this a holy person?"

Jeane laughed. "When we get back to Chicago, we're going to Blockbuster, first thing."

"I understand your perspective, Jeane," he said, apparently realizing she was having some fun with him, "but where I come from, we hold men like Erwählen in reverence. When they are good, we honor them. When they are evil, we fear them."

"No offense, Ngan," she said, "but this isn't Tibet. This is Outside Nowhere, Illinois, and I don't believe in wizards."

"Before we met," he said, "did you believe in aliens or ghosts?"

There was a clatter of metal on pavement that made them both jump. They looked to their left and saw a shopping cart

in fluid silence

overturned where the parking lot of the motel gave way to the parking lot of the laundromat next door. A woman was standing over the cart, holding a laundry basket full of neatly folded clothes. She bent down slowly, stiff, old, and in obvious pain. She grabbed a corner of the shopping cart and righted it quickly, then herself a bit less quickly.

She was black, her tight hair dusted with grey. She weighed easily as much as Jeane and Ngan put together and was wearing a green paisley housecoat. Her shoes were new, plain white canvas tennis shoes that seemed odd on the little feet at the ends of her massive legs.

The old woman looked up and caught Jeane's stare. A brief flash of uncertainty—not fear—passed across her face. Jeane was about to look away when the old woman winked, then smiled. Jeane realized her own face was blank as she watched the old woman put her laundry basket back into the shopping cart and start pushing it into the motel parking lot.

"She noticed you," Ngan said. "You should speak with her."

Jeane turned to him and asked, "Why me?"

"She saw you," Ngan told her. "She smiled. You are a woman."

"You're a minority," she said before thinking.

"I am Tibetan," he said. "There are far too few of us in America to be considered a proper minority, Agent Meara."

She hated it when he called her that.

"And woman," she said, "is nigger of the world."

Ngan smiled, said, "A wise Asian woman said that, I believe," and turned back to the motel room door.

Jeane didn't watch him go. She strolled as casually as she could, intercepting the woman as she passed in front of the motel doors. The woman watched Jeane approach with a welcoming, knowing look.

"Hi," Jeane said lamely.

"Good evening to you, ma'am," the woman said.

"Lovely night," Jeane said. She stopped a few feet from the woman, who stopped walking as well.

"Tornado sirens were blowing," the old woman said. Her voice had a tired, smoke-gravel edge. "Not a cloud in the sky."

"Yeah," Jeane said, looking down. "That was weird. What was that?"

The old woman smiled and let her eyes hang on Jeane. "You're a pretty thing, aren't you?" she said.

Jeane blushed and looked away, feeling like a three-year-old. "Thank you," she breathed.

"You're not from Lesterhalt," the woman said.

Jeane looked up at her. The woman's eyes were wide, expectant. "No," she said. "You can tell?"

This made the old woman laugh. Her teeth were yellow, and she was missing one on top and two on the bottom.

"Not that hard?" Jeane asked.

"Darlin'," the woman said, "a woman don't get to your age and keep a figure like that in Lesterhalt, Illinois. You might have been born here, Miss, but you been livin' city."

Jeane smiled, nodded, and said, "That's very observant of you."

"My name is Edith, darlin'," she said, "and besides all that, you're standing in the parking lot of a motel."

Jeane laughed and held out her hand. "My name is Jeane Meara."

Edith took Jeane's hand and said, "Very pleased to make your acquaintance, Jeane Meara. So what brings you to Lesterhalt, much less to this spot of blacktop talking to an old lady like me?"

Jeane stopped smiling. She hated the drama of the gesture and the change that came over Edith's eyes.

"Was that your friend back there?" Edith asked, her voice slow and deliberate. "The Chinese man . . . the one who went back into the motel to give the womenfolk their privacy."

Jeane nodded and said, "We work together."

"He's not safe here, Jeane Meara," Edith said quickly.

"I know," Jeane said. "A teenage boy put a gun to his head in the diner earlier today."

Edith nodded and looked down. "They'll kill him next time," she said, almost whispering. "They're at their meeting now. Y'all had best be on your way."

in fluid silence

Jeane's heart sank. She felt profoundly sad, though she wasn't sure precisely why. "What's going on here, Edith? What meeting?"

Edith looked up, smiled, tipped her head, and asked, "Are you with the police, Jeane Meara?"

"No," she said. "No, I'm not."

"Too bad," Edith replied, smiling.

"Do you need the police?"

Edith put her hands on the cart and seemed about to take a step forward, away from Jeane. She paused, though, and said, "No, I guess not. Not in so many words. Is there a law against going backward?"

"Going backward?" Jeane asked, honestly not sure what the old woman meant by that.

Edith looked at her with wet eyes. "When I was a young girl, my daddy moved us all up from Tennessee after my uncle was lynched. Hung this good, honest, hard-workin' man from an old tree in the yard outside our church. I never knew why they did it. My daddy, he never did say. 'Crackers are crackers,' that's what Momma used to say, and that part of Tennessee was full enough of them boys.

" 'Illinois,' my daddy said, 'fought for the North in the Civil War—was the home of Lincoln himself.' Daddy said we'd find peace here, and you know what, Jeane Meara? We did. We did find peace. A good many years have passed since then, I'll tell you that, and it's been a fine place to live. A fine place."

"But?" Jeane prompted.

"You never did say why you were here," Edith said.

Jeane was taken aback by the question. She opened her mouth to say something, but nothing came out. What could she tell this woman? What did this woman already know?

"I work . . ." she said, pausing to think, "for a civil rights group . . . sort of."

Edith laughed and said, "Girl, you lie like a possum plays chess."

Jeane blushed again and said, "It's actually not too far from the truth."

"Well," the old woman said, "if you're here with that Chinese fella, I guess you're not from the hotel at least."

"The hotel?"

Edith nodded, the smile disappearing from her face and the laugh disappearing from her voice. "Camp Clarity, they call it. It's some kind of whites-only country club or something outside town. It wasn't long after that place opened up that things started to change around here. For the worse, I can tell you."

Jeane nodded and said, "That's why we're here."

She wanted Edith to know that someone cared enough to come here and do something. Of course, Jeane didn't know what they were actually going to do. The look on Edith's face made it evident that the old woman didn't hold out much hope for their success.

"Well, good for you, honey," she said quietly. "You and that Chinese man are going to do what? Expose them? Put them on the TV?"

"No, no," Jeane said. "Nothing like that."

There was a moment of hesitation where it was obvious to Jeane that Edith wanted to hear more. Jeane had nothing more to say.

"What about you?" Jeane asked. "Have you ever had a run-in with these teenagers or anyone from Camp Clarity?"

"Oh, no, darlin'," she replied. "They don't have anything to say to an ol' woman like me. There's been no cross burnin' or anything like that. It's the same old same old in some ways, y'know? Little intimidations here and there—looks, whispers, the word 'nigger' when you turn your back." She scoffed harshly and said, "Little boys think a colored woman my age ain't never been called a nigger."

Jeane forced a smile, then nodded for her to continue.

"Ain't much else to say, darlin'. Town's up and gone cracker is all. Guess it just happens sometimes, especially in a little town like this that's seen its last factory boarded up and shipped off to China or some such place. Ain't a lot for a white man in Lesterhalt to do but feel sorry for himself."

"That sounds like an excuse," Jeane said.

Edith looked surprised. "It is what it is, darlin', and it'll be what it'll be."

"Sounds like a Bible passage."

Edith laughed at that. "No, just horse sense. 'Sides, if they all want Lesterhalt for their lily-white selves, they can up and have it. I have a daughter lives in St. Louis. She's the manager of a book store there. She went to college in Carbondale, got an education, and kept the sense she got from her momma—enough sense to leave this town behind. She told me I could stay with her. I hate to be a burden on my baby and all, but things here have . . . Well, things here are what they are."

Jeane didn't know what to say.

"It's all right, darlin'," Edith said.

Jeane was embarrassed that this woman felt she had to be comforting when she was being driven out of her home by the sort of open racism most Americans thought had disappeared a long time ago. "I'm sorry, Edith," she said. "Is there anything I can do?"

"I don't know, darlin'." Edith said. "*Is* there anything you can do, you and your Chinese friend?"

"We'll try," was all Jeane could say.

Edith smiled and said, "Well then, that's the best news I've had in a while now."

"Edith, if there's anything you can think of that might help us, anything you've seen or heard that's out of the ordinary, that seemed . . . I don't know, impossible or strange, you come here and find me, okay?"

Edith stared at her for twenty seconds or so, then said, "They ain't just clansmen up there in that hotel, is they?"

"No," Jeane said, before she could second-guess herself and not say what she was about to say. "No, they're not just clansmen up there, and it's not just a hotel."

Edith looked into the distance in the direction Jeane knew Camp Clarity lay. "I didn't think so," she said to the horizon. "I've seen clansmen before. Seen my uncle . . . But this one, this time . . ."

"What is it, Edith?"

143

"Darlin'," she said, "these boys have a plan. Know what I mean, dear? A plan."

A cold sweat dampened Jeane's forehead as much as from what Edith said as from the look in her eyes. "A plan?"

"Good night to you, darlin'," Edith said, pushing her cart a step forward. "It's getting chilly for an old woman, and I still have half a mile to walk home. You and your Chinese friend, you be careful with these boys. They might not kill you, but they will, sure as my great granddaddy picked cotton, kill him."

"Good night, Edith," Jeane said.

"Good-bye, darlin'," Edith replied.

chapter 6TEEN

Erwählen's speech went on for another twenty minutes or so. McCain couldn't help feeling it was the perfect length—practiced and efficient. When he finished there was a thundering standing ovation that just went on and on. Erwählen finally walked off the stage, and Secretary Barrington went back to the podium.

"Wonderful," he said, the audience fidgeting with used up excitement. "Just wonderful. Thank you all, and thank you *Herr* Erwählen. A couple of quick announcements before we break up. Blue Group, you should proceed from three to four. Group leaders, don't forget to file your monthlies with the clerk. We'd hate to see anyone miss out on anything. Regional group leaders should be aware of new spread protocols. If not, please see Mr. Lemon."

McCain had no idea what any of that meant. He looked around the auditorium and saw men taking notes, some nodding, others whispering to each other. Some had stood up. Still others were already filing out of the various exits. The senators on the stage had stepped down and were glad-handing and back slapping at the foot of the stage with a churning crowd of white men.

"And that ought to just about do her for tonight, gentlemen," Barrington concluded with a stiff wave. "Thanks again, and we'll see you next time."

Barrington stepped back from the podium, smiling widely, and there was a smattering of applause. McCain stood up when the man next to him did, and he realized he had no idea where to go. He knew he'd never be able to find his way back to the little dorm room the way he'd come, and he wasn't sure he should go back there anyway. He found himself hoping that Nichts would show up.

The man next to McCain nudged him with an elbow and said, "Looks like Barrington would like a word with you, son."

McCain looked at the man who'd nudged him. He was easily eighty years old, dressed in a three-piece black suit and wire-thin tie. He smelled of mothballs and stale cigars.

"I'm sorry?" McCain asked lamely.

The old man's eyes, sparkling with misplaced vigor, glanced at the stage, and he nodded. "The secretary," he said.

McCain looked at the stage and saw the labor secretary looking up at him, smiling. When McCain caught his eye, Barrington waved him down, his face welcoming and warm.

McCain looked down at his feet, negotiating the breaking-up crowd carefully and slowly. He passed Tom Casale, and they made brief eye contact, nodding to each other. Casale flashed him a tiny smile, but McCain was still too out of sorts to return it. In time he made his way to the stage, and Barrington held out a hand. The secretary, still on the stage, towered a good three feet above McCain. McCain reached up and took the man's warm, soft, almost feminine hand and shook it firmly. Barrington smiled and said, "Matt McCain."

"I'm sorry?" McCain asked.

"Matthew McCain?" the secretary repeated. "You're Matt McCain from Chicago."

"Michael," McCain corrected. "It's Michael McCain, but people call me Fitz."

Secretary Barrington, still smiling, stepped off the stage and landed lithely on the busy carpeting. Something about the way his body came to a stop from the short fall made McCain feel uneasy.

"Michael," Barrington said. "Sorry about that. Twenty years in politics, and I still get people's names wrong. I should ask Erwählen to toss me back in and work on the short term memory, eh?"

He winked, and McCain forced a smile.

"Erwählen wants us to get to know each other," Barrington said. "Did you have plans for this evening?"

The question was so preposterous McCain had to laugh.

Jeane stepped back into the motel room, pushing the door closed behind her. She reached back and turned the deadbolt.

"What did she have to say?" Ngan asked.

He was sitting straight on the edge of one of the beds—the one farthest from the window. Jeane looked at him for a few seconds, and his face remained passively expectant. She crossed the room to the dresser and picked up her purse. Ngan remained silent as she fished for her cell phone.

"The town," she told him, "has gone cracker. She's moving to St. Louis, and I doubt she's the only person of color who's likely to do that. She said that the boys are going to kill you unless we leave now."

Jeane found her cell phone, flipped it open, and looked down at the lighted display.

"I'm not sure what it means to 'go cracker,'" Ngan said, "but I assume she meant that minorities are no longer welcome in Lesterhalt."

"Who's Lieberman?" Jeane asked, still looking at her phone.

"From the ADL?" Ngan prompted.

Jeane looked up and nodded. "He's left an email message for you on my account."

"Yes," Ngan said. "I apologize. You know I dislike carrying a computer, but I knew we would be together and you would have yours."

Jeane sighed and said, "That's a rather convenient form of Luddism. Reject technology, but always make sure you have a wired friend nearby."

Ngan smiled and asked, "What does he have to say?"

Jeane turned the phone off, set it on the dresser, and crossed to sit on the bed near the window. She picked her duffel bag off the floor, reached in it, and pulled out a slim black laptop. She glanced at Ngan, who was still sitting on the other bed smiling at her, and woke the computer up. She clicked a little, typed a little, and clicked a little more, then set the computer on the bed next to Ngan.

Ngan read the email from Ira Lieberman, then frowned.

"Bad news?" Jeane asked.

Ngan shrugged and said, "Surprising news. It seems that our Mr. Erwählen actually advised against the Final Solution."

"*A* Mr. Erwählen," Jeane muttered, then said more clearly, "That wouldn't get him killed back then?"

"Indeed, it very nearly did," Ngan said. "The Gestapo was convinced they'd assassinated him very near the end of the war, but Erwählen apparently escaped and found himself in the hands of American intelligence officers."

"Good for him," Jeane said.

Ngan nodded and stared at her computer screen a little while longer.

"I'm hungry," she said. "If we're not going to go after Fitz, can we at least order a pizza? I take it you never got your dinner."

"You're still working on Bachelor's Grove?" Ngan asked.

He didn't look up at her, but Jeane looked at him. The only sound for a while was the faint hum of the laptop and crickets chirping outside.

"I'm not satisfied," she said finally, "with the conclusions drawn by the investigation."

"I drew the correct conclusions," Ngan said without the slightest trace of wounded ego or defensiveness.

"I have a degree in chemical engineering, Ngan," she said,

with more than a trace of wounded ego and defensiveness. "I used to investigate arson, bombings, very serious crimes for the federal government. If you thought I'd be satisfied with 'it was a ghost,' why did you hire me?"

Ngan smiled.

"I'm not a blind cynic," she continued. "That thing in the sewers in D.C.—tell me it's a creature from another planet and, seeing what I saw, I'll happily accept that. After all, there are billions of stars in our galaxy and billions of galaxies . . . blah, blah, blah. The mystery of the ages solved. But now I have to sign my name at the bottom of a piece of paper that ends with a ghost."

"Isn't that precisely what it was?"

"Maybe," Jeane said, "but that's not good enough. That's not an explanation. That's like saying the Lindbergh baby was kidnapped by a human. An investigation should specify exactly which human and why."

"But the Lindbergh baby wasn't kidnapped by a h—"

"Just . . ." she interrupted, holding up a hand, "don't. Please don't finish that sentence if you want me to stay on this freak show merry-go-round."

Ngan smiled, and Jeane found herself laughing.

"Jesus," she breathed.

"So you're examining the nature of ghosts?" Ngan asked her. "How they do what they do—live on after death, affect the world of the living?"

Jeane sighed, staring at her reflection in the black TV screen. "I think it's something electrical," she said. "A kind of transference or looping of electrical impulses from the brain into some other closed system . . . the roots of the trees in the cemetery, for instance. The . . . um . . . ghost—Jesus . . . never really exhibited any independent creative action. I think it was acting somehow on pure instinct and base emotional responses that were somehow transmitted from . . ."

She trailed off, noticing the way Ngan was looking at her.

"I'll submit a new report when I have something more concrete," she said.

"I look forward to reading it," he told her with real sincerity.

"A similar report on Erwählen's peculiar brand of alchemy will be most interesting as well."

"Alchemy, now?" she asked, irritated. "He's a wizard *and* an alchemist?"

"These two things go hand in hand more often than not," he said.

"Of course they do," she sneered.

"If you could see this magic—experience it for yourself," he asked, "like you saw the alien in Washington, D.C., or the ghost in Chicago, would you believe?"

"That depends," she non-answered.

"Fenton falling all that way and surviving. . . ?" he said.

Jeane smiled and said, "There are ways that something like that could be possible. Unlikely, sure, but more likely than magic and alchemy."

"Indeed," he admitted, "and you are quite right that this is why we hired you. An English inventor and author once said that any suitably advanced technology would be indistinguishable from magic."

"Arthur C. Clarke," Jeane said.

"Yes," Ngan said, smiling, "that was him. He is certainly correct. Maybe there is a scientific explanation for what we encountered in Bachelor's Grove. Perhaps there is simply some mixture of chemicals that Erwählen is using to create this heightened physical nature. If that is indeed the case, the Institute will be very happy to hear that explanation."

"Ngan," Jeane said with a sigh, realizing as she did it that she'd been sighing altogether too much that night, "the *only* kind of explanation is a scientific explanation. By definition, everything else is mythology."

"Or faith?"

She smiled, shrugged, and said, "And the conversation ends there."

"I am a Buddhist," Ngan said. "In my country they would call me *gomchen*. I know that doesn't mean anything to you, and it doesn't need to. It informs me, though, in the same way that your degree in chemical engineering informs you."

"Look, Ngan," Jeane said, "I'm not trying to convert you, or de-convert you, or whatever. Science isn't a religion. It doesn't do the same thing religion does or answer the same questions in the same way. We live in a universe that has laws, that has rules that really work and act on us every day. I saw what I saw in that cemetery, and though I'd like nothing more than to write it off as a hallucination, I can't. I have to figure out what was really going on there. If this guy Erwählen is creating Nazi supermen out of yuppie cosmetics company chairmen and teenage wrestlers, fine. I'm going to figure out how—*exactly* how."

"Perhaps we should order a pizza after all," Ngan said, then winked at Jeane with good humor and bad timing.

She fought down the urge to slap him and said, "Fine. Where's the phoneboo—?"

The gunshots shattered the window into a tinkling shower of sparkles and punched one, two, three, four holes in the thin, cheap plaster walls. One came through the door. There was a handful of distinct whistling sounds in the still air of the motel room and a whole lot more less distinct ones.

Jeane threw herself sideways off the bed, landing on the floor between the two beds. The carpet was rough and smelled bad. She heard at least one bullet lodge in the bed and another ping off the metal frame. She heard Ngan fall to the floor on the other side of the inside bed, between it and the wall. The shooting stopped, and there was a squeal of tires.

"Damn it," she said, angry with herself for not hearing the car pull up. "Ngan, are you—?"

She stopped when she looked under the bed at Ngan. He was laying on the floor, his head across from her feet. He turned his head to look back at her, and their eyes met. He was breathing in short, rapid gasps. Jeane looked at his chest and saw blood soaking into his shirt on at least two spots, growing like blossoming roses.

"Damn it," she said, and she stood up.

The secretary of labor maintained an office at Camp Clarity. It was in the same building, down a carpeted hallway from the auditorium. The secretary led the way there. The teenage boy named Jerry had come down from where he was manning the spotlight and followed them, carrying the submachine gun and eyeing McCain with pissy suspicion.

The office was big, the furniture new. There was very little in the way of personal items there—the knickknacks that fill most people's workspaces. It had a temporary feeling but was comfortable. A wide picture window with venetian blinds pulled up to the top looked out into a dark night sprinkled with distant lights. Barrington sat at the wide teak desk and motioned McCain to a comfortable leather chair. McCain sat. Jerry stood behind him.

"Does he have to stand there like that?" McCain asked, letting his eyes shift to one side to indicate Jerry. "He's making me nervous with that thing."

Barrington looked up at Jerry and made a shooing motion. McCain looked back and saw Jerry reluctantly shuffle to one side. The gun was still pointed at the back of McCain's head.

"Kids with guns?" McCain asked facetiously, eyeing Secretary Barrington.

"Jerry's eighteen years old," Barrington said, "aren't you, Jerry?"

"Yes, sir," Jerry answered dully.

"Old enough to be tried as an adult," McCain said, "but that's not much of a comfort."

"No, no," Barrington said calmly. "What I meant was that Jerry's old enough to exercise his second amendment rights, that's all."

"There should be an amendment that makes pointing a gun at the back of someone's head illegal," McCain replied. "Could make for a less anxious citizenry."

"All in due time, I'm sure, Mr. McCain," Barrington said cryptically.

"Please," McCain said, "call me Fitz."

"Fitz it is," Barrington replied. "Where'd that come from?"

"The nickname?"

Barrington nodded.

"A bad joke," McCain replied. "An inside joke—a family thing."

Barrington nodded, brushing the answer off and making it obvious he didn't care where the nickname came from.

"Why am I here, Mr. Secretary?" McCain asked. "And why aren't I dead?"

"Mr. Erwählen thought we might have a nice chat," Barrington replied. "And Mr. Erwählen thought we might have a nice chat."

McCain laughed.

"Seriously, Fitz," Barrington said, "we don't kill people here."

"I see," McCain said dryly. "So Jerry's in charge of what—opening cans?"

"Jerry's in charge of doing what he's told," Barrington said. "He's here to protect me, not to kill you."

"A step down from the Secret Service."

Barrington smiled and said, "You're quite an accomplished smartass, Fitz. My compliments. Can Jerry fix you a drink?"

"No, thank you," McCain said. "Something tells me I should stay sober."

"Good for you. A Diet Coke or something then?"

"Nothing," McCain said flatly. "Thanks."

Barrington set his chin on his hand and his elbow on the desktop. He stared at McCain for a few seconds, his brow knitted in earnest, concerned interest. "What did you think of the speech?" Barrington asked.

McCain shrugged and said, "Bullshit, delivered well."

Barrington smiled at McCain's honesty. "Very good," he said, "most people in your situation would be kissing my ass."

"You want me to kiss your ass?" McCain asked sincerely.

"No, thank you," Barrington replied. "I really do want your honest thoughts. I understand that what Erwählen said was controversial. You know who I am, right? You know the position I hold?"

"You're a cabinet member," McCain said. "You're the secretary of labor."

"That's right," Barrington said. "I'm sure you have some idea what would become of my career if all this came out on *Hard Copy* or *Nightline*. I'd be run out of Washington on a rail—by some of the men in the auditorium tonight, in fact."

"So, why are you here?"

Barrington sat up straight, then leaned back in the big leather desk chair. His eyes never left McCain's. "Why are *you* here?"

"I asked you first," McCain shot back.

Barrington laughed loudly, slapping the desktop. "That's terrific, Fitz. Really."

McCain smiled, noticing how oddly at ease he felt.

"Fine, then," Barrington conceded. "I'm here because I have a measure of foresight. Things are changing, and I believe in being ahead of the curve. I get a sense that you're the kind of guy who likes to be ahead of the curve too, Fitz."

"You sound like an insurance salesman," McCain said, meaning it as an insult.

"I used to sell insurance," Barrington replied without missing a beat. "That was years ago, though, and I don't relish the idea of doing it again."

"So you jumped in with the Nazis for the long haul," McCain finished sarcastically.

"We're not Nazis, Fitz."

"Then what are you?"

Barrington's lips thinned. For just a second he was rattled, angry. McCain knew he'd asked a question Barrington wasn't prepared to answer.

"There's a question," Barrington said slowly, "that's often asked in job interviews. I'd like to hear your answer to it."

"If you're going to ask me why I want to work at the Gap, Mr. Secretary," McCain said, "it's because of the chicks."

Barrington laughed loudly, the sound of it echoed against the office's bare walls. "No, no," he said. "Nothing so specific. I'd like you to tell me where you see yourself in five years."

McCain thought of a couple jokes but knew enough not to

poke Barrington too much, too hard. "That's a difficult question for someone from my generation to answer, Mr. Secretary."

"Give it a try."

McCain let a breath out through his nose. He looked at the completely ordinary office furniture and said, "I'd like to not be at a cross burning."

"Good enough," Barrington said. "How about ten years? Twenty?"

"I guess my answer would be the same," McCain answered. "I'm not sure why you need to know this."

"Will you still be working for the Hoffmann Institute in ten years?" Barrington asked. The question sent a chill down McCain's spine. "Will you still be working for them in twenty years?"

"Maybe," McCain answered. "Unless some high school wrestler shoots me in the back of the head first."

"Our high school wrestler won't shoot you in the back of the head unless I tell him to," Barrington assured him, "and I have no intention of telling him to."

"In that case," McCain said, "when I grow up I'd like to be Don from *Lost in Space*."

Barrington squinted at him, obviously aware that McCain was having some fun with him, but not really picking up on the reference. "Don?" he asked.

"Sure," McCain said. "He was the pilot, really cool, dated Judy."

Barrington shook his head, smiling, and said, "Dan from . . ."

"*Lost in Space*," McCain provided. "And it's Don."

"Don it is then," Barrington said with a tip of his chin. "What about thirty years, forty years, or fifty years?"

"If I'm alive in fifty years," McCain said honestly enough, "and I am still able to go to the bathroom by myself, I guess I'll have to be satisfied with that."

"An admirable goal, Fitz," Barrington replied with a knowing smirk. "Where will you be in a hundred years?"

Not that anything about the conversation so far had been normal, but this question stopped McCain dead in his tracks.

"2101, Fitz," Barrington said with the sort of knowing smile

Ronald Reagan used to be famous for. "Where will you be the first year of the twenty-second century?"

"Driving my jet car to my new job at Spacely Sprockets?" McCain said, shaking his head at the absurdity of the question. "I'd be a hundred and thirty-two years old."

"Hans Reinhold Erwählen is over two hundred years old," Barrington said, with a weight in his voice that he obviously intended to convey the gravity of that silly assertion.

"Who told you that?" McCain asked.

"Erwählen," Barrington answered.

"Do you believe everything Erwählen tells you?"

"Yes," Barrington answered simply, "I do."

"Why?"

"Because he always tells me the truth."

McCain let Barrington sit there smiling at him for a few seconds.

"You still haven't answered my question," Barrington said after those few seconds had passed.

"Are you saying you can make me live to be a hundred and thirty-two?" McCain asked.

"No," Barrington replied. "I can make you live a lot longer than that—or, actually, Erwählen can. To be honest, I don't have his . . . skills."

"How will he manage to do that?" McCain asked, really wanting to know.

"Do you use a computer?" Barrington answered.

McCain shrugged grandly, letting Barrington know he was getting aggravated by the ambiguity of the interview. "Yes, I do."

"Do you know exactly how it works?"

"No," McCain answered, understanding the point.

"Erwählen can do it," Barrington said.

McCain shifted in his chair and said, "Why don't you answer that question, Mr. Secretary. Where will you be in a hundred years?"

"I will be at Erwählen's side, Fitz," Barrington answered with no small show of pride. "I'll be one of the masters of the New World Order."

"Commandant of the new concentration camps?" McCain pressed, then cringed inside, wishing he could pull that back. He couldn't use an angry Barrington.

But Barrington didn't get angry.

"I understand what you're thinking, Fitz," he said calmly. "I really do. I thought the same thing when I first came here, when I was still the lieutenant governor of Rhode Island. All that racist stuff, it informs us, but it doesn't rule us."

"So you don't believe all that stuff?" McCain asked. "All that stuff about black people being genetically inferior?"

"Oh, no," Barrington said. "That's all quite true. They are genetically inferior. You're not convinced of that, after tonight?"

"After the speech?"

Barrington nodded.

"No, I can't say I am," McCain replied. "I heard a lot of arguments, but no evidence, no real science."

Barrington smiled and said, "And if you had heard some real scientific evidence, Fitz, would you have believed then? Would you have even understood it, if Erwählen had started getting into chemical equations and all that?"

McCain smirked and said, "I would have tried to understand. Maybe I wouldn't have. Maybe I'd still believe we're all just people who do the best we can. Maybe I'd still believe that no one deserves to die for the color of his skin."

Barrington put up a cautioning hand and said, "Easy, there, Fitz. No one here said anything about killing anybody."

"They didn't have to," McCain answered, letting the anger he was feeling soak through into the words. "Once you decide that some group of people, whoever they may be, aren't as human as you, the killing starts soon enough."

"What if I told you Hans Erwählen had the ear of Hitler sixty years ago and fought against the camps, argued strenuously against the Final Solution?"

McCain sighed and said. "Well, he'd have been . . . what . . . ten? Most likely Hitler gave him a gummy bear and sent him on his way."

"I told you," Barrington said earnestly, "Erwählen is over two hundred years old."

"Two hundred years old and a humanitarian racist?" McCain pressed.

"I suppose so," Barrington answered, chuckling. "We don't hate the lesser races, Fitz, and we're not asking you to. We understand their place, and want to help them understand their place as well, that's all."

"That's your New World Order?" McCain asked, shaking his head. "Sounds more like the Confederacy."

Barrington literally brushed the comment aside with a wave of his hand. "We won't go any further into that, okay?" he said. "There will be all sorts of time, and I can assure you that when you've completed the course you'll understand."

"And what if I don't 'complete the course'?" McCain asked.

"You will," Barrington almost whispered. He leaned forward and looked deeply into McCain's eyes. "How do you feel, Fitz? Physically, I mean."

"I feel fine."

"No," Barrington said, shaking his head. "You feel better than fine, don't you?"

McCain swallowed, disappointed to find his mouth and throat dry like sandpaper. "I feel terrific."

"You aren't afraid either, are you?" Barrington pressed gently but firmly. "You've forgotten about Jerry, haven't you? You're not afraid of the teenager with the M4 pointed at the back of your head. The thought of him back there interests you, maybe offends you, but it doesn't frighten you, doesn't panic you."

"No," McCain admitted, trying to look away from the too close, too serious Barrington.

"How do you feel about Erwählen?" the secretary asked.

"Erwählen?" McCain repeated, hoping to avoid the question.

"Does he frighten you?" Barrington asked, sitting back quickly, breaking the heaviness in the air.

"No," McCain answered quickly, but honestly.

"Does he offend you?"

McCain found that he couldn't answer that question as quickly. He wanted to say yes but didn't think he could.

Barrington didn't give him a chance to answer—or so McCain would tell himself later.

"Have you had a chance to see much of the grounds?" Barrington asked.

"The grounds?" McCain answered. "No, not really. I remember a lobby, a reception desk, when I first came here, but after that . . . no, I haven't seen the grounds."

"*Herr* Erwählen would like you to look around, talk with some of the guests, attend some of the seminars and workshops," Barrington said. "Would you like that?"

"You know why I'm here," McCain said, feeling he needed to remind Barrington, though common sense dictated that he shouldn't.

"We know why you're here," Barrington said, "which is why Jerry or one of his friends will be with you at all times. That aside, you'll be free to roam the grounds. You see, Erwählen knows why you came. It's why you'll stay and how you'll leave that interests him now."

"What does he really want?" McCain asked, his voice quivering ever so slightly.

"Erwählen?" Barrington asked.

McCain nodded, not expecting an answer.

"A better world," Barrington said. "That's all."

chapter 7TEEN

Jeane burst out of the motel room, drawing the .380 automatic up and in front of her with both hands.

She held back the urge to start firing blindly into the night and did what she was taught to do. She looked, she listened, she identified a target.

But there was no target.

The tail lights of the car were pinpoints on the dark road outside the pools of dull light in the motel parking lot. A dog was barking. Jeane's jaw clenched.

She put the gun away and went back inside.

When she came around the bed and saw Ngan laying on the floor on his back her first thought was that he was dead. His eyes were open.

"They might come back," he said. Jeane jumped, startled. "If they saw you run out, if they know you're not dead, they might come back."

Jeane was at the door in two long strides. There was a switch on the wall next to the ineffectual-looking chain. She slapped it down, and the lights went off. An orange glow from behind the cheap curtains and shafts of light from bullet holes in the wall and door lit the room, but only barely.

"We need to get you to a hospital," she said, scanning the dresser, the bed near the door, then the floor for her cell phone.

"I'm not sure," came Ngan's quiet voice from the space between the bed and the wall, "that is a . . . a good idea."

Jeane tried to look at him but could see only the bed, the wall, and a shadow between. "What do you mean? You've been shot. You're bleed—"

She was discussing it—having another infuriatingly circular conversation with Ngan. She realized she was standing no more than eighteen inches from the motel room phone.

"I will be fine," Ngan's voice drifted up again.

"Put pressure on the wounds, Ngan," Jeane said, and reached down for the phone. "Press down as hard as you can."

"Do not call the police," he said.

Jeane lifted the receiver and began to put it to her ear. "I'm calling an ambulance."

"Can you be sure that Erwählen doesn't control the ambulances, the paramedics, firemen, and police?" Ngan asked.

Jeane again looked over at the dark spot in which he lay, the receiver still in her hand, but she hadn't yet put it to her ear. The thought made her wince. She was embarrassed and angry by how often she was getting embarrassed and angry. She was talking to the floor next to a cheap motel bed, negotiating with a man who'd just been riddled with automatic weapons fire about the nature and immediacy of his medical care.

Jeane put the phone to her ear and ignored Ngan when he said, "I have to insist that you not contact the authorities here."

There was a dial tone, sharply reassuring in Jeane's right ear. She reached a finger to the phone, aiming without thinking for the nine. It would have been a simple thing. A shift in space of a quarter of an inch or less. It would have taken virtually no effort at all, normally. How many times had she dialed a phone? She could believe a million times.

in fluid silence

Her finger wouldn't touch the nine. Her elbow wouldn't straighten. Her arm wouldn't move.

"Trust me, Agent Meara," Ngan's voice drifted to her.

She was in no pain. Her arm was not numb and was not paralyzed. She wanted to move it, wanted to dial 911, but her arm wouldn't do it. Her arms wouldn't obey. It was as if her one limb had achieved some level of separate consciousness and was simply unwilling to dial the phone.

"Ngan . . ." she whispered.

"Yes," he answered, "it is me."

Jeane slammed the phone down, growling through tightly clenched teeth. "Stupid, damned—"

"We have no time for that," Ngan interrupted her outburst. "Get me up. They'll be back."

Jeane walked around the bed and stopped, looming over the still prone form of Ngan. His shirt was soaked with blood that looked black in the wan light. "Oh," Jeane breathed, "for God's sake."

"Help me up," Ngan said.

"You'll bleed to death," she warned.

"The bleeding is already beginning to stop," he said. "We need to get out of here before they come back to finish me and start on you. I can take care of myself, but not here, not wedged on this dirty carpet. You have to get me outside."

Jeane sank to her knees quickly, her hands in front of her. Even as she tried to figure out the best way to get him out of that tight, dark space, she said, "I'll get you to a hospital."

"Where?" he asked. "Just drag me out by my feet."

"Won't that hurt you?" she asked, ignoring his question.

"Yes," he agreed. "I am sure it will hurt me quite a bit. Please do it, so you can pick me up."

Jeane grabbed his ankles and looked at him with eyes wide, needing to hear one more time that it was the right thing to do.

"Jeane," Ngan said, "I need your help, but I need your trust just as desperately. If you take me to a hospital the doctors will be compelled to report the gunshot wound. The police will be notified, and I think it's safe to assume that Erwählen has agents in the police department here. He might even possess the entire department. Besides, I am not at all fond of western hospitals."

Jeane pulled hard and slid Ngan out of the space between the bed and the wall. She could see him grimace even in the dim, uneven light.

"I have to ask you to trust me," he said, his voice weaker now, but his words carrying the clear tones of sincerity. "There are ways to heal the body other than hospitals. From now and for the next several hours I'm going to need you to trust me. If I am wrong, and I die, it will still not be your fault. Those boys shot me, probably on Erwählen's orders. You did not. You also tried to help me in the—"

"For Christ's sake, Ngan," she blurted all at once, "shut up and tell me what you want already before you bleed out."

Ngan nodded but didn't lift the back of his head off the carpet. Jeane cursed herself for going along with any of this. She was entirely certain that she was making a mistake that would prove fatal to Ngan. She also knew he was probably right about the police and hospitals. Who could know how far outside Lesterhalt they'd have to drive in order to escape Erwählen's influence. She'd nearly been killed by an Erwählen-owned cop herself, and that was in Chicago, over three hundred miles away.

"Lift me up," he told her. "I know you're strong enough. Pick me up and take me outside. Be sure to bring your bag. Leave mine. Bring your telephone and your computer. Leave your car."

Jeane reached over and grabbed her duffel bag and her purse. She unzipped the duffel bag and stuffed her purse into it. She found her phone and computer there.

"I need you to take me somewhere where there is real earth, not floors or pavement," Ngan continued. "I need to be under an open sky. You should find some trees, someplace where we can be hidden, where people won't be able to see us."

Jeane slipped her hands under Ngan's slight form. His eyes closed. She lifted him, rolling him into her chest.

"You're light," she grunted, standing.

in fluid silence

"I will appear to have passed out," Ngan said, his eyes still closed. "I will seem unconscious—even comatose, but please do not panic."

Jeane felt warm, thick blood on her hands, soaking into her top.

"I am not dying," he said. "Do not think I'm dying. Trust me. Trust me, and wait."

Jeane sighed, and carried him out into the cool night air.

chapter 8TEEN

"Get a lot of action, Jerry?" McCain asked the teenager following him. "The Uzi work for you?"

"Just shut up, man," Jerry scowled. "This way."

McCain glanced back to see Jerry nod at a side corridor. McCain turned the corner, and Jerry, gun in hand, followed him. At the end of the little blank corridor was a glass door, revealing darkness beyond.

"They let you in the bar here, Jerry?" McCain asked.

Jerry was taking him, at McCain's request, to Camp Clarity's bar. Barrington had, after all, given him the (escorted) run of the place, and the bar was always the best place in any hotel to get a sense of the clientele. McCain couldn't wait to get a load of the bar in this place.

"Jerry?" McCain pressed when the boy didn't answer.

McCain pushed the door open and let it close on the teenager, who caught it with a grunt and the clatter of the gun on the steel door frame. The air outside was cool, and there was a nice breeze. McCain realized he couldn't remember the last time he'd had a lungful of fresh air.

They crossed the short space between two buildings, their feet scraping on gravel.

"Hey," McCain said, "you never told me if the Uzi worked for you. If it does, I might pick one up for myself. What do you think, the young ladies dig on that?"

"It's not an Uzi, asshole," Jerry grumbled. "Just go."

"Really?" McCain asked, not looking back at the kid. "I thought it was an Uzi."

"Uzis are crap," Jerry said, "designed by a Jew. This is a SITES M4 Spectre, man. Mr. Erwählen wants us to have the best."

"Who said that was the best?"

"Mr. Erwählen."

McCain got to the door at the end of the gravel path and stopped, his hand on the handle. "You want to shoot me, eh, Jerry?"

Jerry stopped, brought the gun up to his eye and sighted slowly, carefully down the barrel. McCain locked his eyes onto the kid's. He wasn't afraid. He knew Jerry wouldn't shoot him unless he was ordered to.

"Why aren't I dead?" McCain asked him quietly.

Jerry stared at him across the gun sights.

"Oh," McCain said, "that's right. You only do what you're told, right, Jerry?"

Jerry's right eye began to close just for a second, but not all the way, then opened again. McCain leaned in toward the boy, who edged the tip of the gun barrel up half an inch. His eyes narrowed in warning. McCain could see sweat beading on the teenager's forehead.

"The New World Order," McCain whispered in mock confidentiality, "needs punks too, I guess."

Jerry let the gun fall, then looked down at the ground. He glanced back up at McCain and his face flushed. McCain turned and opened the door into the subdued, dimly lit bar area. He was pleased to see that Jerry hesitated before following him in.

McCain put Jerry out of his mind easily enough and took

stock of the room. The bar was as ordinary and unremarkable as the rest of what he'd seen of Camp Clarity. It was small, almost utilitarian in its simplicity. It was dark, and the few seats were all deeply padded leather armchairs. The bartender was a tall, thin man with a shaved head. McCain crossed to the bar casually, hands clasped behind his back. He got to the bar and made eye contact with the bartender. McCain was about to open his mouth to order a drink when he realized all at once that the bartender was black. The man looked at McCain with dull, beaten eyes.

"Scotch," McCain said, the word hissing out of his mouth on a single breath.

The bartender nodded and turned his back, reaching for a bottle. McCain couldn't bring himself to understand how this man could be working here, then remembered what Barrington had said about minorities knowing their place.

He turned and scanned the bar. There were six men sitting in armchairs. No one was sitting at the bar. Two of the men were sitting alone, the other four speaking quietly in groups of two. McCain ignored the men who were talking. He'd come to the bar to talk to someone, not intrude on a conversation.

It had occurred to him that other than Nichts bringing him the cell phone, he hadn't spoken with anyone Erwählen hadn't arranged for him to talk to. Though it would have been easy enough to assume McCain might try the bar, then stack the deck with a handful of specially selected drinkers, McCain couldn't think of a better option.

Of the two possibilities McCain picked the oldest. The young one was a stern-faced yuppie nursing a bottle of mineral water and staring intently at the screen of a laptop computer. The older man was sitting next to a low table on which sat a snifter with half a finger's worth of brandy in it. He was smoking a Cuban cigar, the blue smoke curling lazily around his head. He was dressed in a pale yellow polo shirt and stark white golf pants. His new tennis shoes were neither gaudy nor old-mannish, and McCain was happy to see that his socks were white, not black.

"Sir," the bartender said from behind him.

McCain turned, saw his drink on the bar in front of him, and the bartender's receding back.

All inclusive, McCain thought wryly.

With a silent Jerry in tow he approached the man with the cigar.

"Hi," McCain said jovially. The man looked up, smiled, was a bit unsure. "This might sound a little dopey, but this is my first time here, and I'd really love to have someone to talk to. Can I buy you a drink?"

The man glanced at Jerry, who was standing several paces behind McCain, staring at him, holding the gun.

"Kids," McCain said with a shrug.

"Even now in heaven," the man said, "there are angels carrying savage weapons."

He indicated the seat across from him, and McCain sank quickly into the soft leather chair.

"Jerry's no angel," McCain corrected, glancing back at the boy. "Are you, Jerry?"

Jerry was looking down at his gun, obviously attracted to its cold, black steel lines. It didn't seem to McCain as if the kid could hear him.

"Name's Pemberton," the man said, holding out his hand.

McCain leaned forward, took the man's hand, and lied casually, "Widen. Greg Widen."

Pemberton sat back and folded his newspaper carefully, setting it on the little table next to him. "You said this was your first time here at Camp Clarity. Where are you from?"

"New Mexico," McCain lied again, choosing the most unlikely place he could think of, a place it didn't look like Pemberton could possibly have ever visited, much less be from.

"New Mexico," Pemberton repeated.

"Ever been?" McCain asked.

"To New Mexico?" Pemberton answered. "Can't say I've had the pleasure. That's where the flying saucers crashed, isn't it?"

A chill rippled through McCain, and he could feel the color drain from his face.

"Hey," Pemberton said, leaning forward and setting a hand gently on McCain's knee, "I didn't mean anything—"

McCain recovered quickly and said, "Sorry, no . . . it's no big deal. It's just that as soon as you say you're from New Mexico . . . Anyway, I'm from Portales. That was Roswell where the flying saucers crashed."

Pemberton laughed in a way that made McCain think the older man didn't believe in flying saucers. "Let me get that drink," he said.

Knowing it was paid for anyway, McCain smiled and nodded. "Scotch," he said, "neat."

"Ah," Pemberton replied, "a gentleman's drink."

Pemberton held up one hand and snapped his fingers once, loudly. The bartender looked up, and Pemberton held up two fingers. The bartender nodded and poured from a very expensive bottle of single malt scotch.

"So, Greg Widen of Portales, New Mexico," Pemberton said, picking up the snifter with the little bit of brandy still in it. "what do you want to know?"

McCain shrugged and, while Pemberton swallowed the rest of the brandy, said, "I don't know. I mean, I heard the speech tonight. It made sense. I mean, it spoke to me, and there's Erwählen. There's . . . you know. He has that quality. I mean, thank God for Erwählen, but . . ."

McCain couldn't really come out and ask all the questions he wanted answered, so he hoped that Pemberton would ask the questions for him, then provide the answers.

"I'll tell you this, Mr. Widen—" Pemberton said wistfully.

"Greg," McCain cut in, "please."

"Greg it is. People call me Skip."

"Skip?"

"I know," Pemberton said with a laugh. "I'm a bit old to be called Skip, right? Well, thanks to a promise made to an army buddy on the battlefield of Appomattox, my great-grandfather called his first son Clembert, and the Pemberton men have been named Clembert ever since."

"That's quite a handle," McCain said with a chuckle.

"No shit, Greg," Clembert Pemberton III concurred. "My grandfather went by Clem, the poor bastard, and my father claimed Bert, so I was left, from a very young age, with Skip. Oddly, it hasn't seemed to have had any adverse effect on my success."

The bartender appeared with the drinks on a small engraved silver tray. He placed Camp Clarity cocktail napkins on the table and set the drinks down on top of them. Pemberton didn't look at the bartender the whole time, but he stopped speaking when the black man was within earshot. McCain looked at the floor, and the bartender walked away soon enough.

"So," Pemberton said, "what do you do there in Portales?"

"I sell used office furniture," McCain lied, taking the occupation from an old Tom Waits song.

"Any money in that?" Pemberton asked.

McCain shrugged, "Once you get past the tenth store, yeah."

Pemberton held up his scotch, said, "Good for you," and drank it down.

McCain smiled and took a small sip, wincing at the potent whiskey's burn. Pemberton hardly seemed to notice his.

"So, Greg," he went on, "you've come to Camp Clarity for the first time. You've spent a little time in the vril?"

McCain nodded.

"You've spent a little time in the vril," Pemberton continued, "and you're feeling good. You're a like-minded individual, you admire Erwählen, but you're looking for the inside scoop, eh?"

McCain shrugged and said, "I don't know, Skip, I'm just feeling kinda like the new guy."

Pemberton smiled, nodded, and said, "We were all new guys at one point, Greg, but that won't last long. I think you'll find Camp Clarity to be the most welcoming place you've ever experienced. There is practically no place in the world I'd rather be."

"It's an exclusive club," McCain tested.

"And it's not just that," Pemberton said. "Camp Clarity is a refuge, a school, a hospital . . . everything all at once. I can tell you, Greg, that I've been to so many places that were, on a base level, pretty similar to this. This executive retreat business is

in fluid silence

getting bigger all the time, but at those places I learned crap like time management and how to work with difficult people—like I need anyone tell me stuff like that. Here, though, it's like a whole different world. There's a richness to this place, both spiritually and emotionally. It's very personal and can be very powerful.

"Anyway," Pemberton added, "I'm not even sure how exclusive it is anymore. Lots of new faces . . . Would you believe the other day I was on a flight from Chicago to D.C., and I see a guy in coach reading a pamphlet—a Camp Clarity pamphlet. I said something to him, and he looks up, and would you believe it's a goddamned Chinaman? A bald little Chinaman with blue eyes! I about shit my pants."

McCain made himself laugh and was sure he pulled off the required level of genuineness. Blue eyes. An Asian man with blue eyes. Pemberton was describing Ngan. But how could that be?

"So," McCain said, changing the subject, "you're from Chicago?"

"Just passing through. I run a company in Detroit you might have heard of—especially if you like SUVs."

McCain lifted an eyebrow and said, "Not bad. What brought you to D.C.?"

"Damn EPA," Pemberton scowled. "I've got a car powered by rechargeable batteries that'll go ninety miles an hour for six hours at a stretch. I can make 'em for four thousand dollars and sell 'em for twenty, but the EPA is giving me problems about the batteries."

"I thought the EPA liked that sort of thing," McCain said naively, "electric cars."

Pemberton scoffed, saying, "Like hell. See, there's a certain group of oil guys from Texas and Oklahoma who would rather not see the internal combustion engine go away, and they *own* the damn EPA."

"Can you do anything about that?"

Pemberton shrugged and said, "We'll see. Actually, that's why I'm here. These particular oil guys are members."

McCain squinted. "They're here?"

Pemberton nodded and said, "Erwählen's going to help us work something out."

McCain blinked, smiled, and said, "He does that sort of thing?"

Pemberton laughed in a way that made McCain dizzy. He felt his face flush, sweat break out on his forehead, and something in his stomach twist.

"Ah," Pemberton said, "I get it. That's what you didn't understand. Look, kid, this isn't some redneck hate group. This is the future of the United States of America. This is the big time, my friend."

"I never realized," McCain ventured, "that he had that kind of reach." Pemberton simply shrugged, waiting for McCain to go on. "Can I ask you something, Skip?" he said, leaning in. "I mean . . . something maybe a little personal, but I swear I don't mean any offense."

Pemberton frowned, but his eyes smiled. "I'm all ears, Greg."

"Okay, so I'm doing pretty well with the stores and all, making a decent buck, but you . . . I mean . . ."

"I've made a couple dollars," Pemberton said with a smirk.

"You run the biggest corporation on Earth," McCain said.

Pemberton held out a hand, wobbled it back and forth in a so-so gesture, smiled, and said, "Fortune Five."

"Okay," McCain said, making Pemberton believe he admired him. "So, why do you need all this? Why do you need this whole 'New World Order.' I mean, you're already on top."

"They say it's lonely at the top, Greg," Pemberton said, reaching for the cigar that had been burning in the ashtray next to him. " 'They,' in this case at least, are full of it. It's crowded at the top. It's packed with wild dogs biting at each others' balls every God blessed day. I started in the mail room. I honest to God did. That was 1960. I was twenty-two years old. Forty-one years, Greg. It's taken me forty-one years to achieve the position I have. Now look at me. I'm an old fart. I've got lines of guys half my age who can't wait for me to drop dead. Is that what success means to you, Greg?"

in fluid silence

"I'm not sure what you mean," McCain said.

"You work your life away to gain a certain position," Pemberton said, "and when you finally achieve those goals, you have how many decent years left? Ten? Five? One?"

McCain felt his skin crawl. Gooseflesh broke out on his triceps. "So if you can live . . ."

"If I can live as long as Erwählen has lived," Pemberton finished for him. "I get to stay on top, not just get there, look around for an inadequate handful of months, then drop dead. I get to stay. I get to stay forever. All this 'blacks this' . . . 'Jews that' . . . I couldn't give a rat's hindquarters for."

McCain sighed and dropped his head, hoping Pemberton couldn't see his face.

"How do you feel, Greg?" Pemberton asked.

McCain looked up and saw Pemberton smiling down at him like a knowing big brother. "It's actually getting harder . . ." McCain improvised. "It's getting harder for me to understand where I fit into all this, that's all. I mean, I sell used office furniture in the ass-end of nowhere."

Pemberton offered a knowing smile, a shrug, and said, "Erwählen knows. Maybe—"

Pemberton stopped, looking up and past McCain's shoulder. McCain turned around in the big chair and looked over his shoulder. He saw Jerry look up, then stand up, fidgeting with his weapon.

"Well," Pemberton said, "looks like a friend of yours is here."

McCain turned around the other way and saw Secretary Barrington crossing the bar. Jerry almost stood at attention. Barrington ignored the teenager, his eyes set on McCain. Something about the look on his face made McCain's skin crawl. Barrington looked serious and dire, and all at once McCain was sure he'd overstepped his bounds somehow. Maybe the conversation with Pemberton had gone too far. Maybe he wasn't supposed to talk with Pemberton at all.

Barrington said he had the run of the place, but McCain couldn't remember if he'd said it was all right to talk with the other guests. Certainly a man like Pemberton was special.

McCain was sure he was about to be punished somehow.

"Michael," Barrington said, his voice heavy and obviously nervous.

McCain felt his blood run cold again, and he shivered. He'd just had a long conversation with a very important and powerful man who thought his name was Greg. McCain stood as Barrington came within reach of him. The secretary reached out, and McCain made himself not flinch. Barrington put a hand on his shoulder. The grip was both firm and gentle.

"Sit down," he said, "please."

McCain sat, still not looking at Pemberton.

"Listen, Michael," Barrington said, "I have something to tell you, okay? It's bad news."

"What do you mean?" McCain asked, laughing uncomfortably. "If I did anything wrong . . ."

"No, no," Barrington said, smiling in the way people do at funerals. "That's not it at all."

Barrington sighed, then looked up at the bar, lifted his chin, made eye contact with the bartender, and nodded.

"Your friends . . ." Barrington said gravely. "Your Asian friend and the woman were killed earlier tonight."

McCain felt his fingers and toes go cold. "What?" he asked feebly.

"You had two friends," Barrington said, looking him in the eye, "from the Hoffmann Institute. They were staying at a motel in town, and there were some problems. I know this is going to be hard for you, and you're going to have some trouble keeping this in perspective and understanding our point of view."

The bartender appeared and put a shot glass in McCain's numb hand.

"They're dead, Michael," Barrington said. "You're going to feel bad about that. You're going to hate us all, but there will come a time when you understand why that had to happen and understand why there was nothing we could do."

"They?" McCain asked.

"The Asian man and the woman," Barrington said quietly.

McCain downed the shot, and his eyes blurred with tears.

"Fitz," Pemberton said from behind him. "If there's anything I can do. . . ."

McCain's head spun. His vision blurred. Pemberton had called him Fitz. Barrington had called him Michael, not Fitz. Pemberton had never heard the name Fitz.

"Ngan," McCain whispered. "Jeane."

His eyes stopped tearing and all at once felt dry, his eyelids heavy and soft. He closed his eyes, and flashes of yellow and purple blazed through the darkness.

"Michael?" Barrington asked.

McCain felt the shot glass slip out of his stiff, numb fingers.

"Michael?" someone, either Barrington or Pemberton, said.

He tried to answer, though he had no idea what to say, but his mouth wouldn't open.

He was tired, and he wanted to go to sleep.

They drugged me, he thought. That's it.

chapter 19TEEN

McCain awoke with a headache worse than he'd ever experienced in his life. He was laying on his stomach on a soft leather sofa, his left arm draped off the side, hand resting on cold linoleum tile. His eyes were dry, and they hurt.

He sat up, using both hands to muscle his body up and around to sit with his feet on the floor. He was still wearing the same clothes from the night before, the clothes he'd found waiting for him in the little dorm room.

He looked around the room, wincing once when his eyes first moved. It was dark, but not completely. Along one wall of the big room was a row of cabinets and a black countertop that made him think of high school chemistry class. There were sinks, a Bunsen burner, something that looked like a little centrifuge. In the center of the room were two steel gurneys with no mattresses. Next to them was a wheeled tray on which sat a gleaming array of surgical implements. It took

McCain a blink or two to realize that there were bodies lying on the gurneys.

McCain put a hand to his throbbing forehead and tried to understand how he came to the conclusion that the people on the gurneys were dead. Could you just look at someone and realize that? He looked up at them again. They were still, not breathing. That must have been how he knew they were dead.

The corners of the room were dark, filled with shadows that seemed almost solid. He looked up and saw that only a single fluorescent tube was glowing. The room had no windows. The light was directly over the gurneys.

McCain stood up, groaning, the room spinning. He stood in front of the couch for a few seconds, his eyes closed, his hand on his forehead. He breathed a few times, then took a step forward. His head was beginning to feel better. He could walk without falling down, so he did, to the edge of the nearest gurney.

"Oh, no," he whispered. "Ngan."

The man McCain had called "UncleAgain" was lying face up, naked and pale. McCain didn't bother counting the bullet wounds. There were dozens of them, black and red, swollen pink around them. The blood—and there must have been a lot of it—had been cleaned up. McCain took a deep breath. Half of Ngan's head was gone, but it was definitely Ngan. One blue eye was staring straight up at the ceiling, dull, lifeless, and dead.

McCain stepped to the other gurney, though he knew what he would find there—who he would find there.

Jeane was also laying in her back, also naked, her large breasts hanging limply to the sides, her chest, all of her, still. She'd been shot only a few times, but there was a hole in her neck that McCain could have passed his fist through.

"Damn it," he said. "We made a mess of this one didn't we, partners?"

A man cleared his throat from one of the dark corners of the room, and McCain startled back, flipping the tray of instruments with one hand and sending it clattering violently to the floor. His already frayed nerves were stripped to the core by the shrill clatter that echoed in the big, mostly empty, windowless room.

"I beg your pardon," the man said, his accent thick. "I didn't mean to startle you."

"Who is that?" McCain asked, his voice shaking and uncontrolled. "Who's there?"

Erwählen stepped into the weak light next to Jeane's dead body and looked down at her, his face sad, his eyelids heavy. "This is not right," he said, passing a hand over the dead woman.

McCain opened his mouth to scream a string of obscenities at the man, but he stopped himself. He was alone now, surrounded by the men who had already killed his closest friends in the world. He was all that was left of what must have been the most botched investigation in the eighty-four-year history of the Hoffmann Institute.

"You are angry with me," Erwählen said, his voice soft and condescending. "I understand that. I am sorry to tell you that these are not the first people who have died. These are not the last people who will die in the service of the future."

"The future?" McCain almost sobbed, not sure what to say.

"The future of humanity," Erwählen said. "The woman. Were you in love with her? Did you have a relationship with her?"

McCain squinted at him, shook his head, and said, "Jeane? No . . . no, I didn't."

"And the man?"

"His name was Ngan," McCain said. "Her name was Jeane."

Erwählen just stared at him.

McCain took a deep breath and said, "Ngan was like a . . . like an uncle to me."

"Grow up, Michael McCain," Erwählen said.

McCain shuddered like a child and said, "You're going to kill me too."

Erwählen laughed. "Not today, Michael. Not ever if you take a deep breath and start to listen to the people around you." He waved a hand over Ngan and Jeane. "You're not in their club anymore. You're in mine. Mine is better."

McCain said nothing but nodded because he wasn't sure what else to do.

"I want you to have a look around," Erwählen said. "You still haven't had a chance to see what we do here."

"That's what Barrington said," McCain said, looking at the floor.

"Secretary Barrington was correct," Erwählen replied. "You may see something that will help you forget this unfortunate sadness."

McCain looked up at him and asked, "Can I leave here? Can I go home if I want to?"

Erwählen looked at him for a long time, then said, "No. I'm sorry. If you let yourself understand Camp Clarity, you won't want to."

"What am I going to see?" McCain asked, looking back down at the floor. He realized then that he was avoiding the bodies more than Erwählen's eyes.

"The truth," Erwählen said. "Isn't that why you came here in the first place?"

"I suppose it is," McCain admitted.

"Then follow me."

Erwählen turned to the only door and walked out, his back to McCain. McCain hesitated, but Erwählen never slowed. McCain sighed and knew he was actually afraid of being left behind. Without looking at the dead bodies of his friends, McCain followed Erwählen out.

They went down another featureless corridor that ended in a stairway up. McCain lost sight of Erwählen again going up the stairs. He heard a door open, then close, and came around the top of the stairway. He went through the glass door there and into bright sunshine and a cool spring morning. McCain didn't look back at the building he came out of. In front of him was a cement sidewalk that led to the edge of a big flat field of green grass. It could have been a soccer field, maybe football, but with no goals on either side or stripes on the grass.

About two dozen men in casual clothes, some in sweats, were gathered on the field. They were mostly broken up into small groups, chatting with each other, obviously waiting for something. When they caught sight of Erwählen striding up to them in that solid, strong gait of his, they actually burst into applause. McCain hesitated, missing a couple steps behind him, but the clapping men didn't seem to notice McCain at all.

Erwählen shook a few hands, smiling in his typically jovial manner, and McCain came up behind him.

"Very well, gentlemen," Erwählen called out to the men on the field. "Let us begin with two lines, facing each other."

The men scattered and quickly formed into two lines, separated by about forty feet of freshly cut grass. They all seemed anxious, excited, maybe a little scared. McCain recognized Clembert Pemberton and a few men from the speech, including Tom Casale. Jerry was there with two other boys, again armed with submachine guns. Jerry was wearing a shoulder holster over a Lesterhalt High School football T-shirt. A chrome-plated automatic hung from under his arm.

McCain watched Erwählen smile at Jerry, who beamed at the attention. The older man held out his hand, and Jerry, smiling sheepishly, pulled out the gun and placed it gently onto Erwählen's outstretched palm.

Erwählen turned and addressed the anxiously waiting men. "You've all attained a level of ability that makes me so proud. *Ich liebe Sie alle.* We have a very special guest with us today. He is new to us. Michael . . ." Erwählen turned to McCain and waved. "Michael McCain, come over here."

McCain scanned the faces of the men on the field. They were all staring at him expectantly. He had been singled out by Erwählen, and that obviously meant a lot to them—meant everything to them.

"Kommen Sie her, Michael," Erwählen said again, still smiling.

McCain sighed and walked up to within arm's length of Erwählen. He kept his eyes mostly on the ground.

"Take this," Erwählen said, holding the gun out to him, grip first.

McCain took the gun without even thinking about it. He looked at it as if he wasn't sure what it was, but really he just didn't understand what he was supposed to do. Of course, there was a moment when he thought he could just shoot Erwählen, avenge the deaths of Jeane and Ngan, take out this Nazi, this hatemonger with one twitch of a finger and put some kind of an end to it. McCain didn't shoot, though, because even though there was one really good reason, there were dozens of reasons not to shoot.

"Please go over there, Michael," Erwählen said. "Stand in line over there."

Erwählen pointed to the line of men forty feet away, and McCain walked slowly there and took a place in line. The men, including Pemberton, smiled at him and made room in the line. Erwählen moved to stand in the line across from McCain, the other men parting to make room for him too.

"Aim carefully," Erwählen said, "and shoot me."

"What?" McCain said, hoping his voice would carry the distance.

"You heard me, Michael."

McCain tipped his head, glanced at the smiling, anxious men around him, and said, "I don't, uh, I don't think so."

There was a smattering of chuckles along the two lines of men, and Erwählen grinned.

"You can't shoot me, Michael?" Erwählen asked.

"Go ahead," one of the men next to McCain said. "It's okay."

"You're stronger than that, Michael," Erwählen said. "I killed your friends. That doesn't make you angry enough to shoot me?"

McCain looked up and met Erwählen's cheerfully taunting gaze. "That's not funny," he said.

"I'm asking you to shoot," Erwählen said. "All these men here have heard that. It's all right. You can shoot the man who killed your friends. You haven't forgotten what they look like already, stretched out on those gurneys with holes all over them. *Gerade die Frau mit die großen Busen.*"

McCain lifted the gun, leveled it at Erwählen, and held it there.

A silence descended over the field, and McCain could feel the tension of the men around them. They were excited, not afraid.

in fluid silence

McCain let his arm fall and dropped the gun by relaxing his hand. It fell to the grass without a sound. McCain could hear two men near him sigh in disappointment. Erwählen smiled knowingly and said, "Tom, you take it."

Tom Casale bent down and picked up the gun.

"Fire when ready, yes," Erwählen said, then started to mumble something in a language McCain thought at first might be German, but it wasn't. He didn't recognize any of the words—didn't even recognize the language.

The gun went off, and McCain flinched, putting both hands up to his ears in an instant. Erwählen put up a hand, and McCain tensed, sure that the man would drop within that single second that seemed to be stretching on well past its boundaries.

McCain could see the bullet hanging in the air a foot in front of Erwählen's outstretched hand. Casale whispered, "That so kicks ass. That is so kick-ass."

McCain looked at Casale as if he was an idiot, then turned back to Erwählen, who winked at him, still smiling, still holding off the bullet with his palm. McCain felt his legs start to move. He walked toward Erwählen, his eyes fixed on the bullet.

No one said anything. McCain reached out, still not believing it, and took the bullet between the thumb and forefinger of his right hand. It was just hanging there. It burned his fingertips but he didn't drop it. He pulled it closer to his face, looked at it closely, then let it roll lifelessly into his palm.

"There's more," Erwählen said.

McCain was still staring at the bullet resting on his outstretched palm when it floated up off his skin and hung in the air.

"There's a man here under false pretenses," Erwählen said loudly, so that all of the men gathered there could hear him.

McCain's heart skipped a beat, and a cold sweat broke out on his forehead. The bullet hung in the air in front of him.

"I've told you all," Erwählen continued, "that there are few rules here, but what few rules we have must be followed very closely so as not to endanger all of us. Is there anyone here who can come to the defense of this man?"

The silence that followed was painful and endless for McCain, who was sure that any one of the men might betray him. Pemberton . . . why not? Casale . . . quite easily.

Erwählen sighed and said, "Please close your eyes. All of you. All of you except Michael McCain."

As if they were hypnotized, all of the men on the field closed their eyes. Erwählen looked at McCain and smiled, then glanced at the bullet.

McCain swallowed in a dry throat and winced. "I—" he started to say.

Erwählen shook his head and held up one finger. The eyes that had been so welcoming, warm, and paternal were cold now, hard as diamonds. He pointed at Michael, then a few of the men standing with their eyes closed. He pointed at Pemberton and glanced at McCain.

McCain shook his head, and Erwählen smiled coldly.

"No," McCain said quietly, letting his voice sound pleading.

Erwählen shook his head and pointed at Tom Casale.

"He didn't know," McCain said quickly. "It's not his fault!"

Erwählen's face went solid and flat, his expression like the face of a corpse. McCain shuddered.

Erwählen's eyes flicked to Casale, and the bullet that had been hanging in the air was gone. Tom Casale's head exploded in a burst of dark red blood. A mass of grey jelly burst into gobbets of blood-soaked tissue as the man's skull scattered like shrapnel. Shards of bone pinked against the faces, arms, and chests of some of the men standing nearby. They flinched but didn't open their eyes.

McCain looked away. The sound was actually worse than the sight of it. There was no bang. No gun had been fired . . . this time. Casale's head just popped.

"Darryl, Melvin," Erwählen said, "you can open your eyes now."

Two men opened their eyes and looked down at the still-twitching body of Tom Casale. Their faces were impassive, as if nothing at all out of the ordinary was happening. They both looked at Erwählen.

in fluid silence

"Take that away," Erwählen said to the two men, then looked up, addressing the others. "Keep your eyes closed until they've cleaned up."

McCain put a hand to his mouth and worked at not throwing up.

chapter TWENTY

Ngan was drifting off, chanting deep in his throat and being carried by Jeane, her voice fading. His body was a blazing series of waves of agony. He couldn't even feel the bullet holes anymore, nothing that specific, just pain wrapped around him like a burning blanket.

"This is nuts, Ngan," Jeane said clearly. "You're passing out."

The sound of his own chant made it almost impossible for him to hear more. It felt good to do it, and he was happy to be able to concentrate enough through the pain to maintain the chant, maintain the concentration necessary to save his own life.

"You're bleeding too—" was the last thing he heard before his secret spring fell into existence around him.

The Ascended Masters of the Monastery of Inner Light in a secret corner of the Himalayan nation of his birth had taught him a secret few *gomchen*—few lamas even—knew. In this plane of existence that existed nowhere but in his mind he had built a place to come for reflection, as a stopping-off point not unlike an airport for his travels through an inner universe forgotten by "modern man." It was a place where he could leave his body behind.

Everyone's secret spring was different. Ngan's was a cave.

Ngan had spent some of the most important moments of his life in a cave in Tibet. It was a hermitage inhabited by a long line of lamas for century after century before Ngan was born and before the Chinese came. Ngan's cave was based on this hermitage, but it changed every time he came here, based on his needs for it.

This time, though, it looked too different.

Something's wrong, Ngan thought. This isn't right.

Every time, whether he came disturbed, content, curious, or afraid, the secret spring was set in the same place. There were walls—a natural cave on three sides, brick on the first with a door so low even he had to duck through it. There was the uneven floor littered with Tibetan linens, and the oil lamps loosing a greasy smoke into the frigid air.

This time, though, the walls were gone and there was a garden. The sun was shining, and though it was a Tibetan sun it felt warm. He was in a garden of cherry trees and rose bushes. It was an English garden but not an authentic one. It was based on a fleeting memory from a glimpse of a picture from a crumpled, windblown magazine, but to Ngan's eye it had always been perfect. He had been there before.

He looked around and saw that he was standing in a circle of topiaries delicately carved from cherry trees. The ground was littered with white blossoms. The trees were carved in the shape of men. He remembered the topiaries from the last time he'd been here, but they looked different. Then there had been a circle of figures holding hands, locked in a child's game. This time the topiaries were men, not children, taller than Ngan. They were in rows, standing still and straight up at attention, looking into the sky, as if waiting for orders from someone or something.

Ngan stepped around one of the topiaries. He was curious about the trees but less interested in them than the very living person he knew he would find in this secret spring that was not his own.

in fluid silence

"Are you here?" he called gently.

"Over here," a voice answered.

Ngan turned and saw, kneeling among the fallen cherry blossoms between rows of topiary men, a tiny girl. She was beautiful, wrapped in a clean linen dress, her skin smooth and pink. She looked different than the last time he'd seen her. She looked healthy and safe and content. Ngan wished she were real.

"Leah," he said, and she smiled at him. "How did you get here?"

She shrugged and smiled, her blue eyes glinting in the light. "You brought me here."

"This was supposed to be *my* secret spring," Ngan said, folding himself down into a lotus position in front of her, "not yours."

"It is yours," she said with a giggle. "It just looks like mine. You're bleeding."

Ngan almost flinched at the abrupt change in subject. He looked down at his own chest and saw the blood soaking his clean white shirt. He had been shot. Ngan unbuttoned his shirt and slipped it off. There wasn't a mark on him.

"They're on those guys," Leah said, pointing with a straight arm behind him.

Ngan looked over his shoulder and saw three of the topiary men set off from the rest. He slid around and watched them solidify into flesh. The leaves folded into themselves and turned the color of Ngan's skin. In a few seconds Ngan was sitting facing three nearly perfect duplicates of himself.

They were smooth, not completely formed. Each one had a single bullet hole in a different part of its body. Ngan stood and approached them. They seemed awake, and all three turned their faces from him, averting their eyes.

Ngan stepped in front of the first double and looked closely at the gunshot wound.

"Deep into the triangularis sterni," he said, touching the wound on the left side of the double's chest. "It missed the mammary artery."

Leah giggled behind him and said, "You talk like a doctor."

He turned to her and smiled.

"Is that all you see?" she asked, tipping her head in a way that made it clear the question was rhetorical.

Ngan tuned back to the doubles and stepped to the right to stand in front of the second double. This one had a bullet hole much lower in the front of its body, on the abdomen.

"The liver," Ngan said. "The bullet entered straight through the sixth and seventh ribs and into the right lobe of the liver, lodging in the lobus quadratus. This should have killed me."

"It might yet," Leah said calmly, "but is that all?"

"No," Ngan told her, "there's the third one."

He stepped to the third double and touched the red, swollen hole that would have been only an inch or less from the second double's wound if, as on Ngan's real body, all three wounds were on the same midsection.

"That was a painful one," Leah said, her voice calm and as devoid of sympathy as it was fear.

"Yes," Ngan said, not looking back at her, "that one hurt. It tumbled in, tearing through the skin and shattering the seventh rib and bouncing down into the place where my stomach attaches to my duodenum. It ripped my pylorus apart, taking the hepatic ducts with it."

"Where did you learn all that stuff?" Leah asked.

Ngan turned to her, opened his mouth to answer, then couldn't. He had no idea where he'd learned it, that sort of western anatomical minutia.

"What are you going to do about those holes in you?" Leah asked, apparently not requiring an answer to her first question.

"I can fix them here. . . ." Ngan started, then realized, "but I'm not where I thought I was going to be. I thought I was going to my secret spring, not yours."

Leah smiled, giggled, and said, "I told you, this *is* your secret spring. See? There's the tree thing."

The little girl glanced to her right, and Ngan followed her eyes. Off to one side a section of the stiff topiary men was gone. In its place was a tree, strange in shape and pattern, with leaves and limbs of yellow and green. It sprouted up from the ground from a base of fine, twisted roots in four stemlike trunks from which sprouted numerous branches. The leaves of the tree were teardrop shaped, paper thin, and each as long as one of Ngan's forearms.

"It's beautiful, Leah," Ngan said. "Thank you."

Leah shrugged and giggled.

He had expected to see this in his own secret spring, but as a finely woven tapestry hanging on a reassuringly dank cave wall. Instead, here it was growing and alive before his eyes, perfect in its breeze-tickled reality.

"Better than a copy of *Gray's Anatomy*," Leah said impishly. "This is what you really came for."

"The *thangka*," Ngan said. "Yes, Leah, I came here for the Tree of Treatment."

"That's silly," the girl said, "to hear it in English like that."

Ngan smiled and stepped to the tree.

"You know how to read it," Leah said.

Ngan nodded and took one leaf in his hand. On the leaf he saw two seated figures, one in a blue robe, one in an orange robe. The man in the orange robe was taller and was reaching out to the man in blue, whose back was to Ngan. The image wasn't painted onto the leaf, though. It was part of the natural pigment. The leaf grew that way. There was a similar but different picture on every one of the other leaves. The *thangka* was a teaching device used in Tibetan medicine to remind practitioners of the art's major divisions.

Ngan sighed and said, "Triangularis sterni . . ."

He turned back to the doubles, and all three of them made a half-turn in his direction before slowly flinching away again. He looked at Leah and saw that her blue eyes had turned to green.

"You recognize them," Leah said.

Ngan stepped to the first double, touched the wound with one finger, and said, "Phlegm."

He pushed his finger into the hole and felt warm, wet flesh pull it farther in. The tip of his finger brushed hot metal, and he drew the finger out slowly. The bullet, stuck to the tip of his blood-drenched finger, came with it.

He held it up to Leah, and they shared a smile.

"The next one?" she asked him.

Ngan stepped to the second double and said, "Bile."

Again he pulled the bullet out with the tip of his finger, and again he showed it to Leah, both of them beaming.

"He remembers," she giggled happily. "That's so good, Ngan!"

Ngan turned to the third double, stood in front of it, and said, "Wind," and drew out the last bullet. "It is the three humors. The three humors."

He dropped the third bullet to the cherry-blossom floor and smiled at Leah. Her eyes were brown now.

"What color are your eyes really, Leah?" he asked.

She shook her head and leaned back, resting her weight on both her thin arms, her hands bent behind her. "You don't remember," she said.

Ngan's smile faded, and he said, "You're right, I'm sorry."

Leah smiled and shrugged, saying nothing, but her eyes held all the wisdom Ngan had ever attained, all the patience and purity of thought and spirit.

"How did you get here?" he asked.

She shrugged again and answered his question with a question. "Who shot you?"

"A boy not much older than you," Ngan answered.

"Why?" she asked. "Drugs?"

Ngan was taken aback by that until he remembered where Leah came from: the hard, drug-ravaged streets of Washington, D.C.

"No," Ngan told her. "A very bad man is teaching some other men to be as bad as him, and I want to stop them."

Leah smiled, a mischievous grin crossing her face, and said, "Erwählen tried to kill you because he's sensitive to the other. He knows he needs to give his people an enemy to rally against, or they will rally against each other. He's not afraid himself, and he isn't teaching his people fear. He is beyond that. He saw that fail in Germany sixty years ago, didn't he? Then again during the Cold War. Hate alone is a weak motivator, but if he combines hate for the other with real, personal power, he builds loyalty, and with the loyalty of the right people there is little he couldn't do. If they follow him because they love him and because he can give them something they can't get from anyone else, added to the perceived necessity to combat the other, they will do anything for him. It's simple, brilliant, and most likely it will work."

Ngan stared at her silently, and she giggled. It was a uniquely girlish sound that came in sharp contrast to what she had said—a speech of the sort Leah couldn't possibly have the background and maturity to form on her own.

"You never told me why you're here, Leah," Ngan said, forming several possible answers of his own to that question.

"I needed to remind you of the three humors," she said, "and the *thangka*."

"How could I have forgotten that?" he asked, ashamed of himself.

"You didn't," she said. "You've been in America for a long time, and they think differently. You were raised to ask questions, Ngan. You know . . . What is the sound of one hand clapping?"

She held up one tiny, thin-fingered hand and slapped her fingertips against the butt of her hand. There was a faint slapping sound not unlike a clap.

"I'm an American," she said, "from the capital city. Can you tell? I don't ask questions and ponder, I am asked questions to which I devise an answer, one way or the other. It's that mindset that's responsible for the American flags still stuck here and there on the surface of the moon, or the airplanes whizzing over your head every day. A Tibetan might wonder what is on the mind of a man on the other side of the world and look for the meaning of that within himself. An American invents the telephone, calls the man up, and asks him."

"Are you saying I've become an American?" he asked her.

"Would that be so bad?"

Ngan looked back at the three humors and saw that the wounds had healed. The first one seemed smaller somehow. It started to collapse on itself, and with a dull crack it split in the middle.

He turned back to Leah and said, "You're not you, then. This isn't your secret spring. It's mine."

Leah shrugged.

"You're a safe image," Ngan said, not trying to mask his disappointment. "You're here to make me feel better."

"Or," Leah said, winking, "you're the safe image for me, and this is my secret spring." She raised a hand to indicate the topiaries.

"Leah," he asked, "are you all right?"

The smile went away from her face, and she looked down at he floor of cherry blossoms. "You don't know," she said.

Ngan nodded, understanding that this wasn't Leah.

"You're not just an image, though," he said to the top of Leah's head. "You have to have been brought here."

"I was brought here by you," Leah said. "You'll remember my name."

Ngan said, "I should go."

"Not yet."

Ngan looked at the little girl with wide eyes. "Not yet?"

"Things out there move at different speeds," she explained. "You need to wait here for your wounds to heal a bit more."

"You're right, of course," Ngan said, turning again to look at the three humors.

The first one had transformed back into a topiary man, its cherry-branch neck slowly bending back to look up at the sky like the rest of the topiary men. The second was splitting open, leaves folding slowly out from inside it. On the third, the bullet hole was still closing, less red, smaller now.

"I'm worried that Jeane will take me to a hospital," Ngan said.

"You asked her not to," Leah said, "and she promised she wouldn't."

That seemed to be enough for Leah, but it wasn't quite enough for him.

"She thinks you're killing yourself," Leah said with a wicked smile.

Ngan smiled, glancing down.

The name came to him on a gently rushing wave, and he tipped his head in awe at the little girl sitting on the floor of cherry blossoms.

"*Grwa pa mngon shes can*," he whispered. "The Monk Learned in Abhidharma. The Medicine Buddha."

Leah winked at him and giggled. It was a sweet, musical sound.

chapter 2WENTY-1NE

The sun had come up to find Jeane on the verge of passing out. Under this patch of trees in southern Illinois, she had sat in one place on a blanket of dirt, dried leaves, moss, and the collected detritus of hundreds of seasons. Her right hand was pressed over two bullet holes in Ngan's abdomen, coated with blood that was warm on her palm, cool and drying on the back of her hand. Her left hand pressed down on a third wound in Ngan's chest, coated with blood the same way. She had been sitting like that for almost eight hours, and just about every part of her body was quivering with pain and stiffness.

Ngan was still breathing, regularly and deeply. He was asleep, but Jeane was still sure, had been sure all night, that he was dying. He had three bullets in his gut somewhere, and though it was possible—indeed had happened—that he could be lucky enough that all three had missed killing him instantly, it was impossible for him to simply recover on his own.

She'd tried periodically to wake him up, but he never stirred. His face was perfectly serene, as if he'd somehow abandoned it. The thought crossed Jeane's mind more than once that he was already dead, that his body was still breathing out of some autonomic habit.

Truth be told, she'd forgotten half the things that had crossed her mind. The fact was that Ngan had told her to be patient, and she had no choice but to be patient, but her brain had been racing all night. He might have been right that the local hospitals couldn't be trusted, that the local cops might be nothing more than a private security force for Erwählen. If she called the FBI they'd either decide she was a crank or descend en masse on Camp Clarity—another Waco. The Institute wasn't big on calling the cops in any case, and Jeane didn't have a whole lot of friends left in federal law enforcement anyway. She knew only two people to call at the Hoffmann Institute: Emma, the secretary; and Lily Adler, Ngan's boss. What could either of them do from an office three hundred miles away in Schiller Park? And they wouldn't even be there until much later in the morning. Beyond that, the Hoffmann Institute was still largely a mystery to her. All she could do was sit and wait, but for what she had no idea.

Her muddy head reeled, and she almost passed out. Her head bobbed down once sharply, sending a jolt of pain through her neck that made her wince, woke her up a little, and made her say, "God *damn* it," out loud.

She put a hand to her neck and felt the warm, thick wet of Ngan's blood, and she flinched again. The movement didn't hurt as bad this time. With a pained sigh, she put her hand back on Ngan's seeping wound.

Her palm touched something solid when she expected something soft and wet. She jerked her hand away, afraid she'd picked up something like a pebble when she'd moved her hand. But that couldn't be. She'd only touched her neck—an earring? She wasn't wearing any.

Jeane picked something shining and wet with Ngan's blood off the edge of the wound. She held it close to her dry, stinging, exhausted eyes. It was a bullet.

"What the . . . ?" she whispered, then cringed at that ridiculous response.

She looked down at Ngan and saw one of the other bullets rise to the surface of its black-red hole and slip in some collected blood. She went to pick it off, but it slipped more in the blood, avoiding her fingertips, and rolled off the side of Ngan's bare stomach.

Jeane shook her head and blinked, hoping on some level that she had fallen asleep and was dreaming this. It wasn't possible that this was happening. Gunshot wounds didn't pop the bullets out. On the other hand, it could mean that Ngan actually *was* healing himself. A tired, groggy Jeane wasn't entirely sure if it was all right with her that Ngan was somehow managing to manipulate the laws of physics, even if it meant he wouldn't die. The third bullet came out, and she brushed it off.

Something—something big—moved in the trees behind her.

Jeane tried to spin but succeeded only in wrenching her back and nearly falling over. She put her hand down to catch herself, and Ngan's blood on her palm picked up a thick layer of dry dirt. By the time she got her head around, she'd heard movement again but still couldn't see anything.

She didn't know what kind of trees they were, but they all looked the same. They were only just beginning to bud, and the woods had a curiously black and white quality. She'd carried Ngan for less than a mile from the motel. Their motel was on the edge of town, and one didn't have to go too far out of Lesterhalt, Illinois, to find open country. Trees had been a bit hard to come by. The perfectly flat landscape had been given over almost entirely to soy beans and was inconveniently devoid of hiding places.

She'd found this all-too-small stand of trees and stumbled under the low branches, laying Ngan on the ground in the first place she found that was big enough to accommodate them both. She'd spent the rest of the night putting pressure on his wounds. During that time she'd heard the occasional odd rustling of a squirrel here and a bird there, had brushed a decent-sized spider off Ngan's leg, but hadn't seen or heard anything that really startled her.

She stared out into the trees but still saw nothing. She listened intently and heard only a faint dry rustling in the weak breeze, and the sound of Ngan's soft, regular breathing.

"This sucks," she said in a clear voice that echoed in her own ears.

She'd been up all night, and her body had pretty much given up on her. Her legs were stiff, her neck was *really* stiff, her back hurt, her elbows hurt, her shoulders burned, and her head throbbed. Now, apparently, her mind was going on her too.

She turned back to look down on Ngan and realized that she'd stopped holding the wounds. The bleeding had stopped, though, and she squinted at the bullet holes. They looked smaller.

Something big moved behind her again.

She had left her gun on the ground next to Ngan in case she needed it in a hurry, and this counted as needing it in a hurry. She grabbed the gun and turned, the weapon out in front of her at the end of a straight arm.

There was nothing there now, but she had heard something.

She inhaled, about to call out to whoever might be moving around in the woods, but stopped herself. She scanned the woods and realized she couldn't see Ngan, who was behind her now. Jeane didn't like not being able to see him.

She came up on her knees, ignoring the pain. Her gun shook. She sucked in a deep breath, trying to steady herself, but only marginally succeeded. She walked on her knees, then rolled onto her behind, crossing to the other side of Ngan. A tingling started in her legs. It was the most she'd moved them in too many hours.

"Ngan," she said quietly but with force.

Ngan didn't stir in the slightest. His face was still perfectly passive.

"Crap," Jeane whispered, strictly for her own benefit.

It moved again, just off to her right, and she brought the gun that way fast. She didn't see anything, just the trees and dirt and brown underbrush.

A smaller rustle came from in front of her, and she corrected the angle of her gun back in that direction. Sitting on the ground in front of a tree maybe six feet away was a skinny grey squirrel. Its bushy tail twitched once, and it looked off into the woods with its black eyes at nothing at all.

A breath she didn't realize she'd been holding passed through Jeane's lips. Her finger tensed on the trigger. She wanted to blow that damned squirrel to smithereens just for having put her through the last couple minutes—just on principle—but she didn't. She closed her eyes and raised the gun, pulling her finger out of the trigger guard. She changed her grip on the gun so she was holding it by the barrel and clicked the safety on with her thumb.

The sound was behind her. She looked up at the squirrel, and it was running in the opposite direction. It leaped onto a tree and scurried up into its highest branches in the time it took Jeane to turn and see nothing again.

She was still holding the gun by the barrel and realized that might be a mistake. She let the gun slide through her palm, and when the sound came from her left and right sides simultaneously she jumped and dropped the gun.

"Jesus," she breathed and grabbed up the gun.

Something moved behind her, and she fumbled for the safety.

She turned and saw nothing but trees. The sound was behind her again, and she turned.

She expected to see a teenager with a submachine gun, or a jack-booted Nazi with a Luger, or hooded clansmen with shotguns, or an army of angry squirrels bent on evicting her and her messily bleeding companion from their little slice of squirrel heaven. She expected anything, but got nothing. There was nothing there.

"For God's sake, Ngan," she whispered, still scanning the empty woods, "what did you get us into here?"

It was behind her again, then almost immediately to her right. She stopped turning all the way around. She counted maybe three of them, whoever they were. The sounds were always two or three short rustles, like footsteps in the dry underbrush. Jeane had never encountered someone—let alone a group of someones—who were so bad at keeping quiet and so good at not being seen. Most of the trees were no bigger around than the thickest part of one of Jeane's trim thighs. Whoever was using them for cover, Jeane thought, must be—

It peeked at her from behind a tree, and Jeane's blood went instantly cold. She drew in a breath sharply that had a high, panicked edge to it. She took in the face of the thing all at once. Its skin was black, and its mouth was hanging open limply, revealing two rows of tiny triangular teeth, glistening in the bright morning light. Its eyes were red and piercing but small, its nose flat. It made a sound like fingernails being drawn across a chalkboard, and Jeane knew she'd seen eyes like that before—on a goat, on a man in a compound in Texas, in a painting in an old church—and she screamed and fired her gun at the same time. Then the thing was gone, and someone was holding her wrist. She screamed again.

"They're here for me," Ngan said under the fading echo of Jeane's scream and the single gunshot.

She looked down at him with wild eyes and saw that he was holding the gun now. She had no recollection of his having taken it from her.

"Ngan," she all but barked. "Ngan!"

"Yes, Jeane," he said, looking into her eyes.

"What the—" she started. "What the f—"

"Demons," he said simply, and her vision actually blurred. "They're here for me, but there's nothing to worry about."

"W-what the . . . ?" she stammered, knowing she wanted to say something but having no luck getting her brain to function on the level of conversation. "What . . . ?"

"They sensed that I was weak," he said, pulling himself up into a sitting position. "They knew I was on the edge of worlds, and they made an effort to claim me."

"What?"

"They're not significant," he said, looking her in the eyes. "They're angry with me from a long time ago."

"What?"

"You're very tired," he said. "You've been meditating, but you didn't even know it. You were open to them enough to sense them, but they couldn't have hurt you. Still, it *is* unusual for you to have been able to see one."

"Ngan," Jeane said, trying to calm herself, feeling suddenly like she had to go to the bathroom. "What—?"

"What you saw was something I enslaved when I was nine years old," Ngan said calmly, "as part of my training at the—"

"*What was that fucking thing?*" she finally asked, her voice shrill, out of control. "What are you doing? What are we doing here? You popped those goddamned bullets out of you like . . . like . . . How did you do that, and what have you been putting me through all this for? You pass out, I'm sure you're dying—maybe you still are—and then that . . . that . . ."

"Demon," he provided with a smile.

"Shut up!" she screamed at him, lifting her hand to smack him across the face but not actually doing it. "Just shut your damn mouth! Shut up with all that chink bullshit, you—!"

She stopped talking and spent the next three minutes forcing herself not to cry.

"You are angry about one thing, Jeane," Ngan said. "Tell me what it is."

She felt a tear roll down one cheek, and she wiped it off fast, hopefully before Ngan could see it. She forced a smile and asked, "One thing?"

"One thing," Ngan said, "most of all."

Her mind was a complete blank, but still she said, "I'm angry about five things. You didn't tell me how to help you. You got us into something that's obviously too big for us. You sent Fitz in there with no way out. You tell me I saw a demon when you can't know what I saw—there's no such thing as demons. Goddamn it, Ngan! Ghosts, monsters, gods, and de—"

She laughed in place of a sob and put her face in her hands.

"You said five things," Ngan said. "That was only four things."

She looked up at him, meeting his odd blue eyes with hers. She'd never felt so exhausted, so drained of physical energy. "What?" she asked him.

"What is the fifth thing that you're angry about?"

She sighed, looked into the woods, and felt every tiny, downy hair on her body stand on end. There was nothing there.

"I'm angry," she said, "that we're supposed to be a team, but you're not telling us that you're capable of things like this."

"Things like what?"

She looked back at him, her jaw now tight with anger, and almost growled, "You can heal yourself of fatal gunshot wounds. You can stop me dialing a phone. You can . . ."

He looked at her expectantly, waiting for her to finish.

"We're supposed to be a team, Ngan," she said, wiping her nose with the back of her hand.

"See," he said, "I told you you were angry about one thing."

She looked up at him with every intention of smashing his face in, but when her eyes met his she started to laugh. The son of a bitch had the balls to laugh with her.

chapter
2WENTY-2WO

Clembert "Skip" Pemberton knew how to stop a bullet in midair. McCain wasn't sure why he was more surprised by this than Erwählen's having done it. Maybe it was because Erwählen was supposed to be the villain, was supposed to have some kind of, well, superpower, for lack of a better term. It was unsettling enough to think that Erwählen was acting as mediator between Pemberton's enormous multinational auto manufacturing corporation and a cabal of oil company executives who were secretly in control of the Environmental Protection Agency. The fact that he was, by all appearances, teaching these men to use magic made McCain deeply afraid.

Erwählen was spreading more than just racist propaganda.

There was still blood on the grass and bits of brain and skull where Erwählen had caused Tom Casale's head to explode. The two men, Darryl and Melvin, had dragged Casale's body away by the ankles. The rest of the men had stood with their eyes closed, as instructed, the whole time.

McCain couldn't think of anything else to do but try to act "normal" when Erwählen finally ordered the rest of them to open their eyes and begin their exercises.

Pemberton was pleased with himself, though sweat was pouring down his face. He smiled at McCain and wiped a sleeve across his forehead. "Not bad for a sixty-three-year-old company man, eh, kid?"

McCain shook his head, forced a smile, and said, "How in God's name did you manage that?"

Pemberton smiled wider and looked at Erwählen, who said, "By paying very close attention, Michael. Mr. Pemberton is a model student, focused, serious about his studies, and conscientious about returning here on a regular schedule for treatments."

"Treatments?" McCain asked.

Erwählen and Pemberton exchanged a knowing glance.

"So," Pemberton said, "you're name's not really Greg?"

Erwählen and Pemberton roared with laughter, slapping each other on the back.

"Funny," McCain said, feeling a bit like a cow who'd been tipped over in a field by drunk teenagers the night before being led to the slaughter.

Erwählen obviously noticed McCain's change in mood. "It will be all right, Michael," he said. "You've seen a few things today that you weren't expecting to see, a few things that shocked you, but never fear, they'll seem ordinary, even comforting, soon enough. In time, you'll see."

"What do I have to do," McCain said boldly, "to get you to stop saying that?"

"I am simply trying to reassure you," Erwählen said.

"What do I have to do," McCain said, maybe a little less boldly, "to get you to stop reassuring me?"

Pemberton held up a hand and said, "Easy, now, Mike. Let's not say anything we'll regret."

McCain looked at him, and Pemberton looked so serious, so offended on Erwählen's behalf that McCain found it ridiculous enough to laugh at. He laughed, and Pemberton and Erwählen joined him. McCain felt like a fool, felt like he was over his head, which he had been for some time.

"Ah, Michael," Erwählen said, Pemberton hanging on his every word, "don't be so upset. It's all really rather simple. You're seeing conspiracies all around where there are none. It's this simple: Over several decades I have worked very hard at perfecting a process whereby I refine a very ancient source of energy we call vril into a liquid form. When a suitable human subject, a pure homo sapiens, is exposed to liquid vril he becomes imbued with that energy to the extent that after some training he is able to focus that energy outward to do things ordinary people would consider impossible. I understand how to make vril, and I can teach people how to use it so that they can live longer, healthier, stronger lives, and harness some power to use as they see fit. In exchange for that they render certain services and cooperate with other like-minded individuals for the betterment of the human race.

"Now," he finished, "is that so bad?"

McCain found himself standing there with his mouth open, quite literally struck dumb. How could he have been expected to have any kind of a response to that?

"Mike?" Pemberton asked, looking honestly worried.

"Why me?" McCain finally said. "Why weren't Darryl and Melvin dragging me away?"

"Because people like you," Erwählen said. "They trust you. They do things for you. Tom Casale got you in here, didn't he? Why? Because you asked him to."

"So I'm alive because you like me?" McCain asked.

Erwählen chuckled and said, "The word needs to be spread, Michael. I need to identify proper candidates and get them here. I need people like you."

"After I'm brainwashed," McCain grumbled.

"Cleanliness is next to godliness," Erwählen said with a smile.

McCain opened his mouth to say something but found he had no words.

"Jerry," Erwählen said so quietly that McCain was sure the teenager couldn't possibly hear him over the gunshots of the men practicing stopping bullets.

Jerry ran toward them dutifully, though, and without hesitation. He came to a halt near Erwählen and looked at the man with wide, accepting, eager eyes.

"Jerry, my boy," Erwählen said, "take Mr. McCain to the cisterns and allow him an opportunity to see the vril. Take Patrick with you."

Jerry nodded once, then looked at McCain. Only a teenager could be capable of the sort of instantaneous mood shift Jerry accomplished just then—from adoration to contempt. McCain didn't shudder enough for anyone to notice, and opted not to say anything. Jerry waved to Patrick, who was holding a submachine gun, and the teenager ran to Jerry's side.

"Michael," Erwählen said as McCain started to turn and follow the teenager, "I won't tell you again that you will see."

"Thank you," McCain said, keeping his eyes on Erwählen as long as he could before turning and following Jerry.

McCain could hear Erwählen and Pemberton talking behind him but not what they said.

McCain didn't bother taunting Jerry or Patrick as they walked. His mind was spinning with all he'd seen and heard. He obviously had enough to report now, had enough to bring back to the Institute. He could leave now knowing that though the investigation was a failure on an enormous personal level. He had learned enough to . . .

To do what?

What would the Hoffmann Institute actually do about this? What *could* it do? What did the Hoffmann Institute actually do about anything? Could they stop Erwählen? Kill him? McCain was no assassin. Would they expose him? McCain couldn't imagine the story he had to tell making it past *Hard Copy*.

They passed along a sidewalk that bordered a wide parking lot. McCain had lived in enough apartment complexes to know that cars told you everything you needed to know about a neighborhood.

in fluid silence

There was a row of nearly a dozen long, black limousines, none with livery plates. There was a good collection of European and Japanese luxury sedans, not a single minivan, and more than one of the big SUVs Skip Pemberton's company was so well known for. As they went on a little longer, McCain started to notice a few other, less expensive cars, a pickup truck that might have cost eighteen thousand dollars brand new, a few domestic full-sized cars—Camp Clarity's charity cases.

Before long they came to a huge, steel-sided building. There was something very familiar about it, though McCain was sure he'd never seen it before—at least not from the outside. It was all very ordinary. The building would have been at home in any industrial park, might have been used on a big commercial farm, or as a warehouse. There were garage-style doors, but Jerry led McCain up to a smaller steel door and opened it. Patrick hung back behind them. It struck McCain as unusual that the door wasn't locked. If this was the so-called "vril," it was the backbone of Erwählen's entire operation, yet here it was in an unlocked building next to a parking lot where anyone could walk in.

Still not sure what they'd do about it, McCain filed that fact away for the Hoffmann Institute and followed Jerry in. Patrick didn't follow.

McCain realized he had been here before. It was the huge room where he'd first come back to consciousness. It was the room with the three huge pools of golden, flowing liquid, and the rows and rows of orange plastic barrels lining the sheet metal walls.

"That's it," Jerry said, his voice quiet and full of that dense admiration.

"The magic goo that's going to change the world?" McCain asked.

Jerry kept his eyes on the vril as it slowly churned, almost caressing the insides of the huge cisterns. "People are going to change the world," Jerry corrected.

"Erwählen tell you that?"

"Who else?" Jerry asked, then turned to McCain and smiled knowingly.

McCain nodded and smiled back.

"You're not going to confuse me?" Jerry asked. "You're not going to ask me a bunch of questions and try to screw with my head?"

McCain scoffed, and said, "You're head's been screwed with enough, kid."

"I'm not that much younger than you," Jerry said petulantly. "Don't call me 'kid.' "

"Gee," McCain said sarcastically enough that even Jerry could pick up on it, "I didn't mean to offend you."

Jerry looked back at the vril and sighed. "Fine, then. You seen enough?"

"Not quite," McCain said. "How many times have you gone in there?"

Jerry shrugged, not looking at him, and said nothing.

"It's okay," McCain impatiently. "Everybody else has been spilling their guts. Erwählen wants me to be a member of this club, and has been encouraging . . ."

He trailed off, realizing Jerry wasn't even listening to him.

"Er geht jeden zehn Tagen dahin," Nichts perched atop one of the orange barrels.

The homunculus was wounded again, stained with his own blood. One wing seemed broken and hung down limply at the little grey man's side. McCain still understood German. Nichts had said that Jerry went in there every ten days.

"Nichts," McCain said, his voice reflecting his genuine happiness at seeing the homunculus again. *"Ist alles bei sich in Ordnung?"*

"Yes," Nichts answered in German, "I am fine."

"Hey stubby," Jerry said, also in German. McCain was surprised by the teenager's ability with the language, but then why should he be? McCain could understand the language and speak it fluently having only been submerged in the vril twice.

The homunculus looked at Jerry with narrow eyes and nodded. "You are missing the drills, Mr. Jerry," Nichts said.

Jerry shrugged. "Erwählen wanted me to keep an eye on *Urinerstreckeansteckung* here."

in fluid silence

"Urinerstreckeansteckung?" McCain asked with an irritated smirk. He was pretty sure that meant "urinary tract infection." What a bizarre epithet.

"I can do that," Nichts offered.

Jerry looked at the little man and chewed the inside of his cheek, saying nothing.

"This guy is kind of—" Jerry started to say, but was interrupted by Nichts.

"Where's he going to go?" Nichts asked, spreading his stubby arms out wide.

Jerry sighed, looked at McCain, back to Nichts, and said, "I don't know."

"You love me too much, Big J," McCain said, smiling suggestively at Jerry.

The teenager made it known that his skin was crawling, and McCain tried not to take offense.

"I will explain it to the master," Nichts said.

McCain looked over at the vril. It was easy enough to let it seize control of his attention. If he was too forceful in trying to get rid of Jerry, even the inexperienced teenager would pick up on it and resist.

"Fine," Jerry acquiesced fast enough. "I want to sit in on levitation."

McCain pretended not to hear that.

"To be safe," Nichts said, "we can keep this between us. An impromptu change in personnel allocation—"

"Can dangerously imbalance carefully planned resource management," Jerry repeated by rote. "I'll be back in an hour. Patrick is right outside."

Nichts nodded, and McCain didn't turn. He heard Jerry leave while he was still wondering about the things Nichts was saying. He seemed more intelligent since they'd spoken last, only twenty-four hours ago. That had to mean something.

"Why are you here?" Nichts asked when Jerry was gone.

"I wanted to see it again," McCain said honestly, "now that I know a little more about it."

"Vril is everything," Nichts said simply.

McCain turned his back on the cisterns and looked Nichts in the eye. The homunculus shrank slightly from his gaze, his claws scuttling on the top of the plastic barrel.

"Vril," Nichts said, "made me. Or I was made by Erwählen from vril. Can you understand that?"

"I think so," McCain lied.

Nichts smiled and shook his head. "I'm getting better at knowing when people are lying," he said. "Imagine looking at three cisterns like this. One is full of your mother's blood, another your father, and the third God's."

McCain thought of a few answers to that, but rejected them all. Instead, he hoped to capitalize on the intimacy and make a request. "Can you get me a phone?"

"A telephone?" Nichts asked quickly, obviously at a loss.

"A cellular telephone," McCain said, "yes."

"Erwählen stepped on it," Nichts answered.

McCain smiled and said, "You're breaking free of him, aren't you?"

"He ignores me more and more," Nichts said, his eyes wide, wet. "When he first created me, I was his favorite. He taught me, he protected me and relied on me at the same time. I would have done anything for him as much because I wanted to as because I was created to. He was my master, and I could refuse him nothing, but why should I? Why should I refuse one such as Hans Reinhold Erwählen?"

"Because that's what a slave should do," McCain said quietly.

"You don't know anything about being a slave," Nichts said.

"No, I don't," McCain replied, "but I know something about being created. I know something about owing my life to someone I'm not sure I can trust."

"You are a human," Nichts said. "You are a complete being—a born being. You can chose."

"You might be surprised," McCain said. He turned back to look at the undulating vril, his back to Nichts. He could feel the homunculus staring at him, wanting to say something.

"Some of them only have to go in once a year now," the homunculus said. "They're getting stronger."

"Is that okay with you?" McCain asked flatly.

"If they get stronger?" Nichts asked. "No, but I'm not sure why."

"There's a story," McCain said, "about angels in heaven fighting a war for the attention of God. Are you one of Erwählen's firstborn angels thrown over in favor of fickle, independent men?"

McCain expected Nichts to think about that for a long time and was startled when he answered quickly, "I am Erwählen's only begotten son."

"I need a phone," McCain said just as quickly. "I need to get word out. I can put a stop to this."

"No," Nichts said sadly, "I don't think you can. This isn't the first time he's tried, and with every failure he's learned. He will not be defeated this time."

"Can I try?"

Nichts looked at him with fear filling his strange eyes.

"Nichts," McCain said, "he killed my friends. Maybe the only two real friends I had. Erwählen had his boys kill them."

"You know this?" Nichts asked. "It would be unusual. Murders attract attention—leave people missing who will be missed."

"Erwählen showed me the bodies," McCain said. He could feel his throat tightening.

"Are you sure?" Nichts asked.

McCain nodded, wanted to say, "It was them," but he couldn't. His eyes grew hot and wet.

"Did you touch them?" Nichts asked. "Did they feel right? Did they vibrate?"

"Vibrate?" McCain asked. "What are you talking about?"

"Did you touch them?"

"No," McCain answered forcefully. "I didn't. I didn't touch them."

"Then you don't know if they're really dead or not," Nichts said.

"I saw—"

"What Erwählen wanted you to see," Nichts told him. "Erwählen has a way with phantasms."

"Phantasms?"

"You may be right," Nichts said, ignoring the question. "They might be dead, but they might not be."

McCain sighed at the ray of hope that felt so false. "If they're still alive," McCain said, "I need that phone even more."

Nichts stepped back again, his feet once more scraping the top of the orange plastic barrel. "He beat me last time," Nichts said. "I can get into the storeroom where he keeps everyone's telephones, pagers, computers, and such. I crawl in through the ceiling. It angers him when I do this, and his punishments are . . . severe."

"Nichts," McCain almost pleaded. "What can I do? I need that phone—any phone that works."

"Can you take me with you?" Nichts asked quickly, obviously wanting to get it out fast.

"Yes," McCain answered. It was a knee-jerk response, but he damned well needed that phone.

"You have a place for me?" Nichts asked.

"The Hoffmann Institute," McCain said gently, "the place I work for, the people . . . they have experience with this kind of thing. They could help you."

"To be their slave instead of Erwählen's?" he asked.

"No," McCain said, "never a slave. Never a prisoner."

Nichts looked at him for maybe the space of two or three heartbeats, then said, "Wait here."

chapter 2WENTY-THR3E

Jeane looked at her blood- and dirt-caked palm and sighed. She looked down at herself, wondering how and where she could wipe the mess off. Her loose-fitting blue jeans were dirty and wet in spots. The white T-shirt that was already a bit tight on her was plastered to her now with sweat and dew. It wasn't so much white anymore as greyish-brown with a huge smear of Ngan's blood from when she'd had to carry him. Her white shoes were likewise caked with mud, bits of leaves and small pebbles, and drops of blood here and there.

She wiped her palm on her jeans and closed her eyes. She was a mess. She could feel the blood she'd gotten on her neck drying, and she didn't even want to know what her hair looked like. It wasn't in her eyes, so she let it be.

Ngan looked even worse, if that was possible. His shirt was bundled up on the ground next to Jeane. Once white, it was now soaked with blood and spotted with dirt. There were holes ripped in it where the bullets passed through, and some of the buttons had popped off when Jeane all but ripped it off him to get at his gunshot wounds. His pants, simple grey linen suit pants, were wrinkled, torn at one pocket, dirty, and bloody. One of his shoes had fallen off, and torn pieces of dry leaves were stuck to his sock. His other shoe was a remarkably clean black wingtip—not surprising since he hadn't walked into the woods.

Ngan was sitting against a small tree, breathing deeply and touching the wounds lightly with the index finger of his right hand. He seemed pale, was sweating, and was otherwise not entirely well. His eyes were puffy and red.

"It's not coming back," Jeane said, "that thing?"

"No," he answered. "It is gone, and I doubt you'll see anything like it ever again."

"Good, because I'd hate to have the same hallucination twice."

Ngan smiled, and Jeane tried not to look at him. "You seemed so sure it was real," he observed.

She stood stiffly and stretched her back. There was a loud pop that was followed by a surprisingly pleasant feeling. "Oh," she groaned. "I've been up all night. It's not at all unusual to have hallucinations from sleep deprivation. In school, my roommate once stayed up for seventy hours straight to make up a term paper she forgot about. She was sure she saw Godzilla from the window of our dorm room."

"Godzilla?" Ngan asked, groaning as he continued to inspect the gunshot wounds.

Jeane sighed and allowed herself a relieved, if tired laugh. Ngan had never heard of any such thing, and though Jeane had been irritated by that in the past she made the conscious decision right then to start finding it charming.

"Godzilla," she said, "is a giant dinosaur-monster from the movies."

"Ah," he breathed. "So she was mistaken about seeing this dinosaur at your college?"

Jeane laughed and said, "It was a tree across campus."

"I see," he almost whispered, brushing some dried dirt from his hands. "So it wasn't any sort of chink bullshit?"

in fluid silence

Jeane's face went red, and it seemed as if someone had dumped a bucket of warm water over her head. She looked at him, but Ngan didn't look up at her. He was brushing at his pants in an offhand manner that made him look somehow noble, like a character from a David Lean movie.

"Jesus, Ngan," Jeane said. "Look . . . I'm sorry about that, okay? I was feeling strung out, a little pushed to the edge, so I lashed out. It was stupid. I was stupid to say that. That's not me."

"I believe 'chink' is an epithet for 'Chinese,' " Ngan said. He looked up at her with a sly grin and the first hint of normal life in his blue eyes. "I am from Tibet, so it turns out that's a different sort of insult after all."

Jeane smiled and sighed in relief. "I'm sorry," she said. "I didn't mean to imply that you were Chinese."

"Apology accepted, Jeane," he said cheerfully. "Thank you."

"You are some piece of work, Ngan."

"Thank you," he said, "I think. Would you hand me my shirt, please?"

Jeane bent, her back protesting all the way, and grabbed his shirt. She threw it, and he reached for it. Ngan winced in pain and failed to catch the shirt. Jeane moved forward as quickly as her exhausted, stiff legs would allow, scooped the shirt up, and handed it to him. He took it without looking her in the eye and frowned at the torn, bloody mess it was.

"Good thing you didn't drag us out here in the winter," Jeane said.

Ngan didn't respond. He slipped the shirt on and winced when the still wet, cold blood touched his skin.

"So," Jeane said, stepping back from him as much to stretch her legs as to give him space to deal with dressing himself, "now what? You're alive—barely—but everything's gone to hell, and here we are in the woods, exhausted, wounded, cold, stiff, and screwed on so many levels I've lost count of them all. What do we do?"

Ngan, again wincing with pain, took the shirt off and set it on the ground next to him.

"Ngan?" Jeane prodded.

"We will need to put an end to this," he said. "We need to find Michael, get him out of there, then get back to Chicago and file a report."

"A report?"

"Yes," Ngan confirmed, "a report. We are investigators, sent here to gather information."

Jeane laughed. "That's rich."

"You disagree?"

Jeane didn't answer. She knew that he knew what she was thinking.

"Do you feel up to fighting for your life, Jeane?" Ngan asked. "I am still in some considerable pain and will not be entirely well for many days. You have not slept. Michael is perhaps dead. Shall we assault Camp Clarity? Face down the armed teenage boys with your one pistol?"

Jeane knew he was right, of course, and had never intended to "assault" the place. The fact was, though, that if she filed a report now, what would it say? She killed one man after getting no real information except the poisoned makeup, which was now sounding a bit more like urban legend. She'd shot a second man—a cop—who was going to kill her. The town of Lesterhalt, according to the only one of its residents she'd actually interviewed, had "gone cracker." And all of it was the work of a guy who might or might not have once hung out with Adolf Hitler and was now running a corporate retreat.

That particular report would not only be unacceptably devoid of useful, well-researched facts, but it would not be the slightest bit flattering to any of the three of them. This report would be as good as a letter of resignation. She knew Ngan knew that too.

"We'll need—" she started, then stopped when Ngan tried to stand.

He didn't get very far before he sank back down onto his behind, his face pinched and wet with perspiration.

"You can't walk yet," Jeane said, allowing the disappointment to show through.

in fluid silence

"Not quite," Ngan admitted. "Forgive me."

Jeane stretched her arms up over her head, listening to her elbows and shoulders grind and pop. "I could go back to the motel," she suggested. "Get some clothes for you, the rest of our stuff, my car . . ."

Ngan shook his head.

"No?" she asked him, though she knew he was right to refuse.

Shots had been fired. They'd left the room in a shambles with blood and bullet holes all over the place. Even if the cops weren't working for Erwählen, they'd probably be there. Jeane could spend as much as a week or so in jail while McCain was God knew where and Ngan was dying in the woods.

She looked over at Ngan, and his chin was resting on his bare chest, his neck limp. Jeanne's heart skipped, and a tingle ran across her hairline.

"Ngan!" she barked.

He came awake fast, his head lolling back fast enough that he almost banged it on the tree behind him. "Yes?" he said, blinking. "I'm thirsty."

Jeane was thirsty too, of course, and was working hard at trying to ignore that.

"You passed out," she told him.

"Yes," he said very quietly. "I will do that from time to time for the next few days or so."

"Great," Jeane sneered sarcastically. "Maybe I can just—"

A phone rang and both of them startled. Jeane looked around the ground in their little patch of trees. It rang again.

"Come on." Jeane scowled. "Where the hell . . . ?"

"There—" Ngan said.

She looked at him, and the phone rang again. He was pointing, so she followed the tip of his finger and saw her duffel bag pressed against the base of a little tree. The phone rang a third time as Jeane stepped to the bag, bent, and reached inside it. Her hand came out with the phone, she flipped it open and said, "Jeane Meara. Talk to me."

"Jeane," the voice on the other end of the phone said.

Her body sagged all on its own, and she was afraid she was going to fall.

"Fitz?" she asked. "Is that you?"

"Michael?" Ngan, still sitting on the ground, said.

"It's me," McCain said. His voice sounded strange, somehow relieved in a way that made Jeane confused, made her have to think about it. "You're alive."

"Alive?" she asked. "We're alive. How about you?"

"He told me you were dead," McCain said.

"Who?" Jeane asked. "Who told you that, Fitz?"

"You're all right?" McCain asked, ignoring her question.

"Ngan's been shot," Jeane told him. "He's managed to keep himself alive, but he's lost enough blood that he could still be in a lot of trouble. He needs help, but we're afraid to take him to a hospital. Where are you?"

"Where are you?" he asked. "I might be able to help Ngan, but you'll have to come here."

"Where?"

"Hold on," McCain said flatly.

"Hold on?" Jeane almost shrieked. "What do you mean? Fitz? Fitz!"

Jeane felt as if her blood were suddenly boiling. She took a step forward, took her left hand off the tree, and balled her fingers up into a fist.

"Fitz!" she shouted into the phone. *"Michael!"*

McCain ignored the static-filled squawk coming through the borrowed cell phone and looked over at Nichts. The little man was crouched on the cement floor at the edge of one of the huge vril cisterns.

"I need your help," he said.

Nichts took a step back and looked at McCain suspiciously. His broken wing twitched. "I brought the telephone to you," the homunculus said.

McCain smiled, held up the phone, and said, "Thank you. It's already been a big help. You were right. My friends are alive."

Nichts nodded. "Erwählen is skilled with phantasms."

"Illusions?" McCain asked. "Is that what you mean?"

Nichts rubbed his hands together and squinted. "Phantasms. Making the unreal appear real . . ."

McCain shrugged and shook his head. "I guess. Anyway, can you help me get my friends here?"

"Here?" Nichts asked, his gravelly voice almost shrill.

McCain stepped forward and squatted down in front of the homunculus. They weren't quite at eye level. "They're not dead, but one of them has been hurt."

"This would be a bad, bad idea," Nichts whined, shaking his head and wringing his hands.

"We've come this far, Nichts. . . ." McCain said.

"Too far already," Nichts almost whispered.

"My friend has been hurt," McCain said, "and hurt very badly. The vril will help hi—"

"*No!*" the little man shrieked. His leathery wings unfurled, and McCain startled back, falling on his backside, his hand coming off the phone.

Jeane plainly said, "Damn it, McCain, you—!" before he slapped his hand over the little speaker again.

Nichts wrapped himself in his wings, peering out at McCain with one eye. "You have become insane here, Michael McCain of Chicago. You will see to it that we are killed in a grisly, medieval sort of way that will hurt and make us both afraid of—"

"Nichts," McCain tried to interrupt.

"You don't know what Erwählen is like when you make him angry," Nichts continued. "You said you were going to leave and take me with you, so let's go! I never agreed to help you use the vril. Only Erwählen can decide who is immersed in vril. The vril—"

"The vril," McCain said loudly. "The vril may be the only chance my friend has. Erwählen is just a man, buddy. He's just some guy with a knack for chemistry or something. He's not God Almighty. You've made steps to finally break away from him. This is it, Nichts. It's time to break all the way away."

Nichts closed his eyes and said, more calmly, "Erwählen is not just a man, Michael McCain. Have you learned nothing in your time here? He is possessed of great power and influence. He created me."

McCain sighed and looked at Nichts, really looked at him. The little man had wings. This was no midget or "little person." Were Nichts's wings an illusion? Was Nichts himself just an illusion? Jeane and Ngan weren't really dead on gurneys riddled with bullet holes. McCain understood why Erwählen would want him to think his friends were dead. He'd want to cut McCain off from his real life in hopes of replacing it with a new life more suited to Erwählen's own goals. But McCain couldn't think of a reason why Erwählen would create an illusion like Nichts. It seemed to be having the opposite effect from the illusion of Ngan and Jeane. Why would he give McCain a phone or create this illusion of a little winged man? To trick him?

"Are you a . . . phantasm?" McCain asked.

Nichts slid his wings from around him and stepped closer. He closed his eyes and bowed his head and said quietly, "Touch me."

McCain swallowed and reached out with one hand. Jeane had stopped talking. When McCain's hand came off the phone there was no sound. The tips of his fingers brushed Nichts's shoulder. The homunculus's skin was rough but warm. He was solid. He was real.

McCain blinked and said, "Sorry, Nichts."

"Erwählen," Nichts told him, "is capable of more than merely phantasms."

"You say that," McCain said, "and I don't know what you mean. Erwählen 'created' you, Erwählen is the 'creator.' . . . What do you mean by that, exactly?"

"I am a homunculus," Nichts answered. It was plain from his tone that he thought McCain was a little slow for asking. "You don't know what a homunculus is?"

McCain shook his head.

"I believe he started with some pieces of a human or more than one human."

"Pieces?" McCain asked.

"The little pieces," Nichts tried to explain. "The invisible bricks that—"

"Cells?" McCain suggested.

Nichts nodded fervently and said, "He immersed these cells in vril and by a process I could never understand, he grew the shape you see before you now. Using another process that was ancient knowledge a thousand years ago, he imbued the body he created with a mind. He . . . wrote my thoughts into my mind, gave me the spark of life and the ability to hear, to see, speak, feel, taste, and—"

"Come on. . . ." McCain shook his head.

"You can believe," Nichts told him, "or not believe, but here I am all the same."

"But . . . why?" McCain asked.

"I am his familiar," Nichts explained. "I am his servant, in all things. He created me because he could. He created me because I had no will and so could be trusted implicitly."

"But something changed," McCain prodded.

Nichts nodded. "I will be bound to Erwählen in many ways," he said. "When he dies, I will die too. At the same instant. Still, I have been able to think on my own more lately, as Erwählen grows more and more bored with me. He has students now. What need will he have for a familiar? What need will he have for Nichts?"

McCain opened his mouth to speak, and he heard Jeane shriek his name. His face turned red, and he held the cell phone to his ear, but not too close.

"Hold on," he said into the phone and put his left hand back over it as Jeane started yelling at him again.

"I told you before, Nichts," he said to the homunculus, "that I can get you out of here, and I can. But I'll need your help. My friend who is hurt is a very important person in the Hoffmann Institute. Nichts, you have to trust me that I will bring you with us, but to get out of here, I have to get them in first."

"Erwählen will kill us both," Nichts said, nodding.

"Damn it, Fitz," Jeane growled into the phone. "What in God's name is going on? I've had enough of this. This damned thing runs on a battery. I can't stand here all day and—"

"Jeane?" McCain's voice sounded in the phone finally. "Is that you?"

Jeane's blood boiled. He was doing it again. They were in a very serious situation, and McCain was goofing around. Meanwhile, Ngan was just staring at her weakly, patiently.

"Damn it, Fitz." She scowled.

"Okay," he said, "listen up. I heard these things run on batteries, so we don't have a lot of time to chit chat."

Jeane exhaled, pinched the bridge of her nose with two fingers, and tried desperately not to burst into flames with anger and outrage.

"I need to get you guys in here," he said. "There's this stuff I can't really explain—so you'll have to trust me—but it should heal Ngan, make him as good as new—better even—but you're going to have to get inside. Describe where you are, and we'll see if we can't get you here."

"There?" Jeane asked. Ngan looked up at her, not having heard what McCain said. "Fitz, that doesn't sound like a real good idea. They shot at us. We need to get you out of there and back to Chicago. Ngan managed to get the bullets out. He's still alive, but hurt—"

"There was some internal damage," Ngan said. "It will take a long time to heal completely."

Jeane looked at Ngan as she said into the phone, "We need you out of there, and we need to get out of here."

"Jeane," McCain said, "I know it sounds nuts, but you have to get him in here. I doubt you've ever heard of this stuff, but I can tell you from experience it's turning these guys into supermen, and it could fix Ngan fast enough. All you need to do is get in here, and we'll stick him in for . . ." McCain mumbled something Jeane couldn't hear, then came back on and said, "A couple hours, maybe less—just to heal a gunshot wound or two, then we can be on our way. All four of us, back to Chicago."

"Four of us?" she asked.

"I met a friend in here," McCain answered. "He's the one who's going to help get you in. Again, you're going to have to trust me."

"Fitz," Jeane said, still looking at Ngan, who nodded at her, "the thing in D.C.—what did the girl call the thing in D.C.?"

"Buddy," he answered quickly. "It's really me, Agent Meara. Describe where you are."

"It's him," she said to Ngan. Then, into the phone, she said, "Hold on."

"Jeane?" McCain said, obviously taken by surprise.

Jeane moved a step toward Ngan and asked, "Can you walk?"

Ngan nodded and, practically climbing the tree with both hands, his knees shaking, he stood.

"Are you sure?" she asked him. "It might be a long way."

"I can walk," Ngan assured her. "Let's get Michael and get this settled one way or the other."

Jeane smiled and put the phone to her ear. "Fitz," she said, "we're in a little copse of trees about a mile and a half straight south of the only motel in Lesterhalt, at the edge of a soy bean field. Where are you? Do you have enough time for all this?"

Jeane could hear him talking to someone, the cadence making her think he was repeating what she'd just told him in some other language.

He came back on and said, "Okay, this won't be easy, but we can get you here. Do you know which way is southeast?"

chapter 2WENTY-4OUR

Hours and dozens of short, battery-saving calls later, Jeane said into her cell phone, "Okay, we're at the fence."

Jeane could hear McCain breathe a sigh of relief. She looked over at Ngan, who forced a smile. He didn't look good, but he didn't look much worse than when they'd started. Their route through the bean fields of southern Illinois had been a series of stops and starts as whoever it was—Jeane thought McCain had called him "Neeks"—reevaluated their position from Jeane's detailed descriptions of fence lines, tree stumps, distant water towers, and traffic noise. The fact that McCain needed to translate everything she said into what sounded like German didn't speed things up any.

Now they were at the fence that surrounded Camp Clarity, the center of the whole mess. She had been exhausted and barely able to stand when they'd first started out, but the sunny, cool day and the walk—supporting Ngan much of the way—had actually helped her. She still wanted to sit down, and she almost leaned against the fence but stopped herself. There could be security measures: alarms, even electricity, that would make that a bad idea. She made eye contact with Ngan to make sure he didn't touch it either. He was smart enough to draw the same conclusion, and he kept his distance.

Beyond the fence was a parking lot. Jeane wasn't surprised to see that most of the cars were expensive, nice vehicles.

"What do you see?" McCain asked her.

"A parking lot," she answered quietly, scanning for people. She heard voices in the distance but saw no one.

"If you look up," he said, "can you see a big generic-looking building like a warehouse?"

On the other side of the parking lot was a building that fit that description. "Yes," she said.

"Okay," McCain replied. "Go to your . . ." He was listening to his friend again. "Go to your left. Follow the fence, but don't touch it. It's wired."

"I figured that," she said, then looked over at Ngan who was standing on shaking legs. His eyes were puffy and red. "The fence is wired," she told Ngan. "We need to follow it left."

"To the back of the building," McCain added, having heard Jeane pass the information on to Ngan.

"I can hear voices," Ngan said. "Men."

"Me too," Jeane said, then to McCain: "We can hear men speaking somewhere. It sounds like they're outside."

"Over the little hill past the parking lot to your right and behind the low building with the satellite dish is a soccer field where most, if not all, of the members are practicing," McCain explained.

"Practicing?" Jeane asked.

"Practicing what?" Ngan asked her.

"Long story," McCain said. "You'll want to keep an eye out for one kid with a submachine gun. He should be around the warehouse somewhere. His name is Patrick, if it helps. Are you moving?"

Jeane told him they were, then repeated what he'd said to

in fluid silence

Ngan. They started walking along the fence line. Ngan stumbled, and Jeane reached out to help him.

"You're very kind, Jeane," Ngan said, his pale, pained face forming a crooked smile.

She sighed and said, "Thank you, Ngan. You're a . . . you're a gentleman. And you're moving pretty well for a guy who was shot three times less than twelve hours ago."

He smiled wider and increased his pace. She wanted to tell him not to push himself but thought better of it. Ngan knew himself better than she could ever know him. If he could go faster, he should go faster.

They followed the fence around and came to the back of the big building. There were no doors on that whole long side of the warehouse and a good thirty feet of dirt, brown grass, and gravel separated the fence from the building.

"Are you at the back of the building?" McCain asked through the phone.

"We're—" Jeane started to answer, but stopped when a teenage boy walked around the corner of the building.

He had a vicious-looking weapon hanging from a shoulder strap and was looking down at the ground. Jeane pulled her gun, and Ngan touched her shoulder.

"No," he whispered. "They will all hear."

He was right, Jeane knew. One gunshot would bring the whole crowd down on them. She looked Ngan in the eyes, and he gave her a look that made it obvious he had some kind of plan. Ngan stepped forward, almost to the fence, and put his hands on a tree to support his weight.

"We see the kid," Jeane whispered into the cell phone.

"Careful," McCain warned quietly.

As if on cue, Patrick looked up. Jeane's breath caught in her throat, but she kept herself from bringing her gun up to aim at the teenager. Patrick did bring his gun up to his shoulder, though, and aimed at Ngan.

"Who the . . . ?" the teenager called, his voice trailing off even as his left elbow sagged and the gun pointed slightly down.

Jeane followed Patrick's seemingly dead gaze to Ngan's

eyes. The older man had the teenager enraptured. Jeane remembered McCain describing Ngan doing something like this once before.

"I need you to go to town for me," Ngan said in a clear, level voice that echoed against the side of the steel building. "Right now."

"Town . . ." Patrick mumbled. His arms went limp, the gun dangling, pointing harmlessly at the ground.

"Right now, Patrick," Ngan ordered.

The teenager nodded blankly, turned, and walked away, disappearing behind the big building.

"Jesus," Jeane said. "You need to teach me how to do that."

Ngan closed his eyes and staggered away from the fence. "It's not that . . . easy," he murmured.

"Jeane?" McCain asked from the cell phone.

"He's gone," Jeane told him. "Ngan . . . just sort of told him to go away."

McCain chuckled and said, "The goat caught in the gaze of the snow leopard?"

"Yeah," Jeane said, "something like that."

"He really needs to teach me how to do that," McCain said.

"Yeah," Jeane replied. "Anyway, we're clear."

"Good," McCain said. "Nichts should be there."

"Neeks?" Jeane asked. "What does he—?"

The sound Jeane made was part gasp and part scream. She didn't register Ngan's reaction. The creature appeared at the fence line, and Jeane was sure it was another demon. This one was smaller, uglier in some ways, and not as openly menacing, but it wasn't human. It was grey and wrinkled and squat, and it had wings like a bat.

She tossed the cell phone into her left hand and drew the .380 from the back of her jeans with her right hand.

Ngan grabbed her wrist before she could aim, let alone fire, and drew her arm up. She almost elbowed him in the face before she realized it was him. She spun on him, heard McCain say, "Is he there?" from the phone, and was sure that when she'd turn around again the little monster would be gone.

"Jeane," Ngan said, his eyes strong and compelling, "it's all right."

Jeane turned and her lips pulled back from her teeth when she saw that the monster was still there, cowering from her, hiding behind one of its awful wings.

"I think this is Michael's new friend," Ngan said.

Jeane blinked at the thing and shook her head. From the phone McCain said, "Talk to me, Jeane."

She put the phone to her ear and said, "Fitz."

"I'm over here," he said, his voice coming from the phone and in person at the same time.

Jeane looked up and saw McCain come around from behind the building. He turned his cell phone off with a beep and smiled, looking at her first, then Ngan. The smile faded from his face as Jeane turned off her cell phone. McCain looked them both up and down.

"What happened to you guys?" he asked.

Jeane and Ngan both ignored the question. She was happy to see him but was still more than a little unsettled by McCain's new friend.

"What is it?" she asked.

"That's Nichts," McCain said. "Don't be afraid. There's nothing to be afraid of."

"It's a homunculus," Ngan said, letting go of Jeane's arm. Ngan looked at the little creature and said, "You are a homunculus, aren't you, little one?"

The thing McCain called Nichts tipped its head inquisitively at Ngan, obviously not understanding.

"Don't bother, Ngan," McCain replied. He looked at Jeane and said, "Nichts only speaks German. Say, '*Wir wollen eintreten, bitte,*' and he'll start digging."

"*Wir* . . ." Jeane started.

Nichts looked up at her, apparently recognizing the word, and it made Jeane jump. She almost brought her gun up, then stopped herself and quickly tucked it back into the waistband of her dirty jeans. She held her right hand up, still holding the cell phone in her left hand.

"You speak German?" Ngan asked McCain.

"*Wollen* . . ." McCain prompted Jeane. He looked at Ngan and said, "I do now. I have a lot to tell you."

Jeane swallowed in a dry throat and said, "*Wir wollen* . . ."

"*Wir wollen eintreten, bitte,*" McCain repeated.

"*Wir wollen . . . eintreten, bitte,*" Jeane said slowly, carefully.

The little man's face contorted into a smile, and he moved to the fence. Jeane couldn't stop herself from taking a step backward.

Nichts didn't notice. He bent down about eighteen inches from the fence and started to dig, burrowing like a mole. Jeane glanced over at Ngan, who was watching the homunculus with obvious fascination.

"When he's done," McCain said, "you'll need to crawl under, but whatever you do, don't touch the fence."

"I don't know. . . ." Jeane started to protest.

Nichts was already half-buried in the loose dirt and gravel under the fence. The hole was getting bigger by the second.

"We've come this far, Jeane," Ngan said. "It's less a leap of faith than others I've seen you make in the short time we've known each other."

"That . . ." she stammered, "that's, uh, that's not the same thing we saw in the woods?"

"No," Ngan said reassuringly. "This little man is no demon. He's not human, of course, but he is no demon. Michael is an excellent judge of character. If Michael trusts him, I see no reason why we should not."

All Jeane could see now was the homunculus's wrinkled grey feet sticking out of its impressive hole.

"This," Jeane said more to herself than to Ngan or McCain, "isn't going to end well."

chapter
2WENTY-5IVE

There were no demons here.

In the vril Ngan could feel no other presence. The little link in the small sounds and the brushing touches that he had grown accustomed to in the world of solid things was gone. He had studied what it meant to be dead, and this was very much like that. He couldn't use any of his senses. There was no temperature. There was nothing to experience outside himself, so he turned his attention inward.

There were things flying around like pollen or flower petals, and the light had a golden-yellow cast. He couldn't see, but there was a golden light.

Then Leah was there. Perfect again. Clean again. Alive, happy, healthy, and whole again.

The breeze was coming from every direction at once. The topiaries were there, not rigidly looking into the sky again, but all arranged in a circle. Men looking outward so that none of them seemed to be looking at any of the others.

235

"You're back," Leah said, her voice echoing in a way that Ngan found unnerving.

He opened his mouth to reply, but found that he couldn't form words. His mouth seemed full of something thick and warm. He gagged on it, opening his mouth wide.

"It's okay, Ngan," Leah said, smiling at him. "Let it out."

She smiled at him, and Ngan coughed. His knees gave out on him, and he collapsed to the dry grass floor of the topiary garden. His mouth opened wide, and his throat tensed. His stomach contracted, and it all came out.

Ngan had his eyes closed at first, then opened them when he heard a thousand little clicking noises all at once. What he saw made his stomach tighten more. Thousands of ants were pouring out of him like vomit—thousands, hundreds of thousands, maybe millions. They were small, no longer than the width of Ngan's littlest fingernail, and a bright yellow-gold color.

They scurried away quickly the second they touched the ground, splitting off into orderly groups and heading out into the far corners of the secret spring.

"There you go," Leah said calmly. "Now you can talk."

Ngan looked up at her. Ants were already crawling on her, first a few, then a few dozen, then a few hundred. She never flinched, didn't seem to notice the ants at all.

"Busy," she said, an insane gleam in her eyes, "aren't they?"

Ngan opened his mouth to say something, but again he was only able to vomit out another few hundred thousand little gold ants.

When he seemed to be finished, Leah said, "Okay, *now* you can talk."

"Ants?" he asked her, tense and expecting his throat to hurt. It didn't.

She shrugged and smiled. An ant crawled across her open eye, and again she didn't flinch. "They're very efficient," she said, "and very small."

Ngan stood, looking at the ground all around him. The whole circle of topiary trees, the ground all around him, and the ground all around Leah where she sat cross-legged on the moss was covered with ants. Some of them were carrying leaves. Ngan remembered the name for ants like that. Leaf-cutter ants? Not very creative, but clear.

He looked at the topiary trees, and something about them seemed different.

"The trees . . ." he started to say.

Leah giggled and said, "Neat, huh?"

"They're eating the trees?" he asked her.

"Look at them more closely," she urged him.

Ngan did as she asked and realized quickly that the ants weren't taking leaves from the topiaries in Leah's secret garden, they were adding leaves to a new tree. They were building a new topiary tree. The legs were already finished up to the knees.

"How much time has gone by?" he asked.

Leah laughed, and he laughed with her. It felt good. It was then that he realized that the pain in his chest was gone. He touched himself where the worst of the three wounds had been. Leah noticed and stopped laughing.

"You're going to be okay," she said. "I'm glad."

"Michael was right," Ngan said, letting his hand fall from his chest.

Leah nodded.

"This vril of Erwählen's," he continued, "has definite healing properties. If I stay in long enough I will be able to survive a fall like Fenton did. This is extraordinary."

"Yeah," Leah said, apparently bored. "It's swell all right."

Ngan looked at her and offered a smirking grin. "You are not Leah."

"We went over all that, Ngan," she answered.

"The Medicine Buddha?" he asked.

Leah just shrugged, still covered with ants.

"I would have healed in time, no?" he felt the need to ask.

Leah nodded and said, "You know you should have healed faster. You should have been okay in the morning, but you weren't because you knew you had to come here. You needed to still be sick, to still be weak, when you came to the vril. You needed to be submerged. You needed to see it and feel it, touch it and taste it and smell it. You had to experience it."

"Why?" he asked.

"You know why," was her non-answer.

The ants had the topiary man's torso finished.

"What are they building?" he asked.

"A man," she answered.

"What man?"

Leah giggled again. "You know what man."

Ngan could literally hear something click in his mind, and he said, "Erwählen."

"You'll need to stop him," Leah said. "Jeane's gun won't do it, and if Michael's charm was enough, it would be over already. The Hoffmann Institute will not stop him. You know you were sent here to gather information, but you don't know what they intend to do with that information, do you?"

"Leah," he said, "I'm not . . ." He tried to think what he was trying to say, but wasn't he really saying what Leah was saying? Wasn't she really him?

"Will they do anything, Ngan?" Leah asked.

"Or did they just want to know?" he asked himself.

"You already have some skills, Ngan," Leah said. "The vril will give you more. You will have to kill him. You know that."

"That was why I was sent here?" he asked.

The ants had finished the topiary-Erwählen's arms.

"Jeane asked you," Leah said. "Michael thought about it."

"We're assassins?"

"You can be," Leah said. "You have some chance. Jeane will help, Michael too, but in the end it will have to be you."

"I am a *gomchen*," he said. "I am no assassin. I am a monk."

"Not any more, Ngan," Leah assured him. "You haven't been for some time. The Hoffmann Institute is no monastery."

The ants had started building the topiary-Erwählen's head.

"I can't—" Ngan started.

"You have to," Leah said.

Ngan said, "With what? Empathy? *That* will kill this man

who's lived so long, eluding assassins from the Gestapo, the CIA, and how many others?"

Leah shrugged and said, "No one ever said it was going to be easy, Ngan, but it's up to you. Live in Erwählen's world or kill him, because if you don't kill him, the world will be Erwählen's world. He doesn't understand what it is he's brought into the world. No one his age could, I suppose. It's a power the human race will develop eventually, but this isn't something like high density ceramics. It's something fundamental that you're better off figuring out on your own. Now, we need to stop talking about this. He's found a way in, and his ants are almost finished."

"He's found a—?"

"There you are," Erwählen said, interrupting Ngan.

Ngan spun toward the now completely formed topiary. It was a deep green, leafy bush in the shape of a tall man with a square jaw and barrel chest. The voice came from a place in the leafy head where a mouth should be. Ngan could see no trace of eyes, but he felt as if he was being stared at nonetheless.

"Yes," Erwählen said. "Here I am."

Ngan sensed that the tree man was smiling.

"Hans Reinhold Erwählen, I presume," Ngan said to the topiary man.

"That's him all right," Leah said.

Ngan looked back at her. She was completely covered with gold ants. The place where she'd been sitting cross-legged on the ground was a mass, a pile of the insects all crawling all over each other.

"Ants," Erwählen said. "That makes a certain amount of sense, I suppose."

"Will they hurt her?" Ngan asked out of some reflex action.

The topiary-Erwählen replied, "They're trying to."

"I'm fine," Leah said, though her voice sounded different—deeper somehow. "Don't mind me."

"Ah," Erwählen breathed. "She's not real."

"Smarty-pants," Leah teased, her voice deeper still.

"How did you get here?" Ngan asked Erwählen, ignoring

Leah, who was an extension—a more realistic extension in some ways—of himself.

"This is my property," Erwählen replied, his tree arm gesturing to indicate the floor of the secret spring.

"No," Ngan said simply. "This place is mine, based on a friend's, to be sure, but mine and mine alone."

"The vril," Erwählen corrected, "is mine. As is the right to use it as I see fit, and make it available only to those I deem worthy."

"White men?"

"Not all white men," Erwählen corrected. "Not all of them are worthy."

"And who says whether or not they are worthy?"

"I do," Erwählen answered.

"Based on what criteria?" Ngan persisted.

"My own."

Ngan glanced back at Leah. The ants were beginning to withdraw. He could see the top of her head. Her blonde hair had turned black.

"You will answer questions for me," Ngan told the topiary-Erwählen.

"I will tell you what it pleases me to tell you."

"Before I kill you, Mr. Bond. . . ." Leah drawled, her voice loaded with obvious sarcasm, but then it wasn't Leah's voice anymore. It sounded familiar to Ngan, but it wasn't Leah. It was a man's voice.

Ngan looked at her sharply. He had no idea what she was talking about. Who was Mr. Bond? How could she make a reference he didn't even understand if she was just a reflection of him? And who was speaking through her now?

"Questions," Erwählen said quietly, through his leaf and branch throat. "I never said I was going to kill anyone."

"You will," Ngan told him. "You have, and you will again. You will kill, and you will enslave, and you will marginalize, because you are a fascist."

"That's a rash generalization," Erwählen protested lamely. "What do you know of fascism?"

"I am Tibetan," Ngan answered.

"And that makes you an expert?"

"I fled the Chinese," said Ngan.

"Then what do you know of fascism?" Erwählen prodded. "If you'd stayed, you would have found out."

"If it was bad enough to make me leave Tibet," Ngan told him, his anger rising, burning in him, "that's all I need to know."

"So, you were afraid of the Chinese and ran away," Erwählen concluded. "Therefore you know all about what it's like to live in a world unified under one pristine vision."

Ngan felt a chill run down his spine and had to admit he was intrigued at the possible directions this conversation might lead him, but it occurred to him that if Erwählen was here, he must have come into the secret spring through some link in the vril, might even be floating in the golden liquid alongside him. Jeane and Michael were out there, and Erwählen knew he was in the vril.

"It's all right," Erwählen said. "I have no intention of killing Michael McCain or the woman. If I really wanted you dead, you would be dead already. I like this woman you brought. She has a certain quality I find appealing. She seems to come from reasonable Aryan stock. It might be time to begin including women, now that a solid base of strong men have been—"

"She won't have anything to do with you," Ngan interrupted. "And you did try to kill her. You tried to kill us both at the motel. You came close to killing me, but Jea—the woman—survived without a—"

"Jeane," Erwählen interrupted. "You can say her name. I can feel her name in you."

Ngan said nothing. He had to think about the fact that Erwählen seemed to be able to read Jeane's name from his thoughts. Still, he recognized that Erwählen hadn't addressed the fact of the attempted murders.

"Your vril," Ngan asked, "will work on women?"

Erwählen laughed and said, "It will work on anyone. I tell my people it affects white men only because I want people who look like me and think like me around me more than people who look and think differently. Is that so bad?"

"Of course it is," Ngan said.

"Ah," Erwählen returned, "spoken like a true American."

"I am Tibetan," Ngan felt the need to correct him. "I am living in exile."

"Indeed?" Erwählen asked smugly. "The fact that you insist on making that distinction makes it obvious that you'd rather be with other Tibetans, that Tibetans are better than Americans, or white people, or black people or—"

"That is an interesting jump, Mr. Erwählen," Ngan joked, "but there are degrees of comfort and control, and though we all would rather feel comfortable in our surroundings, some of us are tolerant enough to—"

"Tolerant?" Erwählen asked, the tone in his voice even more superior now, as if he'd managed to manipulate Ngan into some kind of incriminating admission. "So, you *tolerate* people who aren't from Tibet? You merely allow them near you? Or do you really welcome them?"

"Why are we having this conversation?" Ngan asked bluntly.

"I'm curious," Erwählen admitted. "Honestly, I know I'm going to win, and I'm curious."

"You want to understand me," Ngan said, "so the better to command me?"

"Oh," the tree in the shape and with the voice of Erwählen answered, "I understand you, Ngan Song Kun'dren of the Monastery of Inner Light. I understand you much more than you realize."

"What could you know of me?" Ngan asked.

"What would a *Bodhisatva* know?" Erwählen asked sharply.

Ngan shuddered and felt the ants flow around his ankles in ripples. The Erwählen-tree tipped its head down to look as well. Ngan wasn't sure how to gauge the tree's reaction.

Ngan was deeply offended that a man like Erwählen would ever identify himself as a *Bodhisatva*. For people of Ngan's persuasion, Tibetan and other Buddhists, a *Bodhisatva* was a most special person. A result of multiple rebirths, this holy man was said to be capable of perfect concentration—a feat few could even imagine, let alone achieve. Ngan knew that a *Bodhisatva*

in fluid silence

was capable of bringing into being ten kinds of magical creations—especially phantasms of people and—

—and Michael had told him about the illusionary forms of he and Jeane dead on tables in Camp Clarity's morgue. A *Bodhisatva* could create something described as a "beverage of immortality" that was something with all the properties of Erwählen's vril.

"So," Erwählen said to the top of Ngan's bowed head, "you don't think someone like me should use that title, or you don't think someone like me should actually achieve that state? Is that reserved for Tibetans? Do you include Indians, maybe, even Chinese? Maybe, but certainly not white people. Certainly not westerners. You have a smaller mind, a smaller scope than you think, *gomchen*."

Erwählen's use of Ngan's title was the thing that almost put Ngan in his place.

Almost.

Michael and Jeane were out there. If this man was—all the heavens help us, Ngan thought—truly a *Bodhisatva*, they were in even more danger than they'd feared.

"How did you know I was here?" Ngan asked.

"Where?" Erwählen played dumb, and Ngan knew it.

Ngan refused to answer.

"The vril," Erwählen said after only a few seconds, "tells me all."

"There was no lock on the door," Ngan said. "It was remarkably easy to get under the fence. You allowed Michael free access to it. For a creation so special, I'd think you would be more protective."

Erwählen laughed, and the leaves of the topiary tree rustled.

"You're not protecting it," Ngan concluded.

"No one can use it as well as I," Erwählen said. "No one can understand it the way I do. No one outside Agharti, where it flows in their air like light flows in ours, will ever be able to destroy or even sully it. I don't need to protect something that will never be anything but mine."

"Agharti?" Ngan asked. "The world within."

"You've heard of it?"

Ngan chuckled and said, "It is a myth."

The Erwählen tree shuddered and said, "So is vril, and yet here we are."

"So the world is hollow and full of vril," Ngan said. "You've been there?"

"I've seen their cities," Erwählen said.

"How do they feel about—"

"They don't care," Erwählen iterrupted. "The surface is mine. They can have the inside."

Ngan hummed to himself and quickly assembled a wall in the inside of his forehead, imagining stones and mortar. Another ripple effect ran through the ants, and there was a loud whistle like steam escaping as some million or so of them were boiled in their own gold-colored exoskeletons.

"What are you doing?" Erwählen asked.

Ngan built a stone room in a corner of his mind, a place he knew Erwählen couldn't go, and in that stone-walled room Ngan thought the word: Pride. That was Erwählen's weakness, and that was how they were going to bring him down, how they'd managed by luck and mistake and sheer force of will to get this far. This man was so supremely self-confident that he left his greatest treasure unguarded because he couldn't imagine the possibility of anyone with the power, brains, and courage to steal it from him. It was the mindset of someone who was already the master of all he surveyed. But the fact was that Erwählen wasn't yet the master of all he surveyed.

Erwählen was no *Bodhisatva*. He didn't create vril. He got it from somewhere he called Agharti. He took it from someone, maybe refined it, but he didn't create it.

"Are you closing off from me?" Erwählen asked.

The tree took a step closer to Ngan, who didn't flinch.

"Does that upset you?" Ngan asked, baiting him.

"It does," Erwählen said, "but for different reasons than you think. I'm really not such a bad person, Ngan. You have jumped to conclusions."

"You hate," Ngan said, "and that has never led to a positive result."

"Not when it's resisted with greater hate, no," Erwählen replied. "You don't have to love everyone to not be consumed by hatred. Hate, used properly, can be a form of enlightenment."

"You are a fool," Ngan said, not masking the pity in his voice.

Erwählen's response was a reedy laugh. "Why are you here?"

"To gather information."

"Tell him," Nakami said, and Ngan jumped.

He'd forgotten—the voice was Dr. Nakami's—but it came from Leah. Nakami, head of the Hoffmann Institute, was there. Or had Ngan subconsciously replaced Leah with Nakami because he needed a figure of greater authority to provide support against Erwählen?

"Tell me," Erwählen demanded. "Why are you here?"

"To kill you," Ngan admitted. "We have to kill you."

"You have to?" Erwählen asked quietly. "This Hoffmann Institute of yours has sent you here to kill me?"

"No," Ngan said honestly.

"Then you decided on your own to kill me," Erwählen concluded. "Why? Because you hate me?"

"No," Ngan answered. "Because I love everyone else."

Erwählen laughed again and said, "I could teach you to be more selective."

"No," Ngan said. "No, thank you."

"Well, then," Erwählen sighed, "I will have to kill you first. That's too bad. I liked your friend McCain. He reminds me of a man I had the pleasure of advising many years ago when I was employed by the American intelligence establishment—such as it was. It will wound me to kill him. It really will."

chapter TWENTY-SIX

McCain and Jeane stood at the edge of the central vril cistern and looked down at Ngan. He was floating, arms spread to one side, legs drifting limply, maybe three feet below the undulating surface of the golden liquid.

"He's been in there long enough to have drowned," Jeane said, her voice betraying her utter lack of confidence in the supposed magical qualities of the soupy liquid.

"I spent a lot longer in there than he has," McCain told her.

"So you said," Jeane sighed.

McCain glanced at her, then looked back down at the hazy form of the suspended Ngan. They'd lowered Ngan into the vril right away, then McCain told Jeane everything that he'd seen, heard, and done at Camp Clarity. McCain could tell by the look on her face when he first saw her at the fence, while he was speaking, and now, that she wanted him to think she didn't believe him. McCain could tell she did believe him, though. She was smarter than that. She'd seen things, experienced things in connection with this case that had to be explained somehow, and Jeane would never allow her cynicism to keep her from being prepared for the unexpected.

"Michael McCain *ab* Chicago," Nichts said from behind them.

Jeane jumped a little, turned her head just a bit, but didn't look at the homunculus.

"*Wie geht's?*" McCain asked the little man.

"*Das ist sehr arg,*" Nichts warned. "*Es geht bevorstehend sehr schlecht.*"

"What did he say?" Jeane asked.

McCain turned around and stepped off the edge of the cistern, dropping heavily to the cement floor in front of Nichts.

"He said," McCain translated, "that things are going to get very bad, very soon."

Jeane chuckled, but McCain kept his eyes on Nichts.

"*Sorgen Sie sich nicht,* Nichts," McCain assured him. "*Jetzt nicht länger.*"

"Do I need to know what you're saying?" Jeane asked, turning herself to face McCain.

McCain looked up at her and held out a hand to help her down. She scowled at him and stepped off, landing more easily than he had without touching his hand.

"I was just reassuring him," McCain said. "He's afraid."

Jeane spared the homunculus a suspicious, unpleasant glance, and Nichts withdrew a step from her. She looked up, studying one of the rows of orange barrels.

"Let me know if he says anything useful," she said. "I need to take a look at these barrels. Seems this place has a security measure after all."

"What sec—?" McCain started.

"*Er wißt, das wir hier sind,*" Nichts interrupted, his voice quivering with unconcealed, unashamed panic.

"Who knows we're here?" McCain asked. Nichts stared blankly, and McCain realized he'd spoken English. "*Wer wißt, das wir hier sind?* Erwählen?"

"*Natürlicherweise* Erwählen!" the homunculus said.

in fluid silence

"Wie?"

The homunculus put a wrinkled, calloused hand to his own face, and his whole body started to shake. McCain could see a tear roll down Nichts's puffy grey cheek.

"Nichts," McCain said quietly. "It's okay. *In ordnung.*"

"Nein," Nichts sobbed. *"Sie werden mit mir grollen."*

A chill ran up McCain's spine, and he almost yelled for Jeane. McCain could tell Nichts was upset, maybe because he thought McCain would be angry with him about something. McCain couldn't think of anything that Nichts had done that would make him angry—unless he'd put Jeane or Ngan in danger. McCain looked up. Jeane was squatting next to one of the big orange plastic barrels reading something written in small white print on the side of the barrel near the bottom.

McCain realized that if Nichts thought he was going to be angry, he was lucky he didn't know Jeane better. The little man might have had a heart attack on the spot.

McCain wanted to reassure Nichts, tell him that he had nothing to worry about, that Ngan was only going to be in the vril for maybe another half an hour, then they would all be off.

"Nichts," McCain said calmly, *"Es gibt nichts um zu sorgen. Ngan wird vielleicht nur eine halbe Stunde im vril sein, dann sind wir alle weg."*

Nichts looked up at him, dropping his hand from his eyes. He only glanced at McCain's eyes, then looked away. McCain had seen ashamed before, but nothing like what he saw painted on the homunculus's face then.

"Es gibt etwas anders bei mich, daß Sie wissen sollen," Nichts said slowly.

Something else McCain should know about him? McCain felt like his heart slowed down as if anticipating a shock.

"Es gibt etwas um einen Familiär zu sein . . ." Nichts continued.

There is something about being a familiar . . .

"Der Schöpfer . . ."

The creator . . .

"Erwählen kann sehen, alles die ich sehe . . ." Nichts almost whispered.

"What?" McCain asked, feeling his face go pale. "Nichts..."

The homunculus told him that Erwählen could see what Nichts saw...

"*Hören was ich höre...*" Nichts continued.

Hear what Nichts heard...

"Nichts..." McCain breathed.

"*Er müßt nur sich konzentrieren,*" Nichts said. "*Er müßt nur wollen.*"

So Erwählen could use Nichts as something like a remote camera. The old man could see what Nichts saw, hear what Nichts heard, and all he had to do was concentrate. All he had to do was want to. All he had to do was be was curious.

"Oh, Nichts," McCain said, forgetting to speak German, "that's just so bad. That's really something you should have told me way, way, way before this. *Sie sollten mich erzählen,* Nichts. *Sie sollten mich sehr früher erzählen.*"

"*Sie haben nicht gefragt,*" Nichts said defensively.

"I didn't ask?" McCain almost shouted. "*Ich haben nicht gefragt?*"

Nichts held up a hand as if to ward off a blow, and McCain was startled by the fact that he actually did have his hand up to strike the homunculus.

"Oh, Jesus, Nichts," McCain breathed. "I'm sorry. *Es tut mir leid.*"

"*Er hatte mich ignoriert,*" Nichts said. "*Vielleicht hört er nicht zu. Vielleicht sieht er nicht...*"

Nichts reminded McCain in a shrill, panicked voice that Erwählen had grown bored with his familiar of late, and might not have been listening, might not have been watching.

"*Es tut mir leid*, okay Nichts?" McCain said, his hands in front of him now, empty of malice or threat. "*Ich bin sehr reuevoll.*"

"This place is wired," Jeane said loudly, startling both McCain and Nichts.

They both looked at her; both looked confused. Nichts didn't understand English. McCain just didn't understand.

"These orange barrels..." Jeane said, casting a cold,

accusatory glance at Nichts before fixing an even colder glare on McCain. "You couldn't guess what they might be?"

"Oh," McCain sighed, his face blossoming bright red, "that's bad."

"Our Mr. Erwählen may be carelessly self-confident when it comes to perimeter security," Jeane said, sighting down the line of barrels with a shudder, "but he's got a hell of a self destruct system set up here."

"What's in those barrels?" McCain asked breathlessly.

"34-0-0 ammonium nitrate," Jeane said. Her face looked pale.

"Ammonium nitrate?" McCain asked. "What's that?"

"Fertilizer," Jeane said quietly, looking all around. There was easily a couple hundred barrels.

"Fertilizer bombs?" McCain asked, also looking at the barrels.

"Was hat sie gesagt?" Nichts asked.

Both Jeane and McCain ignored the homunculus.

"What can that do?" McCain asked, already suspecting the answer.

"Ask the people of Oklahoma City," Jeane said sternly. "It'll take care of the evidence. Or prevent anyone else from using this goop."

"That's great," McCain said, shaking his head to snap himself out of it. "It gets worse. Erwählen probably knows we're here and what we're doing. Nichts told me Erwählen could see and hear everything I thought I've been doing behind his back, or most of it."

McCain was purposefully vague. Jeane had made her mistrust and nervousness of Nichts plain, and McCain was afraid of what she might do if she found out that Nichts was something like a walking surveillance camera that her partner had been performing to the whole time.

"The fact that we're learning this right now, of course," Jeane said, her eyes practically firing lasers into McCain's head, "is less than convenient."

"We need to get Ngan out," McCain said. "We need to get him

out of there and hope he can walk well enough to book from this place right now."

"Was sagt sie?" Nichts asked.

McCain opened his mouth to answer, looked at Nichts, but his voice caught in his throat. The homunculus wanted to know what they were saying. There was a series of loud, echoing, tinny cracks that punctuated the bursts of dark red blood that exploded all over Nichts's squat little body. The force of the submachine gun fire sent Nichts sliding across the cement floor between McCain and Jeane. The little man opened his mouth to scream, but all that came out was a fountain of dark arterial blood. He left a wide trail of gore on the concrete as he slid ten, fifteen, twenty feet before coming to rest after a half spin.

McCain looked up to the source of the gunfire and locked eyes with Jerry. The teenager gave McCain a smug scowl and leveled the gun at him.

McCain caught movement out of the corner of his eye and saw Jeane pull her automatic from the back of her pants, but she kept the gun hidden.

Jerry shifted targets to her and sighted down the barrel as Jeane brought her gun up in both hands, aiming.

Erwählen stepped up next to Jerry and held up a hand to calm the whole room down. "Enough now," he said calmly, like a vet talking to an injured dog. "Ah, now, here we are. All together at last."

chapter
2WENTY-7EVEN

McCain looked up and caught Jeane's eye. He saw her let her right arm slide slowly behind her back. Her eyes widened just a little, and McCain was sure she was trying to ask him a question without speaking. The problem was McCain wasn't sure exactly what it was she was asking him. She might want to know if she should shoot Erwählen, or maybe she wanted to know whether or not this even was Erwählen in the first place.

If he nodded would she know he meant to tell her that this was Erwählen, or would she think he meant to tell her it was okay to shoot him? And why wouldn't it be okay to shoot him? McCain knew full well that either Erwählen or the three of them were going to have to die today, but he'd just seen Erwählen and his people stop bullets in midair. . . .

Jeane narrowed her eyes at him, obviously unhappy with his indecision, though only a second or two had gone by. She looked at Erwählen, her hand still sliding behind her back, and asked, "Who are you?"

Erwählen laughed. Jerry squinted angrily at McCain, staring at him through the sights of his submachine gun.

"You have broken in here to steal my most prized possession, a truly unique and beautiful thing beyond your limited comprehension," Erwählen said in his thickly accented voice, "and you don't even know who I am?"

McCain said, "That's—"

"Hans Reinhold Erwählen," Erwählen finished for him, all fatherly smiles and twinkling eyes.

McCain looked down at Nichts when the homunculus drew one ragged, gurgling breath into lungs filling with blood. McCain looked back up and met Erwählen's stern gaze for just half a second before the man turned to Jerry and nodded. McCain tensed, waiting for the bullets to rip him apart, but instead Jerry turned the gun on Jeane.

With a hissed obscenity, Jeane launched herself to one side and high in the air. The first bullet blasted out of the flashing muzzle of Jerry's weapon and whizzed harmlessly past the bottoms of her feet even as the next one came out of the gun.

Jeane fired back in midair just after the second bullet brushed past her shoelaces and just before the third came out of Jerry's gun.

McCain's mouth fell open in fear and confusion, then he realized what Jeane was diving for. There were continuous thick concrete walls, three feet high, around each of the three vril cisterns. Jeane was diving for cover behind one of them.

Erwählen held out his right hand, and Jeane's first bullet crackled to a stop six inches from the man's palm. Jeane fired once more before she passed behind the concrete wall. Again, Erwählen stopped the bullet in midair, saving himself or Jerry a possibly fatal wound.

Jeane crashed to the floor behind the cistern wall, scraping the skin of her left arm horribly and swearing all the way, "You're shooting in here you goddamn stupid moron—in a room full of explosives!"

One of Jerry's barrage of bullets pinged off the top of the wall, sending a puff of pulverized cement rolling into Jeane's eyes.

in fluid silence

"Gehen Sie um!" Erwählen shouted to Jerry, who flinched at the loudness of his master's voice. *"Erschlagen sie!"*

He'd told Jerry to go around to the other side of the cistern and kill Jeane.

"No!" McCain shrieked, standing and holding his arms up, then immediately feeling ridiculous.

Jerry turned his sights quickly on McCain, but Erwählen grabbed the gun and brought it up and away. Jerry fired a few shots into the tall ceiling and scowled.

"Jerry," Erwählen said, *"nein."*

The teenager looked over at Erwählen, surprised, but he relaxed his arm. Erwählen let go just as Jeane fired another shot at them. Erwählen brushed the bullet aside.

Jerry aimed at Jeane, and she fired at them again just before Jerry got off a four-round burst. Erwählen stopped Jeane's bullet and she had to duck behind the cistern wall as Jerry's barrage gouged into the cement above her head.

"Stop him!" McCain screamed at Erwählen, who looked at him sharply.

The look in Erwählen's eyes turned genuinely warm, genuinely sorry. McCain's heart sank, but his anger quickly pushed that emotion aside.

Jeane ignored the moment and unloaded the rest of her pistol's seven round clip. Erwählen stopped all the bullets in midair and Jerry stood, completely out in the open, firing at will. McCain could tell that the teenager realized Jeane was out of ammo. He let the rest of his own clip drain, then quickly replaced it with another. Erwählen put a hand on Jerry's arm. The teenager slid a cartridge into the chamber, but he held his fire.

"It's all right, Jerry," Erwählen said in English. "Let's give everyone a moment to breathe, eh? Michael?"

McCain looked at him and shook his head, his lips a thin, tight line.

"No?" Erwählen said with no little sarcasm.

Nichts drew in another long, ragged breath, and McCain looked down at the homunculus. Nichts opened one eye, and it

255

rolled lazily to meet McCain's. A tear dripped out from under his wrinkled, puffy lower lid.

"Nichts," McCain said. "It'll be okay. I can still get you out."

Nichts exhaled with a frothing fountain of blood, and he slowly shook his head side to side.

"For goodness' sake, Michael," Erwählen grumbled, his voice echoing in the big room, "please, don't tell me you're about to shed a tear for a homunculus of all things."

McCain looked up at Erwählen when he felt a tear roll down his cheek. Erwählen flinched from the sight of it. McCain turned back to Nichts quickly and said, "We're getting out."

Nichts managed to shake his head again, and McCain realized the homunculus couldn't understand him.

"Nichts," McCain said, *"Ich habe Sie versprechen . . ."*

The homunculus's eyes went first, then his face, his neck, his torso . . . as if he were dying a piece at a time. McCain's eyes blurred with tears, and he sobbed once when he could see that Nichts was dead.

"Yes," Erwählen shouted across the room, "all very sad. Here you're crying, and I'm the one who spent—what?—forty thousand marks in materials alone to make that thing."

"That's enough, Hans," McCain said.

Erwählen brushed McCain's ire aside with a flip of his wrist and said, "Please. Enough now, Michael. You can't help your friends at this point, but I still have a place for you here, a place for you in the future."

McCain sighed and said, "You really are an extraordinary man, Erwählen. You could have been something. When you speak, people listen to you. They want to be near you and part of your vision, but under it all there's just nothing but a bitter, hate-ridden demagogue, drunk with his own self-worth. I wouldn't have anything to do with your future if my life depended on it, you Nazi piece of shit. I guess my life does depend on it, too, so there you go."

Erwählen's face fell, and McCain blushed in response.

"You wound me, Michael," Erwählen said. "You wound me deeply. I'll have to have Jerry kill you now. Though that will delight Jerry, it will make me feel very sad, and I will feel very sad for as long as fifteen minutes. Then I will move on and change the world to suit me. Last chance, Michael."

McCain opened his mouth to speak, but no sound came out. He just shook his head.

"Too bad," Erwählen mumbled, then nodded to Jerry.

The teenager lifted the gun to his shoulder and started to advance on McCain with long, confident, heavy-footed strides. McCain held up a hand to shield his face. He knew he had maybe three seconds at most to live, and he realized Jeane was still—

"Hey! Asshole!" Jeane said sharply, tearing Jerry's attention away from McCain.

She had her left arm up with her bloody forearm in front of her face. Her gun was in her right hand, which was up next to her right temple. Jerry turned toward her and she snapped her right arm out, stepping forward at the same time. The gun actually whistled as it shot through the air, tumbling end over end. Jerry flinched, and the gun hit him in the chin hard and bounced to strike the top of his gun. The weapon came out of Jerry's hand and clattered onto the cement floor, sliding a little bit in McCain's direction when it bounced off Jerry's instep.

McCain dived for the submachine gun. He grabbed it with his right hand, and without thinking he tossed it into the vril cistern. There was a dull, bubbling splash, and the weapon was gone.

"Fitz!" Jeane screamed. "I could have—"

"Bitch!" Jerry shouted over her.

McCain was still moving toward the teenager. With no plan of action whatsoever, he smashed into Jerry's side. McCain's momentum was easily enough to knock Jerry down, but when he saw the result of the tackle he was pleasantly surprised. Jerry sprawled all arms and legs into the low wall of the vril cistern and was forced to back into a little corner. McCain skidded to a halt with a painful scrape, maybe four or five feet from Jerry.

McCain looked up to see Jeane approaching fast. The look on her face almost made McCain worry about Jerry. Her right hand curled into a fist. Jerry turned up and saw her coming. A look of purely childlike terror flashed in his eyes, and it sounded as if he was saying something, but his lips weren't moving.

Jeane stopped in midstep and lurched forward sharply. There was a sound like bending metal, then steel scraping on steel.

Jeane said, "Where did this—"

McCain looked up, rolling onto his back, as Jeane tripped and cartwheeled in the air over him. She was wrapped in shining stainless steel bands. One of the bands was over her mouth. Her nostrils flared. Her arms and legs were trapped, motionless, and she hit the floor hard, rolling like a log and coming to rest next to the still form of Nichts.

McCain couldn't begin to imagine where the steel bands had come from or how Erwählen had managed to do it, but he knew it had to have been Erwählen.

"Jeane—" McCain said, then stopped when Jerry kicked him hard between the legs.

The air rushed out of McCain's lungs all at once and pain seared through his abdomen. Through slit-eyes, McCain saw Jerry unfold himself from the corner of the cistern wall. The kid was angry, incensed, and perfectly capable of killing. McCain had had just about enough himself.

Shaking off the pain, McCain stood and faced Jerry. "Okay, punk," McCain said in his best Clint Eastwood, "come get some."

"Ah," Erwählen said, his voice suddenly cheerful, "this will be interesting."

McCain threw the first punch, surprising himself with the sharp speed at which his arm snapped in the direction of Jerry's face.

The teenager dodged backward with a twist of his neck, and McCain connected with nothing. Jerry immediately returned with a punch of his own, and McCain reflexively launched himself backward. The world spun around him, and he realized he was actually flipping backward. McCain knew he couldn't have done that. He was only now able to shoot a basket from the three-point line. He was no gymnast.

It must be the vril.

in fluid silence

McCain landed on his feet without a bounce. Nailed the dismount, he thought.

Jerry set his feet wide apart and held his hands up in front of him like a boxer. McCain smiled and cracked his knuckles. Jerry wasn't overly impressed. They started running toward each other at the same time and leaped into the air. They met in the middle, Jerry kicking straight out with his left foot, McCain in a spinning kick with his right.

Jerry's foot slipped harmlessly along McCain's hip, but McCain's kick smashed into Jerry's jaw. Bone snapped audibly, and a spray of blood peppered McCain's sweatpants as they passed each other on the way down. McCain hit the floor solidly again. Jerry skidded to a stop with a pained grunt.

The teenager's hand went immediately to his jaw, and he wrenched it hard, snapping the bones back into place. Jerry groaned so loudly it was almost a scream. McCain took advantage of Jerry's moment of weakness and skipped up to him quickly, shooting in a series of fast, low kicks. Jerry dodged the first three, then blocked the fourth, which sent a wave of pain up McCain's leg.

Jerry snuck in a low punch to McCain's stomach and didn't give any reprieve, following the stomach punch with one blow after another to McCain's face and neck. McCain managed to block most of them, but a few got through, and his vision started to blur with pain and sweat. Just to get Jerry off him, McCain grabbed the kid's collar and sat back, bringing his leg up and rolling Jerry over him, flipping him up into the air. There was another dull splash when Jerry fell sprawling into the vril.

Movement to the side caught McCain's attention, and he saw Erwählen approaching the helpless form of Jeane, still wrapped tightly in the steel bands.

McCain spun on Erwählen and had just opened his mouth to warn him off when something hit him so hard in the back of his head that it felt as if his eyeballs were going to pop out. His body lurched forward and hit the cement floor. The air was forced from his lungs again, and his chin scraped painfully on the rough surface.

g .w. tirpa

A knee dug into his back, and he was pushed into the floor. He heard something crack and felt a blaze of pain when a rib broke. McCain brought his right knee up and used it to flip over on his back, sending his opponent sprawling away—but Jerry didn't go sprawling away. He came down with both knees on McCain's chest and smashed his fist full into McCain's defenseless face.

Stars exploded in McCain's vision, but he was still able to tip his head to one side in time to dodge a second punch. Jerry's fist smashed into the floor instead of McCain's face. McCain took some joy in the sound of Jerry's fingers shattering from the impact.

The teenager cried out, and McCain tried to bring a knee up between Jerry's legs. The kid was too fast, though, and McCain felt himself being turned over before he realized what was happening.

Jerry was on his back again and had one amazingly powerful forearm under McCain's throat. Jerry squeezed, and McCain's vision dimmed. Jerry lifted his head, turning his face toward Jeane.

Erwählen was kneeling next to her. He looked over at McCain and took a handful of Jeane's red-brown hair in his right hand. Jeane couldn't speak with the steel band around her mouth, but she rolled her eyes up and found McCain's gaze. Her eyes were more angry than pleading, but McCain could tell she knew she was in trouble.

"I can make it quick for her," Erwählen said, "as a favor to you, Michael."

Jerry's stranglehold on McCain tightened. McCain tried to say something, tried to tell Erwählen what he wanted to hear to save Jeane's life, but the sound couldn't pass his closed throat. He pushed against the rough cement floor, but the teenager's grip was too tight.

"I've been wanting to kick your ass for a while now, dick," Jerry growled into McCain's ear. "You can live long enough to see your girlfriend—"

"Enough, Jerry," Erwählen scolded, still holding Jeane by the hair. "It's time to get this—"

in fluid silence

Erwählen stopped speaking and looked up. His head continued tipping upward as if tracking something moving in front of him. His mouth fell open in undisguised shock. McCain could feel Jerry shift on his back and heard him gasp. Jeane spotted whatever it was they saw and her eyes went wide. A strange yellow glow was gradually rolling up along the surface of Jeane's eyes, like a bright yellow light bulb was being drawn up on a wire behind him.

"*Hans Reinhold Erwählen!*" Ngan's voice echoed in the big room.

McCain twisted his neck painfully and managed to roll through Jerry's vril-enhanced grip and turn his head the other way. It was Ngan. He was standing encased in what must have been some sort of vril bubble. It was a sphere of bright golden semiliquid, like water released in a weightless environment. As it did in the cisterns, the vril surrounding Ngan seemed to pulse and undulate, almost writhing with a life all its own.

Ngan's face was as calm as it normally was. Still wearing only his tattered grey suit pants, McCain could see that the bullet wounds were now completely healed. Ngan's blue eyes appeared black in the gold-yellow vril, but they were wide and alert. His brow was set in the way he set it when concentrating. His hands were at his sides, but not completely, with maybe five inches between his hands and hips.

"Hans Reinhold Erwählen," Ngan repeated. "You are no *Bodhisatva*. You are no *tulku* or *gomchen*. You are hardly even an alchemist."

"Half an hour in the vril," Erwählen scowled, still holding Jeane by the hair, "and you presume to tell me—"

"Yes," Ngan interrupted. McCain was surprised Erwählen let Ngan speak. "You are a thief. Where did you steal this from, *wizard?*" The way Ngan said that last word made it plain that he didn't think Erwählen deserved the title.

"Ants," Erwählen said with a sly smile, "eh, Ngan?"

"You have a tiny mind, Erwählen," Ngan said simply, as if discussing the weather. "This is not for you."

Erwählen let go of Jeane's hair and stood. He looked at Ngan with angry defiance. McCain was starting to feel something like a spectator at a very crowded tennis match, having to twist his neck painfully in Jerry's grip to follow this bizarre exchange.

Ngan stopped his slow ascent when his feet were perhaps eight feet off the surface of the vril pool. Erwählen looked up at him and crossed his hands in front of his chest. He touched his right ring finger to his right thumb and his left little finger to his left thumb.

"Magic . . ." Ngan grumbled. It was as close to a sneer as anything McCain had ever seen from Ngan.

The vril bubble in which Ngan was standing quivered and popped up a good six inches so quickly the motion hardly registered on McCain's vision. Ngan looked down at his feet, then looked sharply at Erwählen when the vril bubble sailed back fast and bounced off the far wall like a rubber ball. Ngan flipped forward when the bubble started coming back toward the rest of them. He looked as if he were on one of those Space Camp gyro rides, but from the look on his face he was neither thrilled nor amused.

"I control it!" Erwählen shouted like a petulant child. "I control the vril! It's mine!"

Ngan held his hands out to his sides, eventually bringing them level with his shoulders. Within three revolutions, Ngan came to rest standing straight upright.

McCain felt Jerry relax just a little. Putting his hands under him, McCain pressed against the cement floor and managed to get a couple inches of air between his chest and the cement. Jerry shifted his grip, and McCain pushed off with one hand. He rolled over Jerry and onto his back. Jerry answered this by releasing what had suddenly become more a hug than a chokehold. He punched McCain in the face again.

McCain's head bounced off the cement floor, and his ears started ringing. Under the ringing there was a low, throbbing hum that sounded out of place to McCain.

He looked up and over at Ngan, who was hovering only a few feet away, still eight or nine feet off the ground. The humming sound was coming from Ngan.

"What's he doing?" Jerry asked in a shrill, barely controlled voice.

McCain wasn't sure if the teenager's question was directed at him or Erwählen.

Erwählen answered first, after a fashion. "Chant all you like *gomchen*, and imagine your ants and your little girls and your trees. The power I wield is real. It has force in this world as it has in Agharti. You can keep your pondering mysticism."

McCain tensed under Jerry, but the teenager turned to look at Erwählen. "You never taught him," Jerry said. "He's never been trained! He's not even white!"

"It's all right, my boy," Erwählen said. "The vril serves me. This liquid exists in no other place, is formed by no other hand. In the world beneath, in the forgotten cities of Agharti, even they don't understand this magic like I do. Vril will power the next stage in human evolution."

McCain had had enough of all this vril stuff. He had no idea what Agharti was, or what vril was, or what it was going to do for who when. He'd had enough of this mysterious syrup that made everyone go mad for it. He'd readily admit that it made him feel good. He'd been able to hear better, see better, fight better since he'd been exposed to it, but steroids could do some of that too, and he wouldn't pollute his body with those either.

McCain wanted whatever was left of the vril in his body out. He wanted to be normal. He wanted to go home, and whether he had a real family or knew where he came from and why didn't matter anymore. Erwählen could embrace him and smile at him and remind him of the father he never had or the twin brother he'd never know. Erwählen could offer him everything from power to acceptance, but so could Ngan and Jeane, if not the rest of the Hoffmann Institute, and they weren't trying to take over the world, or, from what McCain had seen so far, even advance some specific political stance.

If the time had come to make a decision, it was more clear to McCain what that decision had to be than it had been since he'd gone to Camp Clarity posing as the next yuppie corporate white supremacist in line.

Jerry started to stand, his head turned to look at Erwählen. Ngan's chanting had grown louder now. Jerry had to shout over it to be heard. "*Herr* Erwählen?" he yelled, his voice quavering. "He can't—"

McCain tucked his knees to his chest and set the bottoms of his feet between Jerry's legs. With a mind more focused than at any other time in his life, McCain rejected the vril still running in his veins and forced it all to shed its energy through his legs. He straightened both legs underneath Jerry and with an unsettlingly feminine yelp, Jerry was propelled higher into the air than McCain had even intended to throw him. He shot up like a rocket and when he hit the skylight there was a sound like a high-speed car accident.

By the time the first jagged shards of broken glass hit the floor Jerry was gone from sight, having easily cleared the roof in a gentle arc. McCain flipped back over on his stomach, his arm over his head, when he saw the glass coming down. He could hear it falling all around him but couldn't feel any actually strike him. He had a brief but terrifying thought that they had already fallen on him and the cuts were either too big to feel right away or a big piece had managed to sever his spinal cord, blocking the pain from the other shards.

A hand protecting his eye, McCain peeked out and up and saw glass falling all around them but not on either McCain or Jeane.

Ngan's chanting was even louder now, and McCain rolled onto his back again. Ngan's vril bubble was floating directly above McCain's face, so close he could see the leaves stuck to the bottoms of Ngan's socks.

Ngan had extended the size of the bubble to cover both McCain and Jeane and protect them from the falling glass.

When the rain of shattered skylight subsided, McCain sat up and shook his head. Jeane was looking at him with narrowed eyes that demanded he take some action. Erwählen had backed off several steps and was studying Ngan with one eye while maintaining his own invisible umbrella, lest the glass cut his life short at barely over two hundred. When the glass subsided,

in fluid silence

Erwählen held his hands in front of his chest and closed his eyes, obviously gathering strength.

McCain stood, with every intention of rushing Erwählen, vril strength or no vril strength.

Erwählen saw McCain approaching, and with a smug smile born of indecision, he waved one hand out in the direction of McCain.

McCain felt as if he'd been kicked in the chest by a horse. He fell back, sliding to come to a stop again under Ngan's floating vril bubble. McCain coughed, wheezed, and otherwise reacted normally to a blow of that nature and severity—a blow that Erwählen had delivered across a good twelve feet of empty air.

Ngan's chanting stopped abruptly. Erwählen's head snapped toward Ngan, his eyes bulging and his face red. Erwählen held that pose for one heartbeat, then a second, then the top of his head from his top teeth up past the bottoms of his ears, slid off. Blood poured over the sides of the gaping wound like a glass filled too high with water.

McCain could hear himself gasp, the echoes sounding clearly in the now silent room. It didn't seem possible, but Erwählen was most convincingly dead.

The old man's body went rigid but didn't fall. It was ghastly to look at, but it just stood there, not twitching, not falling over, stubborn even in death.

"Damn it," McCain heard Jeane sigh.

Startled to hear her voice, McCain looked over at her. The steel bands weren't there anymore, and it occurred to McCain that, given what he knew about Erwählen's peculiar brand of magic, maybe they'd never really been there at all. She slid to a sitting position and rubbed her face with her hands. When she finally looked at him, McCain could see by her eyes that her exhaustion was close to claiming her. She seemed completely out of it.

"No!" Jerry screamed from the other side of the room.

McCain, Jeane, and the still floating but silent Ngan all looked up at him. The teenager, covered in bleeding cuts, shards of glass, and bits of dirt and grass, was running toward them, his eyes fixed on the still-standing decapitated body of Hans Reinhold Erwählen.

McCain saw Jeane notice that Jerry was going for something in his pocket, and her eyes instantly cleared.

"Gun!" Jeane screamed, her tone making it clear it was a habit drilled into her during years of law enforcement training.

Jerry pulled something small and black out of his pocket as he came to a skidding halt not two steps from where Jeane was sitting. Jerry never looked at her. His eyes were fixed on Ngan.

"Oh," Jeane said tiredly, "crap."

McCain could see she was looking at the little black box in Jerry's hand.

Unable to think of a reason not to, McCain asked Jeane, "What's he got there?"

"The detonator," Jeane answered quickly.

"Damn straight," Jerry coughed, blood trickling out of his swollen lips. "You put it back. Put his head back or I swear to Christ I'll blow this barn sky high."

"He's dead, Jerry," McCain said, forcing himself to his feet. "It's all over."

"Bullshit!" Jerry almost squealed, pointing at Ngan. "You put it back. Right goddamned now!"

Jerry held the detonator in his right hand. He held it up so that Ngan, who was remaining completely quiet and passive, floating there, could see it.

"Jerry, man," McCain said, holding out one hand, "give it to me, kid. It's over. You can't put somebody's head back on. Don't make this any—"

"He can put it back on," Jerry said, still holding the detonator in front of his forehead. "When I first came here, I only had one arm. I was in a car accident, and they took my arm. *Herr* Erwählen grew it back. The vril will make it right. The vril will—"

"It's his *head*, Jerry," McCain interrupted. "Think about it. It's not an arm. There's a difference, vril or no vril."

Jeane stood up on shaking legs, and Jerry took a step back from her. McCain could sense that Ngan was slowly approaching.

in fluid silence

"It's not different," Jerry maintained. "It's not different."

"Michael," Ngan said calmly, "it's possible that our friend Jerry may be right."

McCain glanced at Ngan who was staring at the standing, headless body of Erwählen. He followed Ngan's gaze, and his breath caught in his throat when he realized that there was maybe an inch more head than was there a minute or so before.

"It's growing back!" McCain said, still unable to really believe it.

Jeane took one big step toward Jerry, who was looking at Erwählen, the detonator still held up in front of his face.

"Sorry guys," she said, then landed a solid, echoing head butt onto Jerry's bleeding forehead.

McCain thought at first that she was hitting the detonator on purpose, then he saw her eyes go wide when she realized Jerry had tried to block the headbutt and had placed the detonator between her head and his. The little black box was sandwiched between Jeane's forehead and Jerry's. There was an audible click. Jeane fell backward, eyes closed, having knocked herself out. The teenager fell sprawling the opposite direction, and McCain had just enough time to take in one breath before the world went orange, gold, yellow, and red.

All of the orange barrels blew at once, and from deep inside the inferno, there was no way for McCain to know exactly how big the explosion was, but it was big—at least as big as the whole warehouse. McCain could feel a strong, hot wind, and his vision was overloaded by the brightness of the interior of the explosion.

Like the sight of a glass falling off a countertop, the explosion seemed to take forever though the initial fireball was gone in a matter of seconds. McCain could see both Erwählen and Jerry shredded by the force of the blast, and it was right then that he began to wonder why he wasn't dead too.

He looked around and could see Jeane lying in the floor. Another nice bruise was already beginning to show on her forehead, but she was breathing, wasn't being shredded by heat and concussion. Ngan was there too, looking at him with a knowing, unashamedly self-impressed smile.

"You're doing this?" McCain asked Ngan.

Ngan nodded and said, "I have limited control over the vril," Ngan answered.

The bright fireball was quickly giving way to a thick black smoke that should have choked them to death. Deep in the smoke McCain could see the shadowy outlines of what was left (and there wasn't much) of the big building. Where the cisterns were, McCain could already see mounds of broken cement floor and melting sheet steel—a formidable seal.

"I understand," Ngan said quietly, and McCain looked at him. Ngan was looking out into the ruins at no one.

Ngan met the younger man's gaze and said, "Leah is in the ruins. She told me that the power of the vril is waning. We should be on our way."

McCain looked all around and saw no sign of anyone, let alone the little girl from D.C. What could she possibly be doing there?

Ngan laughed and said, "You're looking at me like I'm mad, Michael, but if I told you I was the only one who could see and hear her would that make you feel better?"

McCain didn't bother pursuing the issue. He could hear fire alarms going off now and knew this would be a popular spot real soon. He went over to where Jeane was lying and after only a few gentle tries, he managed to shake her awake.

"They didn't go off?" Jeane asked, groggy and confused.

"They sure did," McCain said, "and thanks for including us in your very special suicide attempt."

She looked at him as if she was going to start explaining in a loud, stern voice why she had every right to be offended by that, then her eyes just softened.

"Hey," she mumbled, "I was tired."

Ngan led the way out of the still burning ruins, his globe of vril around them growing smaller and more brown, less gold, with every footstep until it simply faded away.

They emerged into the parking lot soon enough. McCain, Jeane, and Ngan, having found their way out of the ruins, watched as a near-endless stream of luxury cars were streaming out of the parking lot. Clembert Pemberton passed by in one of his huge SUVs close enough for him to recognize McCain. Pemberton scowled at McCain, but kept driving. Secretary Barrington was in the passenger seat, trying not to look at them. Jerry's friends roared by in a Camaro and didn't notice the three of them coming out of the barn.

The fence was gone, so after a few minutes watching the invited guests evacuate, McCain and Jeane followed Ngan into the already smoldering woods beyond Camp Clarity.

"Now what?" McCain asked when he felt far enough away from Camp Clarity to speak.

Ngan looked up into the sky and saw stars beginning to show themselves on a deepening sky. "Back to Chicago," he said, "to file our report."

Jeane stumbled a little when he said that, but easily regained her balance.

"Okay," McCain said, yawning widely. "I mean, what *right* now?"

Jeane returned McCain's yawn but Ngan seemed immune to it.

"I have things back at the motel," Jeane said. "My car at least I'd like to get back."

"So," Ngan said. "I believe the motel is this way." He pointed into the woods.

Jeane shrugged and said, "They're all just leaving. If we go back to the motel are there going to be cops there? Teenagers with guns?"

"Perhaps," Ngan said. "But perhaps not."

"Don't you love it when he says shit like that?" McCain said to Jeane.

"Despite its seemingly remote location," Ngan said, "that was a rather large explosion. There will be traffic as all those men flee the area, there will be confusion, there will be attention from neighboring towns. We have a better chance of getting into Jeane's car and driving away than we had sneaking through the back fence into Erwählen's vril cisterns."

Jeane forced a smile and said, "Hey, stranger things have

happened. We can't walk back to Chicago. Maybe Erwählen was as sloppy about sabotaging my car as he was about your access to his private magic goo stash."

McCain enjoyed the first real laugh he'd had in days—maybe weeks—then looked at Jeane and grew concerned.

She was using trees to keep herself standing.

"You're too exhausted to drive," McCain said flatly. "Give me the keys."

Jeane sighed and shot McCain an unhappy look.

"See," she said to Ngan, "I told you this wasn't going to end well."

i'm still here

And so it starts again. Each time a little closer, frustratingly closer, then back here. I don't have to describe it, do I? You've heard it all before. I've seen it from the outside, and from the inside, and now so have you.

I know I'm floating. The sensation is clear. It's moving in every direction at once, but so slowly it's like a long roll up, down, left, right. I could be upside down, but why would that matter?

There is no feeling, no sensation other than that gently undulating suspension. There is no temperature—no hot or cold. Isn't that what people have searched for all along? That state of perfect physical detachment? I remember things like air conditioning and electric blankets. These are things to ward off the invasion of the real world on our fragile, imperfect cells. But here, in the vril, I am protected. I am perfect.

I have no illusions about why I'm here. I can't remember exactly how I came here. But I know why. I have failed, and so here I am again. My invention: an unlimited number of second tries. It may take some time still for me to remember what I was trying to do, but I know I'll have another—

There.

A sensation.

I can remember words that might apply: vibration, hum, tickle, oscillation.

I can feel it in points that might be parts of a body, but it seems unlikely that I have a body anymore.

Why would that be unlikely?

Why wouldn't I have a body?

There—there is some change. It's a differentiation in the vibration, changes in the sensation. There was a word for that.

Ton.

Sound.

I've heard sounds before.

I've heard the stamp of boots and the sound of symphonies. I've heard laughing and screaming and kind words and cruel words.

This sound is like a chant, like Tibetan—

No, that's not it. That's not what it is. Why would I have thought that?

The sound is the sound of voices. Two people are talking. Two people are having a conversation.

But they have no language. It's not people. I must be hearing apes or whales vocalizing, baboons warning each other . . .

". . . believed this in a million years if I didn't see it myself," one of the voices says.

People, not baboons. They're speaking a language I understand. That's English. I understand them.

Do I have ears? I can hear them.

"I'm not kidding," another voice is saying—a woman, "that's a planetary gear."

The other voice is a man. He says, "Jesus, I think you're right. They've solved the short-range repulsive van der Waals interactions problem."

What is he saying?

"Oh, there's more," the woman again. "See that line, there? That set?"

A shuffle of feet. I can hear that.

The man says, "It's an SWNT. Holy crap. Where did they get this stuff?"

What stuff?

What are they talking about?

I understand English, but I can't understand them. They aren't making sense.

"Get a measurement of its resistivity," the woman says. Is she in charge?

"I've got point defects all over this thing and another one in close proximity with precisely the same defects," says the man.

These people aren't talking about anything that has to do with me.

Why am I here? Why are they talking about this in their nonsensical English?

"Are you getting that?" The woman asks.

The man says, "Its voltage-current characteristics . . . these things are semiconductors, right?" But what does that mean?

"Depression near zero bias voltage," the woman tells him.

The man makes a sound like a breathy laugh, and he says, "That's a Coulomb blockade. Oh, man."

"They're so small," the woman says, her voice conveying something akin to rapture.

I can recognize that now?

I guess I can.

These people are excited about whatever it is they're talking about that has nothing to do with me.

I stop paying attention because I know I'll be finished soon. I'll be me again, in time, with a body. I should go back underground. I should go back to Agharti and rest. I should go there to remember the old ways, to feel the pure vril again. I should go there and rest, and plan, and wait, then try again.

In Agharti, vril flows like light in the air, in everything all around you, and it's been there forever and ever and ever.

They accept me there, though there's no reason for them to.

I'll go back down. Deep down and rest, deep down and become me again—whoever that is.

They won't be looking for me there—whoever they are. They don't even believe that Agharti exists. A world under their noses, under their feet every day with power unimaginable . . . and they just forget. It's not even a story now. Legends that were a sort of history have been replaced by fiction now for so long that no one sees truth in anything.

They've made a world of lies, and they hate me because I tell a truth of my own.

I will spend the time in Agharti that I need to spend, and I will return.

I will do this over and over again.

The woman is pretty in a restrained sort of way. The man is—

I can see.

I can see them.

Everything has a golden yellow haze over it. I can see through a haze of vril. It's the vril that's filling the mouth I can feel now. I have one hand—a right hand. I have eyes, and I can see.

The man and woman are both wearing long lab coats. There is a collection of generic putty plastic apparati and a small table on which sits a laptop computer. I can't see too many details, but I can see that they are looking at the computer and at the plastic box machines. A clear plastic tube full of vril snakes past my vision, somewhere outside in front of the people. The woman draws some vril out of the tube with a syringe.

She looks at the liquid with appropriate reverence. The woman is Asian.

Yes, I am disappointed.

They continue speaking about some small things that do something, but I don't want to hear. They seem to be talking about the vril, but they know nothing. They know nothing of my creation.

They're talking about my wonderful elixir as if it's a collection of ants.

It's not ants.

The Asian woman looks Japanese, and she says, "You could get heterostructures like that by successive formation of different sulphides."

The man nods. He's white. He's a white man.

The white man says, "It's in the literature. The Italian guys wrote that up, but . . ."

The woman stops what she's doing and turns to look at the man, who looks up from the computer.

He smiles, and she smiles back, then—yes, here I am. You see me.

I try to speak but can't tell if I've opened my mouth. I can feel the vril on my tongue.

He's looking right at me.

"Freaky, isn't it?" he says, looking at me.

I can't answer him.

The woman glances back at me but doesn't look me in the eye. She looks away and hugs herself, arms crossed across her chest. She moves away and changes shape. I know what that effect is from. It's an optical illusion. She's not really changing shape.

I'm in a glass tank with rounded walls. The tank is full of vril.

I have a name.

I remember it.

You know it, don't you?

Hans Reinhold Erwählen.

I am Hans Reinhold Erwählen.

"Oh, my God," the woman says. She keeps shifting away from where I can see her. "He's here."

"What do we do?" the man asks, moving around like he's all flustered.

He doesn't have time to decide how to handle himself. See there? Someone is walking in.

I know this man.

I've seen him before.

What's his name?

He has two other men with him. All three of them are wearing dark suits.

"Um," the woman says, "Mr. P—"

"We don't have much time," one of the men says.

The man I'm sure I recognize says, "That's him?"

He's looking at me.

Who is this man? Does he work for me?

"Is he . . . ?" the man in the suit asks.

"He's alive," he woman tells him.

Yes, he is relieved. The man in the suit is relieved to hear that I am alive. I feel good about that, but I have no idea why.

The man in the lab coat is standing, and he tells the man in the suit, "It looks like cellular regeneration—way beyond anything you'd call healing—but it's not."

"It's true then?" the man in the suit asks.

The woman nods, glances at me, but still won't look me in the eye.

I want to speak so badly. They're talking about me like I'm a museum exhibit.

"They're putting him back together one molecule at a time," the woman says.

She has to be lying, This is vril. Vril doesn't do that. There is no "they" with vril—just one thing, just vril alone.

The man in the suit asks the man and the woman if I will remember, if I will be normal.

They assure him I will, and that makes me feel better, but I'm sure they don't know what they're talking about.

"It'll take time," the woman tells him.

The man in the suit shrugs, looks me up and down in a way that makes me angry, and says, "Time we have. But not today."

Without addressing the people in the lab coats, the three men turn and walk quickly away. As they recede into the golden hazed distance of the nondescript white room, one of the men next to the man who seems so familiar speaks for the first time.

I can hear him say, "This way out, Mr. President."

[enD of 3

DARK·MATTER

(Four)
Of Aged Angels
Monte Cook

"They've been here for fifty some years, but they were here before, too. Long ago, down the bottomless throat of time, they came to the world, and they walked as gods through the forests. The people of that time had no name for these ancient angels, but they saw their effects. The caress of these gods put ripples in the world like a child's light touch on the surface of a pool."

For a moment—just for a moment—McCain was caught up in his poetry. For that moment, he believed that this really was Jim Morrison.

"But then they left, for there was war in heaven," Morrison said, looking at the ceiling. "Dark were the skies, heavy with the conflict of birds as seen by a snake. When they fled back through the doors, they left behind something cherished among them—and among us since then, at least those few who knew that it truly existed."

"What was it?" McCain asked, his voice barely a whisper amid the darkness and stone.

Without a pause, Morrison told him, "The Holy Grail."

July 2001

©2001 Wizards of the Coast, Inc. All Rights Reserved.

DARK·MATTER

(Five)
By Dust Consumed
Don Bassingthwaite

Ned looked over at Jeane and asked, "Are you sure you're ready for this?"

She snorted. "I was trained as an ATF investigator. I have been shot at, burned, dropped, beaten, and damn near blown up several times. I have been to crime scenes that would make most people vomit. I have seen . . . things . . . that would make *you* wet yourself, Ned." She took a deep breath and produced the key that Hollister had left for her. "No, I'm not ready."

The safe deposit box was larger than she had expected. The top clicked open when she turned the key in the lock. She took another deep breath before lifting it any further. Inside, two envelopes rested atop a plain beige file folder. A yellowed newspaper clipping had slipped partway out of the folder, exposing the date: August 6, 1962. Just slightly less than a month before her birth, the trained investigator in her noted. The rest of her, though, was focused on the smaller of the two envelopes and the words that were written on it in a light, open hand forty years ago:

For Jeane.

December 2001

©2001 Wizards of the Coast, Inc. All Rights Reserved.

MAGIC: The Gathering

Invasion Cycle — J. Robert King

The struggle for the future of Dominaria has begun.

Book I
Invasion
After eons of plotting beyond time and space, the horrifying Phyrexians have come to reclaim the homeland that once was theirs.

Book II
Planeshift
The first wave is over, but the invasion rages on. The artificial plane of Rath overlays on Dominaria, covering the natural landscape with the unnatural horrors of Phyrexia.
February 2001

Book III
Apocalypse
Witness the conclusion of the world-shattering Phyrexian invasion!
June 2001

MAGIC: THE GATHERING is a registered trademark owned by Wizards of the Coast, Inc.
©2001 Wizards of the Coast, Inc.

FORGOTTEN REALMS

Venture into the **FORGOTTEN REALMS** with these two new series!

Sembia
GET A NEW PERSPECTIVE ON THE FORGOTTEN REALMS FROM THESE TALES OF THE USKEVREN CLAN OF SELGAUNT.

Shadow's Witness
Paul Kemp

Erevis Cale has a secret. When a ruthless evil is unleashed on Selgaunt, the loyal butler of the Uskevren family must come to terms with his own dark past if he is to save the family he dearly loves.

The Shattered Mask
Richard Lee Byers

Shamur Uskevren is duped into making an assassination attempt on her husband Thamalon. Soon, however, the dame of House Uskevren realizes that all is not as it seems and that her family is in grave danger.

JUNE 2001

Black Wolf
Dave Gross

The young Talbot Uskevren was the only one to survive a horrible "hunting accident." Now, infected with lycanthropy, the second son of the Uskevren clan must learn to control what he has become.

NOVEMBER 2001

The Cities
A NEW SERIES OF STAND-ALONE NOVELS, EACH SET IN ONE OF THE MIGHTY CITIES OF FAERÛN.

The City of Ravens
Richard Baker

Raven's Bluff — a viper pit of schemes, swindles, wizardry, and fools masquerading as heroes.

Temple Hill
Drew Karpyshyn

Elversult — fashionable and comfortable, this shining city of the heartlands harbors an unknown evil beneath its streets.

SEPTEMBER 2001

FORGOTTEN REALMS is a registered trademark of Wizards of the Coast, Inc.
©2001 Wizards of the Coast, Inc.

About the Author

G.W. Tirpa, the grandson of European immigrants, was born in upstate New York in 1964. He now lives in the foothills of the Cascades where he practices taiji and writes. *In Fluid Silence* is his first foray into the world of DARK•MATTER™. He can be contacted at **gwtirpa@netscape.net**.

The Wizards of the Coast logo is a registered trademark owned by Wizards of the Coast, Inc. DARK•MATTER is a trademark owned by Wizards of the Coast, Inc.
©2001 Wizards of the Coast, Inc.

Your worst nightmares,
the darkest whispers of your soul ... ue.

In the heartland of America, ...e
humanity in its ...

Three agents of the shadowy Hoffmann Institute become entangled in a plot, begun in Nazi Germany, that leads to the highest reaches of world power. As the truth becomes increasingly unbelievable, one agent discovers that the on... way to beat the enemy is to join him.

DARK•MATTER™

9780786916801

Printed in U.S.A. TSR21680

$1.49
868321
A0—
413-P
No Exchange Books
Spy & War